CW01494993

Published in Great Britain by
L.R. Price Publications Ltd, 2024
27 Old Gloucester Street,
London, WC1N 3AX
www.lrpricepublications.com

Cover design by L.R. Price Publications Ltd

ISBN: 978-1-916613-27-0

PITCHFORK

Lester Boyd

Introduction

Neil had a normal upbringing without any major incidents or events occurring. He was a quiet child, more from circumstance rather than design. Living with horses all around him, it was surprising that he showed little interest in them until into his late teens, when a visit with his aunt to a historical building, and a fleeting glance of a string of racehorses, stirred something inside him and ignited a passion causing his life to dramatically change direction. His first visit to a racecourse soon followed, and he was hooked; he started riding, and it soon became clear that he had an aptitude and a talent for it. Riding out at a local racing yard soon followed, and before he knew what was happening, he was riding in public as a jockey in races. Following a few early mistakes, things started going extremely well, and he was being spoken of as having huge potential and a man going places. After a few wrong moves, it all started to dramatically unravel, and following a change of stables, he was soon on a downward spiral, with no apparent way of stopping, and before long, he was fighting to save not only his career but more importantly his life, the more he probed, the deeper into danger he went, with consequences that could prove fatal.

CHAPTER ONE

Daydream Underachiever

Neil Bartholomew was a strange child as he was surrounded by horses but showed no interest in them for the first 15 years of his life, and then slowly, very slowly, the horse bug got hold of him. He lived on a highly successful stud in the Cotswolds, called Lazy Horse Stud, he believed, as someone had once told him that the name derived from the Frenchman who set up the stud many years ago, Baron L'Azee, or something like that. The stud was run by his dad Eric, who was of the old school, strict disciplinarian, stiff upper lip, and an enthusiastic member of the golf club; though his friends used to joke that his handicap was higher than his I.Q., he could never work if this was an insult aimed at his golf or at his intelligence or both? He was always congratulating himself on a job well done, which it was, but as usually is the case, it was down to, in his words, the backroom staff who did most of the work and, in reality, ran the show, Neil's mum Ann, quietly and unassumingly organised the day to day running behind the scenes, while Eric wined and dined

3

clients at the sales and racecourses and many other venues, and lived a life of luxury. Ann was always telling him that if he didn't cut down on the finer things in life, he'd end up suffering from gout, but he took little notice of such things. Ann ran the house, and it wasn't a small house, producing excellent meals three times a day and always had his evening meal on the table at the stroke of seven every night for, as she said herself, as long as she could remember.

Neil wasn't the only child, as he had a sister called Cynthia, a few years older than him. She, from an early age, was completely horse mad, spending ninety per cent of her time on horseback and the other ten per cent dreaming about horses. She entered all the local shows and gymkhanas with great enthusiasm, though sadly with little success, but this didn't dampen her spirits or lessen her enjoyment. She was like a tornado of energy, and the house was very quiet now that she'd gone to University to study dentistry. Neil admitted that he didn't notice when she was there but noticed when she wasn't. All that she'd left behind was a woolly first pony, who was sometimes put with the youngstock at weaning time, as a calming influence, like a surrogate mother. Her last horse had been offered to Neil, but as usual, he'd shown no interest, so she'd loaned it to a friend.

Neil was always deep in thought, and he'd convinced himself that if his parents had a favourite child, then that would have been his sister Cynthia, but of course, no one had ever said anything to suggest this.

Neil had spent his first 14 years in something of a daydreaming state and doing little else. He had been sent to a posh boys-only boarding school, which was quite a long way from the stud, so home visits were usually restricted to the holidays. At school, he'd been hopeless at sport but slightly better academically, though he rarely applied himself to the frustration of his harassed teachers, who could see that he had ability but not the inclination. Parents' evenings never went very well; where Neil thought that the teachers really enjoyed telling his parents about his lack of academic interest, and where his dad used to pace around the room like a raging bull.

He made few friends, as the other schoolboys couldn't really fathom him out and gave up trying; mercifully, the school bullies left him in peace. His sanctuary, and where he spent most of his time when not in lessons, was the school library. It was an extensive library with a huge collection of books that had been built up over many years, some left by Old Boys. Neil thought that if he left them any books, they would cover the subject of Truancy. He whiled away hour after hour there, perfectly content, sat in a corner looking out of the window and watching the world go by or reading book after book, sometimes reading more than one book in a day. All this reading ensured that the one subject that he was good at was English.

During most summer holidays, whilst his mum was carting Cynthia around the summer horse shows, he was sent off to stay with his Aunt Emily, who lived in a very remote part of Yorkshire. Whilst here, he also spent most of his time reading books, but not horse-related books. His Aunt tried to integrate him into village life, with limited success. He did like wandering around the area, as he was fascinated with the hills, they had hills at home, but not as impressive as these, and he sometimes strayed as far as the moors, vast open spaces where he rarely saw anyone, and once nearly trod on a snake. He was shocked when on his return, his aunt told him that it was most likely an adder and that they were poisonous!

On his first visit to Yorkshire, he'd found it a bit disconcerting, as unlike at home, everyone spoke to him. The locals were very inquisitive and wanted to know everything about him and his family, where he was from, what he did, in fact, an endless stream of questions. He once thought that he might make up a fantastic and fanciful story but was sure that the canny northerners would see straight through him!!

His aunt used to take him to watch the local cricket matches. On a nice summer's day, he found this quite enjoyable but didn't have a clue what was going on and was amazed at how seriously it was taken. It whiled away the days pleasantly enough, as long as the sun was shining. After one such cricket match, he was taken to the local and given a big foaming pint of local ale, his protestations that he was too young to drink went unheeded, and he was told that he was in Yorkshire now, and things were done differently, and anyway, they had added, the local bobby was stationed about 30 miles away! He went home with his aunt rather light-headed.

Visiting his aunt happened every summer holiday, and then it was back to school with only a brief period spent at home, where he saw little of his parents or his sister and had never felt that he was properly part of the family. The normality of sibling rivalry past him by, and his sister grew up without him really noticing.

CHAPTER TWO

Into the Woods

He surprisingly passed one or two O levels, doing best as was expected at English, and returned home unsure whether he'd be going back to do A levels; in fact, he had no plans for the future, which worried him slightly, but worried his dad a whole lot more!

The first week of the holidays was spent at Lazy Horse Stud before he went off to Yorkshire again. He was now old enough to be left at home on his own, whilst his dad was out undertaking stud business and his mum was out doing whatever she did.

He always looked forward to his trips to Yorkshire or going up north but realised that this might be for the last time.

At home, he'd started walking around the fields. His favourite location at the stud was the wood at the top of the land; he was allowed here until the pheasants arrived for the local shoot, and even when they were there, he still sneaked up some nights, imagining that no one would ever notice, but of course, they did, as you're never as alone as you think in the countryside. He'd agreed to do some beating this season, something that he'd never fancied doing in the past. His dad was a big shooting man with more shotguns than was strictly necessary and a couple of gundogs who lived out in kennels behind the house. Neil often asked if they could accompany him on his long walks but was always dissuaded from doing so as he was told that he'd spoil them and ruin them for picking up. Poppycock, he thought, but he'd learnt from past experiences that it was best not to cross his dad.

One morning had started badly, with his dad trying to discuss his future with him, He'd started calmly, but after a few non-committal remarks from Neil, he'd got angry and started shouting and making stark predictions about Neil's future.

"Well, that went well," he said to his mum, who was looking on with a worried expression and a furrowed brow.

His dad got him looking through prospectus after prospectus for various colleges, none of which he was even slightly interested in. So he was more than ready for his walk, it was getting a little late by the time he reached the woods, and dusk was falling, and the branches on the trees were swaying and making a slightly spooky sound, or so Neil thought. He went through the gate, stopping when he thought that he'd heard voices, then continuing when all appeared to be silent apart from the hooting of a distant Owl. He carried on but not with his usual gay abandon but with a slower, cautious step; as he went past a gnarled old oak tree, he was suddenly met by a group of men coming the other way, carrying spades and other articles which he couldn't make out.

The taller one, who smelt of stale beer and fags, grabbed hold of him and said, "Oi, what are you doing here? These woods are private, didn't you see the sign KEEP OUT?" this was said in a threatening, menacing tone. Instead of replying that these were indeed his woods, and it was them that shouldn't be there, he just remained silent.

The tall man released him and roughly shoved him forward, and said, "Be on your way".

Trying to be cool, he tried to speak, but no words came out, and as his confidence ebbed away, he just turned tail and ran all the way back to the house.

He burst into the living room where his dad was watching a bloodstock sale from Ireland. He heard the end of a conversation in which his dad was telling his mum that they'd bred the next one for sale and that it hadn't done much on the flat, and he presumed that the vendors were hoping that the jumping men may be interested in it. His mum was trying to look interested but brightened up when her son approached.

"Dad", he shouted, "there are some rough men with spades in the wood".

Expecting his dad to be alarmed, he was rather disconcerted when he replied, "Don't worry, it's the mole men, and anyway, what are you doing up there?" and he carried on watching the tv screen and carried on with his original conversation, "That stallion has fallen out of favour; I wouldn't be surprised if he's not shipped abroad".

Mole men, Neil thought, that's hardly likely in the dark, at this time of night, they'll be in the pub. He, however, slunk off unsatisfied with the answer and went to his room to read one of his books, but he couldn't concentrate, and he threw his book down and went to bed. Sleep was hard to come by, and Neil tossed and turned, going over the events in the wood, with the ugly unshaven face of the man that grabbed him vividly reappearing in his mind. Neil was usually a good sleeper, in the land of nod as soon as his head hit the pillow, but not this night; he only managed to snatch the odd half hour of sleep before waking again. In next to no time, the general clatter and sounds from the stud woke him, and he went downstairs for breakfast, looking like he'd had no sleep at all.

After breakfast, thinking what his dad had told him was poppycock, he decided to retrace his steps back to the woods; he went out of the yard, past fields of horses grazing contentedly and youngstock in various stages of development, but as usual, he took no interest in them if they'd been cows or sheep, it would have made no difference to him. All was calm when he reached the woods, the birds were chattering in the branches, and he could hear the trickling sound of a stream as it made its way down the hill; he walked past the gnarled old oak tree where he'd met the men the night before. It looked different in the daylight, but he noticed that a few steps in front of him that there had been some digging, big moles he said to himself with a wry smile, when suddenly he heard a sound, like a baby's cry, and he could see what looked like some sort of animal, half buried in a hole. He cautiously approached and realised that it was a small dog, some sort of cross-bred terrier, he thought, but in a bad way. It whimpered when it saw him and struggled to free itself, Neil helped it out and was shocked to find it was covered in cuts and caked in blood, with a chunk missing from one of its ears, but the main thing was that it was alive.

Neil wasn't sure what to do with it, but noticing that it had a rough strap round its neck that resembled a collar; he carefully attached a length of baler band as every good countryman has some in his pockets, and took it home, his dad snapped, "We can't have that thing here, it'll upset the Labradors".

Bloody temperamental gundogs, Neil thought as he left and took the dog to the one person, he knew who would help. That person was Steve Carson, the long-serving stud manager. Steve always had a dog of some description, following obediently wherever he went, but sadly he'd just lost his old spaniel. He was at home in the stud managers bungalow, sat reading the Sporting Life, with a mug of tea on the table going cold in front of him, and his wife Lynne listening intently as he unhurriedly told her about some problem with a young colt with ringworm. Lynne, with her veterinary background, was a great asset.

"We don't want them all catching it," he was saying, but his words stopped when he saw Neil. "What on earth," he said, "where did you find that?"

Neil told him the full story and how his dad wanted nothing to do with the dog.

"I don't know why your dad didn't put a stop to this years ago?"

"To what?" Neil enquired.

"Never you mind."

Steve looked the dog over, as did Lynne from a veterinary aspect, and they declared that with a lot of tender loving care and time, the dog would be OK. They agreed to take it on.

"Its real owners will be long gone; they'll have left it for dead," Steve said with a shake of his head, "but you'll have to help with taking it for walks and looking after it when we're away," he said, looking at Neil, who readily agreed and was pleased to have something to do.

However, next week he was off to Yorkshire, but he wasn't looking forward to it as he now had plenty to do at the stud farm and had even, in a moment of rashness, agreed to help Steve with the horses. Luckily so he thought, he was only going away for a few weeks, instead of all of the summer holidays as usual, mainly because he wasn't going back to school, and his dad kept banging on about his future and those blasted prospectuses.

CHAPTER THREE

Northern Knights

As usual, Neil took the train, and as usual, he was convinced that it was a lot colder when he finally arrived in Yorkshire. For some reason, he wasn't full of the usual joy and excitement of going up north, but at least, he told himself, it wasn't for too long.

As expected, a taxi was waiting for him at the picturesque, quaint old Dales railway station, and on arrival, his aunt was genuinely pleased to see him. He reasoned that she couldn't be lonely, as even though she never married, she threw herself into the local social scene, busying herself with the W.I., the local Bowls Club, and making endless supplies of jam, chutney and some very potent fruit wines.

Neil was reading less now than in his younger years, and it was no longer an all of the time consuming passion. As he was beginning to spread his wings, he still enjoyed going for walks, that is, if he could avoid the nosey locals.

He was therefore pleased when his aunt suggested a trip to see Middleham Castle, the only downside being that it was an organised W.I. trip, but she assured him that it would be OK for him to tag along and that it shouldn't bother him too much, being in a coach full of elderly ladies chatting all the time ten to the dozen. Neil intended to research the history of the castle on Google the night before, but sadly the broadband was almost non-existent in this area of the Dales and kept cutting out, and extremely frustrated, he gave up. He, however, found an old book in his aunt's bookcase, and after brushing the dust off, he read about Middleham and its castle. He learnt about Richard the Third residing at the castle, about the Princes in the tower, and how in later years, the stone had been robbed from the castle to build surrounding dwellings. It also mentioned that Middleham was also famous for racehorses, which normally would have passed him by, but for some strange reason, something stirred inside him, which added to the intrigue and excitement of the forthcoming visit.

In the morning, Neil, his aunt and a ragged bunch of elderly jolly ladies gathered at the White Horse Inn car park awaiting the coach's arrival. The sun was trying to break through the clouds as the coach came round the corner, and the W.I. ladies started getting on, which took a lot longer than Neil had anticipated.

It was only a short journey to Middleham, which Neil thought was a blessing; as the cacophony of sound produced by the ladies incessantly chatting deafened him and drowned out his attempts at daydreaming, he only wished that he'd packed some ear plugs. He spent the journey looking out of the window and dodging all of their questions. The scenery as they whizzed past was breathtaking, and he realised why the Yorkshire Dales were such a popular tourist attraction, with the small hilly fields dotted with sheep and surrounded by dry stone walls of all shapes and sizes and in differing states of repair. Neil started wondering how long it had taken to build them. They passed many old and interesting buildings, and one he thought might have been the castle, but was informed that it was an Abbey — Jervaulx — if he remembered correctly.

The coach parked in the large market square, and on disembarking, Neil's first thought was that for a small place, there were a lot of pubs. On enquiring about this, he was informed that the town was overbrimming with a lot of very thirsty stable lads and lasses.

The castle towered menacingly over the surrounding houses and buildings, and Neil could clearly see which ones had been built using stone robbed from it. Imagine if someone tried that in today's climate, he thought, how times change. He thought that it would have been difficult, in the days of King Richard the Third, to attack the castle as it would have originally been surrounded by open spaces and perched in its lofty position, would have been virtually impenetrable. The WI ladies weren't as adventurous as Neil and wandered around the lower regions of the castle and sat about outside, some showing none or little interest in the overpowering building. Neil, however, climbed up as high as was possible, where he could see many sheep and horses contentedly grazing in the lush though hilly surrounding fields, which he presumed hadn't changed much since the King's days of reign here. He was beginning to imagine himself as King Richard riding up to the castle on a prancing charger wearing gleaming armour and surrounded by his loyal knights when he heard a shout from below and could see his aunt beckoning for him to come back down. He sauntered down the worn steps with hardly a care in the world and rejoined the rest of the party, who were heading for one of the many cafés in the town. Walking back down the hill, they came across a small string of racehorses, walking in crocodile fashion. Neil, at this stage of his life, knew virtually nothing about racing but was impressed with their sleek and fit well-toned bodies, how athletic they looked, how thin their legs looked, how they could carry all that weight and jump, he mused. Talking of fit and toned bodies, he was instantly taken with one of the stable lasses, a lithe blonde girl, who was moving rhythmically and in time with the horse's stride, but who was oblivious to his piercing stare as she was animatedly chatting into her mobile phone, wedged against an ear. He gazed in admiration as they all passed.

"Admiring the fine athletic bodies, are you?" his aunt enquired.

"Yes," Neil replied, "and the horses aren't too bad either," he added with a mischievous smirk, as he had one last lingering look as the string of horses disappeared.

His aunt informed him that they were probably returning from the gallops which were up the hill out of the town, the Low and High Moors.

"Would you like to go up there and watch them one day?"

And he surprised himself by saying, "Yes, I would".

They followed the rest down to the café, and Neil was astonished and impressed with the depth of his aunt's racing knowledge; and he knew not why, but an interest in racing was beginning to develop inside him, and he wondered abstractedly if this could be a turning point in his life, or if as usual, he was just being over dramatic. He, however, couldn't get the blonde girl out of his mind but realised that he'd probably never see her again.

That night back in his aunt's cottage, his daydreams about blonde stable lasses were rudely interrupted by his aunt, who informed him that his dad was actually going to come and pick him up this time and take him home. Wow, that's a first, he thought. I wonder why? When he went down for tea, it all became clear as his aunt explained that his dad was going to the local racetrack first and then picking Neil up on the way back. Neil surprised himself by suggesting that he and his aunt could accompany his dad to the races; his aunt warmed to this suggestion declaring it a jolly idea. She wandered off to phone his dad, and in next to no time, it was all arranged.

His dad came off the phone and said to Neil's mum, "I can't believe it. Neil wants to go racing tomorrow!"

His mum replied, "That's good, isn't it?"

"Yes, I suppose it is. It's only taken him 16 years to show an interest!"

CHAPTER FOUR

A Day at the Races

His dad, always an early riser, unlike his son, arrived at the cottage at the exact prearranged time and looked annoyed as Neil wasn't ready, and his Aunt was wandering about getting flustered as she couldn't find her hat. His dad was immaculately turned out, looking every inch the country gent, which of course he was, and his Aunt was looking very smart as well. As expected, Neil had no smart clothes with him and was turned out in jeans, a sloppy jersey and worn trainers.

His dad exploded, "That won't do; I won't be seen dead with you dressed like that, and trainers, really," he snorted derisively.

His aunt was getting more and more flustered but managed to calm the situation. "Don't worry, Eric, we'll stop at Bedale, and I'll sort it."

She'd always been a little bit in awe of her elder brother Eric and had been more of a playmate with her younger brother Harry as Eric had always appeared a little aloof and standoffish, or so she thought.

Eric, like most men, hated shopping, so he sat in his Range Rover, parked on a yellow line, whilst Aunt Emily was dispatched to turn Neil into a racegoer ASAP. His aunt being a good W.I. member, hurried off straight to a charity shop, and in next to no time, Neil was kitted out to look the part in a smart shirt, tie, trousers and a tweed jacket, and all for next to no money. Neil, who was not one for looking smart usually, looked in the mirror and was pleasantly surprised and pleased at the image that stared back at him.

As they set off again, his dad said to his aunt, "Who's that smart young man sat in the back?"

His aunt smiled, a forced smile, Neil thought, who hoped that his dad's humour might be funny one day soon.

It was only a short journey to the races, Eric parked in the Owners & Trainers car park, which was a very grand description for a muddy field, and they all trooped off to the entrance. Neil's aunt had only been racing a few times, and his dad was a regular racegoer, but for Neil, this was the first time. They streamed in after his dad had shown some I.D., and Neil's first impression was that it was very compact, quaint, and a little bit old-fashioned; he'd once glanced at Royal Ascot on the telly, and though he wasn't expecting anything on that grand scale, the smallness of this course surprised him slightly, though it wasn't a criticism, as everything was close by and he felt very near to the action, the saddling boxes, the parade ring, the bookies and the racecourse itself were all very near. His dad soon disappeared, saying that he needed to see someone in Owners & Trainers; his aunt hung around with him and watched the first race, but then she met a friend and said that she needed to sit down; they went off to find some seats and grab a coffee.

"You'll be OK on your own, Neil, won't you?" she called over her shoulder but didn't appear to wait for an answer.

So Neil was left all on his own, except that you never really are on your own at the races, and amazingly he was fascinated with it, not just the racing, but everything in the racing scene; in short, he was hooked!

He watched the horses come across the road from the stables, get saddled up, enter the parade ring, then observed as the jockeys all came out en masse from the weighing room and looked round as they tried to locate the correct connections, then as they stood in earnest discussion with the trainers, as the owners listened on. They always seemed to get some last-minute instructions before being legged up, and then they were off, and what happened next was all down to the man or woman on top of the flighty fidgeting beasts. The bookies were a revelation to Neil, with a lot of action as people darted from one to another and a large amount of money changing hands just before the race was off. Neil didn't have any binoculars, but luckily there was a big screen in the centre of the course, where he could watch all the action, especially when the field was almost out of sight on the other side of the course. He stood up in the stands hemmed in amongst the other racegoers, most of them not unsurprisingly dressed very similarly to himself, Neil managed to surpass his own lowly expectations by picking a placed horse in nearly every race, and even though he was only betting in small amounts, he was making a healthy profit and had more than enough to pay his Aunt back for the clothes that she'd bought him, though he knew that she wouldn't accept any money from him, he thought that he should offer to pay for them.

Neil was actually enjoying himself and having a great time and began to wonder why he'd never gone racing before. In next to no time, the fifth race arrived; as he watched the horses arrive, he suddenly spotted the blonde stable lass from Middleham leading around one of the runners. He scanned the race card and learnt that the horse was called Pride of the North and appeared to have a bit of a chance if the betting forecast was anything to go by. The jockey, the race card informed him, went by the name of Gilbert French-Saunders, pity he thought that the race card didn't have the name of the stable lass as well. Neil watched closely as the tall, gangly jockey was legged up and joined the others on the course, and the blonde stable lass went to watch the race unfold with the other lads and lasses. Watching the races, Neil had become a grandstand jockey, becoming critical about the riding of some of the jockeys. He had to check himself, as after all, it was the first time he'd gone racing, and what did he really know? He particularly watched Gilbert's mount, as he'd put money on it, funny name for a jockey he mused, he sounds like an upper-class twit, a Tim nice but Dim type of character, Neil was smiling at his own sense of humour as the race began to unfold. The racegoer next to him was commenting to no one in particular that Gilbert was a toff who only gets rides due to his dad owning half of Yorkshire. Despite all these misgivings, Gilbert got himself into a winning position, only to set off for home too early; in Neil's inexperienced opinion, then looking like he'd win easily, the chap at the side of Neil informed him that this would be his first winner. However, it wasn't to be as Gilbert wobbled about in the saddle, waving his arms around trying to encourage but actually unbalancing the horse in the process, hindering his steed rather than helping it; the result is that a 33-1 unconsidered outsider, sneaked up on the inside and won by a short head. The jockey looked dejected coming in to fill the place allocated for finishing second, though Neil felt sorry for the connections, especially the blonde stable lass who was fussing over the horse. He was still watching the activity in the unsaddling enclosure when he heard a shout from his dad, who informed him that they were leaving NOW. Neil remembered that he had mentioned that they were leaving after the fifth race but, in the excitement of the day, had completely forgotten. The journey back to his aunts was filled with race talk, with Neil holding his own in the conversations, something that didn't usually happen in his dad's company. On the way back to the stud, his dad asked him if he'd enjoyed himself, and he admitted that he had, but when asked why he'd never wanted to go before, he had no answer.

He asked his dad about the jockey Gilbert French-Saunders, and as expected, his dad was a ready source of information; however, he was similarly dismissive about him, saying that he was an apprentice rider who was just starting out, and he didn't expect him to make much impression on the racing scene. His father, Oliver, had been a very flamboyant debonair amateur riding in the Grand National and the Pardubice race, a notoriously dangerous race in the Czech Republic, but he didn't think that his son possessed the same devil may care attitude. Oliver owned one of the largest estates in Yorkshire, with a fine grouse moor, visited by Royalty and the wealthy from the U.K. and abroad on a regular basis.

"He's sitting on a gold mine," Neil's dad said, with a touch of jealousy.

"What, he's got gold there as well?" Neil enquired innocently.

His dad just shook his head and raised his eyes above. Talking of shooting reminded Neil that he'd agreed to go beating that autumn, but on a pheasant shoot, as there weren't any grouse moors in the Cotswolds.

CHAPTER FIVE

Mistakes

On returning to the stud farm, Neil's life changed dramatically. He still read a lot but was moving away from exclusively reading the classics to choosing books from the vast array of tomes in the farm's extensive library and found horse racing thrillers a great joy to read.

He particularly liked John Francome and Dick Francis novels and could easily read one in a day, as they were real page-turners. Now though, he only read them during the hours of darkness as during the daylight, hours he was to be found out and about on the stud. He spent a lot of time at Steve's house talking over the day's racing and playing with the rescued dog, now named Brock. He took him for long walks; it had taken him a long time to settle in, growling at certain people, especially Neil's dad, and barking at the slightest sound.

"Lucky we've got no neighbours" Lynne had said, but Neil knew that she liked the dog as much as the rest of them.

He exercised it around the farm once or twice a day, and he had started taking an interest in the daily activities and was even beginning to learn the names of some of the mares and even helped out on occasions. Steve had told his dad Eric that he was showing a natural affinity with the horses, a fact which pleased him, but he said nothing to his son.

On one of his daily walks, he bumped into what he could only describe as energetic whirlwinds, Tilly and Dilly Milligan, vivacious tomboys from the neighbouring farm known as Shiloh Farm, which had a large acreage of arable and pigs. The girls were flying around the countryside on horseback without a care in the world; they came round a corner and skidded to a halt in front of Neil and instantly started firing questions at him at the same time.

"You're Neil, aren't you? Do you ride?"

Neil, who wasn't very good at the art of conversation, informed them that, of course, he rode but failed to add that he meant a bike.

"OK then," they excitedly said, "meet us by the ford on horseback tomorrow morning at 10 o'clock".

And before Neil could fashion an answer, they had galloped off in a cloud of dust, like the baddies in an old-fashioned cowboy film. Neil walked back, thinking to himself that there were plenty of horses on the stud; surely it wouldn't matter if he borrowed one? These turned out to be famous last words. The next morning when his dad was out at the sales and Steve was delivering a mare back to its owner, Neil wandered into the stables and got one of the Polish grooms to saddle up a horse for him; the groom muttered something in a foreign tongue which he didn't understand so duly ignored. He'd already snuck into his sister's bedroom and was now kitted out in a pair of very tight, very white jodhpurs so that he was walking in a slightly strange fashion and speaking in a squeaky voice, well, more squeaky than usual. The horse that had been saddled up for him seemed a little surprised when he put his foot in a stirrup and swung himself into the saddle; she jogged rather than walked and tossed her head around, but even so, Neil was enjoying the experience, and surprisingly looked the part, and apart from when he jumped on his sister's old pony about ten years ago, this was his first time on horseback. They jogged past the old Stud manager's cottage, which was being done up as a holiday cottage, but work had come to a halt after recent storms had caused flood damage. He arrived at the ford, the designated meeting place, the twins were already there waiting, and he could hear their voices from some distance off. He was expecting a warm welcome, but when he got there, they gasped in horror.

"What are you doing riding Blue Moon?"

"Why shouldn't I," he rather crossly replied.

"Because she's the studs foundation mare, the one that gave birth to the Derby winner, and she's in foal to no less than Frankel, what on earth are you doing? Your dad will kill you, take her back before anyone notices, and if you're lucky, you may get away with it!"

Finally, they relieved the tension that was building up in Neil by saying, "And you look ridiculous in those tight girly jodhpurs!"

Neil was beginning to realise the magnitude of the situation, so saying nothing in reply, he jumped off Blue Moon and slowly walked her back, but by now, she was going a little short and slightly limping on the stony track. He put her back in the stable, brushed her down, hoping that he'd got away with it, and went off looking for the Polish groom to ask him why he'd let him take this horse out but couldn't find him.

The next day he kept himself to himself but overheard a discussion between his dad and Steve, suggesting that Blue Moon had a bit of heat in a front leg.

"How on earth did she get that?" he heard his dad asking in an annoyed tone.

Thankfully it led to nothing, and in a few days, Blue Moon was fine. Neil presumed that he'd got away with it, but the next time he went to Steve's cottage, he was taken to one side and asked by Steve, "Have you got anything to tell me?"

"No, I don't think so," he nervously replied.

"Last chance or I'm off to your dad," was fired back at him.

Neil then told him everything, saying how sorry he was, but he hadn't known what he was doing.

"Well, if you'd taken more interest in the stud, you'd have known the damage you could have done, she could have lost her foal, and the stud could have lost its reputation!"

"I know now," Neil said, "I won't do anything like it again".

Steve calmed down and said, "Well, we can all make a mistake; just don't make the same mistake AGAIN!" As an afterthought, he said, "If you want to go riding, I suggest that you get yourself a horse".

Getting a horse sounded a good idea, but with very little money to his name, he wasn't sure how to go about it. When he went back to the farm, his sister was there showing off her latest boyfriend. She seemed to change boyfriends' as much as some people change their underwear, he thought to himself. Instead of sloping off to his room with a good book, as he usually did, he stayed and listened to the conversation. It was as normal about horses, about the recent scare Blue Moon had; he knew if they'd all looked at him, he'd have gone bright red.

In a brief break in the conversation, he announced that he wanted to start riding; his dad was dismissive as usual and said, "What's brought this on? You haven't shown any interest in sixteen years?"

His mum looked pleased and said, "Eric can't you buy him a horse? After all, we spent a lot on Cynthia with ponies and riding lessons."

Eric looked disinterested and didn't answer, but Neil noticed that his sister looked as if an idea was forming in her mind.

The next week passed by with little of interest happening, but then one morning, he woke up to hear a horsebox drawing up below his bedroom window, not unusual on a stud farm, but something seemed different.

He was just musing over why when his mum called him, "Neil, come down, your sister has come to see you".

Neil did as he was bid and, with an air of curiosity, walked outside to be met with his sister leading her horse around.

Seeing Neil, she said, "The girl that was loaning him has bought her own horse so doesn't want him any longer, so if you like, you can borrow him, as long as you promise to look after him properly, every single day of the week twenty-four seven".

Neil was overjoyed, though somewhat surprised at her generosity, as it was unexpected.

Cynthia said, "Golden Simba, meet Neil, I'll be watching closely, and he'll be moving on swiftly if you don't look after him".

Neil was beaming now, thanked her profusely and started planning many adventures on horseback. Firstly, he needed some proper riding clobber, so the next time his mum went shopping, he tagged along and headed for the equestrian shop in town. It was a very old-fashioned shop, smelling of soap and leather and run by an old lady who actually looked a bit like a horse; she insisted on helping Neil try on various pairs of jodhpurs, and whilst pulling them round to see if they fitted properly, pinched his skin time and time again, he wasn't sure if she did it on purpose, but it hurt and after trying on four pairs he was getting fed up, he didn't like shopping at the best of times, he decided that he'd take the next pair whatever they fitted like, as was past caring and said to himself that even if the next ones were pink, they'd have to do. Luckily the next pair, in a manly shade of brown, fitted perfectly, and with a proper skull cap purchased, he was at long last ready for action.

CHAPTER SIX

Bridge Over Troubled Water

Showing a rare case of sensibility and perhaps growing maturity, Neil rode Simba around the paddock for the first few days so that he could get used to the horse and vice versa. His dad, whilst passing by, commented that he actually looked surprisingly good on a horse and was getting on well but added that he should have started years and years ago. After a week, he arranged to meet up with the twins Tilly and Dilly and go for a hack around the local countryside. They met at the same place as last time, but this time all went smoothly, and over the following weeks, their friendship grew, and there was a constant babble of talk, mainly nonsense, but just occasionally, something sensible and profound emerged. One day they had just slowed down after a spirited canter, and the banter and jokes ceased as the twins started questioning him.

"Why did it take you so long to find horses? We've been riding since we were three!"

"I don't know," he replied, "I suppose that it was just taken for granted that I would ride, so I suppose that I rebelled. I think that my dad thought that I'd go away and learn another trade and then come back and take over the stud with new and updated ideas".

"Well," they both said, "you've certainly got a talent for horses, and we both think that if you want, you could make a career in it, as you're a natural," and then added with a grin, "you're just a little rough around the edges, but a born horseman".

Rare praise indeed, and this got Neil thinking about what he might actually do with his life.

The twins, who were both very clever, said that they would have liked to have had the opportunity of taking over the family farm but that this was not possible as their brother Jim had already been lined up for this role in a few years. They were both planning on going to university to learn medicine but were unsure where this would take them.

They all agreed that was enough of the serious discussion and were soon back to light-hearted mickey take and leg pulling, with Neil coming off worst as usual.

At the end of the ride, the twins said that they were off to a show at the weekend and that if he wanted, he could tag along. It was a gymkhana with many different events, and it would be lots of fun, and it was just possible that he might just win something. Neil agreed and started looking forward to what would be his first equestrian competitive event. He now felt quite guilty that he'd never been to the shows with his sister Cynthia, though at the time, he'd been many miles away watching cricket in Yorkshire instead.

Their last ride before the gymkhana could have ended in disaster and was Neil's first flirtation with danger in what had otherwise been a very sheltered existence.

The skies had been black and thunderous for the last week or so, with incessant rain falling, and the land was completely soaked through, with the falling water having nowhere else to go apart from the already swollen rivers. Neil sat inside miserably, looking out at the thunderous skies, he wasn't really a fair-weather rider, but even his enthusiasm had waned in these appalling conditions, he'd ridden indoors going round and round a barn, but both himself and the horse soon got very bored with that. So when he awoke one day, and the sun was fighting to get out amongst the clouds, he swiftly arranged a hack with the twins. They met up, as usual, all wearing raincoats just in case the weather reverted to the recent norm. The bridleways were very wet and interspersed with large puddles and deep mud in places but passable with care. Nearing home, they approached by the usual route by the ford in the stream below the old stud manager's cottage; however, as they reached it, they were faced with a roaring foaming surge of water, flowing faster than they'd ever seen it before. In summer, it almost dries up and just trickles silently and peacefully, but now they are faced with a raging torrent. Luckily there was a little footbridge at the side, and the twins decided to pass via this, it was narrow and with a few dodgy wooden panels, and Neil's horse was having none of it; the twins got impatient waiting as Neil, and his prancing snorting horse remained at the other side. Neil shouted to them that he was coming through the water and started wading in, his horse seemed happy with this, and it wasn't as deep as he'd expected, a couple of feet and up to his horse's belly. Simba strode purposely through splashing as he went; Neil could feel him struggling against the current, as they reached the deepest point, with his stirrups touching the dark water when suddenly disaster struck, a large log came floating down in front of them and got lodged against the bridge blocking their way. Whilst Neil was thinking about what to do next and planning on turning back, Simba took matters into his own hands or hooves and, with an almighty leap, launched himself at the log. Neil was taken by surprise and only just managed to stay in the saddle; as the log was cleared, Simba got his back legs entangled with it, and down he came with an almighty splash, and they both went under, the cold hit Neil immediately, and everything went dark and surprisingly quiet, as he landed on the stony bottom of the stream, Simba was thrashing about above him trying to regain his footing, and Neil took a few glancing blows, then suddenly the horse was gone, and all was quiet, and Neil was able to surface gasping for air.

"Oh, there you are," the twins chimed.

Where did they expect me to be, Neil thought. By now, his horse had vanished, as Neil staggered to dry land looking like the creature from the black lagoon, with blood on his face and bruising, where flailing hooves had caught him and ripped in his riding jacket. He was shivering uncontrollably and pleaded to be allowed to ride behind one of them on one of their horses, but all to no avail.

"Nah, you'll make us all wet, and anyway, you'll be better off walking, as it'll warm you up."

So Neil trudged disconcertedly behind them, and as they peeled off to go to their farm, he parted with a limp wave. Luckily when he got back, Simba was waiting, appearing none the worse for his ordeal. So Neil dried him down thoroughly and put him back in his stable, and fed him before returning to the house still frozen to the core. He told his mum and dad what had happened and as expected, was met with little sympathy.

"You've ruined your new riding mac," his mum said, and his dad just said, "were you fooling about again acting the class clown, trying to impress the girls?"

Neil shook his head and walked away whilst his dad was still talking.

"I hope that you've dried that horse off properly. Otherwise, your sister will kill you if anything happens to him!"

Neil had heard enough. If this had happened to Cynthia, they would have been fussing all over her; feeling sorry for himself, he ran a hot bath and sank into the calming and steaming waters feeling a little unloved. I could have drowned, he said to himself, and acting the fool indeed, definitely not!

All was soon forgotten, though, and it gave the twins more ammunition to make fun of him. In fact, when arranging the next ride, their text included an Emoji of a little figure wearing armbands and a snorkel. All too soon, the day of his first gymkhana was fast approaching and excitement, and a bit of tension was mounting.

CHAPTER SEVEN

Born to Lose

Neil wasn't exactly good at getting up early but was improving. Even his dad, who wasn't known for dishing out compliments, especially in Neil's direction, had been overheard saying that he was impressed with the change for the better in his son. Neil had set his alarm for 6:30 am and sprang out of bed, like a gazelle with a lion in hot pursuit; he peeled back the curtains and was pleased to see that it was a bright fine sunny morning and that the recent wild stormy weather had abated.

He was first down to breakfast which was definitely unusual; when his dad appeared, he did a double take and said, "Ann, come quick, there's an intruder in our kitchen," then laughed smugly to himself at his own joke.

Neil smiled through gritted teeth but didn't reply as he wasn't going to let anything spoil his big day.

After breakfast, he groomed Simba, who'd been fed earlier by one of the Polish grooms. He got his shining tack ready, which he'd diligently cleaned the night before so that he was ready and waiting for the Milligan horsebox before it arrived. The show was about ten miles away, so they'd decided that it would be better to be driven there; otherwise, riding there and back would have made it a very long and tiring day for horse and rider. The journey there was uneventful. The twins' mother, Barbara, did most of the talking, as the twins were unusually quiet. Perhaps, Neil thought, nerves were affecting them as well. Barbara asked Neil what he wanted to do with his life, and he heard himself saying that he thought that he'd like to have a career with horses. Where did that come from, he wondered to himself.

"In what equestrian discipline?" she asked.

Neil was stumped as he hadn't gotten that far working out exactly what he wanted to do, so he glibly just said, "I think that I'd like to be a polo player".

The twins just stared at him, and Neil was thankful that the questions stopped as soon as they arrived at their destination.

There was a hive of activity when they got to the showground, with people on foot and horseback dashing all over the place. The earlier classes for the younger age groups had already started, so after the horses were unloaded and tied up at the side of the box, Neil went on his own to watch events and see if he could learn anything, he was surprised at how competitive it all was, and the fast speed that the little ponies achieved and how they could turn on a sixpence, and it shook his confidence somewhat. He then went with the twins to enter, and signed up for the Sack race, Apple Bobbing and Bending and Clear round class. He was hoping for at least one rosette. He remembered how his sister used to be very proud of the rosettes that she'd won, even if they were mainly just for minor places and rarely the red winning ones. He'd been very dismissive and shown little interest, which he was now feeling guilty about. Perhaps, he thought, I've been a poor brother, and he wondered if it was too late to make amends.

There was, however, no time for introspective thoughts, as his first class was fast approaching, and before he knew what was happening, he was riding into the ring with butterflies in his stomach and a feeling that he needed to go to the loo. It all started badly, as in the Sack race, Simba stood on the sack, and Neil came to a sudden halt and fell over, and by the time he'd righted himself and was back on his feet, the winner was being announced. The Apple bobbing was next, and this he thought would be his best race, as he had no fears about dipping his head in a bucket of cold water and retrieving the apple. In the race itself, all was going to plan, he quickly got the apple between his teeth, but when he cleared his eyes of water and looked round, Simba had run off; if only I'd kept hold of him, he thought.

The twins by now had a clutch of rosettes and kept waving them in front of his face, saying,

"Your sister used to win on Simba; do you think that she was a better rider than you?"

This made him more determined when the time came for the Bending race, and he did well; the first six all finished very close, and he was confident that he'd finished fifth, and luckily rosettes went down to fifth place. He felt quite proud to be collecting his first ever prize, but as he went to receive it, they had all gone. Tilly, who'd actually finished sixth, had grabbed fifth. She claimed that it was rightfully hers.

Neil was a little hurt and confused and said, "But I finished ahead of you".

"It was close," she replied, "but you'll have to be quicker in future".

She giggled and rode off, leaving Neil a little miffed and confused. I'd never do that to them. I'll never understand girls, he thought, but I suppose that it might be fun trying to!

His final class was the clear round, and the course looked easy, the jumps low and inviting. It's up to me now, he thought. I'm competing against myself and no one else. Simba jumped beautifully, clearing every jump with ease, and he left the ring on a high. The only problem was that he'd jumped the wrong course, so no rosette again and disqualification.

It seemed like a long journey home after the day he'd had. The twins didn't help, giggling and pointing fun at him. It may have been good honest fun, but it started to get to him.

In exasperation, he said, "I'm a born loser. I'll never make anything of myself".

"Don't be silly," Barbara said, "it took the twins about half a show season before they started winning!"

The twins stopped picking on him and echoed their mum's sentiment. Neil felt a little better and cheered up, and all talk was about next weekend's show. He was determined to sharpen himself up and toughen up, never go home a loser again, and never let anyone, whoever they may be, get one over him or get the better of him!

Back home, his dad said, "So how many rosettes did you win?"

"Not many," Neil replied and hoped that the inquisition ended and luckily, it did.

CHAPTER EIGHT
The Winner Takes It All

From that day on, Neil didn't look back, and all his previous insecurities were forgotten. The very next weekend, the three of them rode to a nearer local show. They'd decided to move on from gymkhanas to the jumping classes, mainly as they'd realised that their horses couldn't compete with the youngsters on their quick and wick ponies. In their first jumping class, they were all placed, but the class was won by a wiry youth, similar in shape to Neil, but that was where the similarities ended, as he had a rough unkempt look about him, as did his horse, but Neil had to admit that they could both jump; The twins told Neil that he was called Frank Boyle and that he had a twin brother called Derek, who wasn't there for some reason.

"Probably helping the police with their enquiries," the twins said, "but they're OK when you get to know them, but don't cross them!"

Mixed messages, Neil thought, and he took an instant dislike to Frank and didn't really feel like getting to know him or his absent brother, not because he'd beaten him in the jumping, but because there was something about him he didn't like.

"He's a wrong un," he declared.

The twins said, "They seemed OK when we first met them, and we've got on OK so far, so have nothing against them, but we think that they could be trouble".

Neil was going to find this out himself before too long!

At the next show, both Boyles were there. All the twins would say was, "Steer clear of them".

Neil observed them from a distance; he could see them by their horsebox, an old wooden one with hardly any paint left on it; he could hear raised voices and could see an elderly man barking orders at them. Neil watched them practising but noticed immediately that Derek had entered his horse in the 14.2 hh (hands high) class and could see that the animal in question was far too big for that event.

He was watching with the twins and said, "That horse is too tall".

"Leave well alone," advised the twins, but Neil wasn't about to back down, "it's not fair to all the other competitors".

He went up to the lads and confronted them, "Don't you think that your horse is too tall for this class?"

"Mind your own business, shove off" came back the reply, and they rode off.

The girls advised him again to just leave it, but he was on a mission now and wouldn't or couldn't stop. He went straight to the judges and made a complaint. They were reluctant to do anything but eventually, with a degree of apathy, agreed to measure Derek's horse, and unsurprisingly it was nearly a hand higher than it should have been, so it got disqualified. So it ended up in the 15.2hh class, the same one as Neil, Tilly and Dilly.

The Boyles were furious with Neil's intervention, who innocently said, "Well, you'd been upset if you'd won and then been disqualified".

This didn't pacify them, and they both sneered and took Neil by surprise by grabbing him by his shirt collar and pushing him up against a nearby horsebox.

"We told you not to interfere."

They slapped him about a bit before punching him hard in the stomach, leaving him winded and slumped on the floor, and kicked him as they left, issuing the warning, "Don't mess in our business again, or else".

The twins found him bent double by the box, red in the face and looking flustered.

"What happened to you?"

"As if you don't know," he replied crossly, "I met those so-called friends of yours and came off second best".

"Well, you look OK and should be fit to ride," they said with little sympathy.

Luckily Neil was fit to ride and more determined than ever and actually managed to win the class, the girls were placed, and the Boyles uncharacteristically knocked a few fences down, and both of them finished mid-division, they stormed off, and the ill-tempered battle had started, and it lasted all season and beyond.

The Boyles were used to winning their fair share of jumping classes, but as the season progressed, they hardly won anything, with Neil cleaning up in virtually every class. At the next show in the Chase me Charlie class (higher and higher), it got near the finish with only three competitors left, Neil, Frank and Derek. The fence was getting very high, with no one giving way. Neil was flying over the obstacle with consummate ease whilst the Boyles were struggling. Derek had the fence down, and then it was down to two. They both cleared the next height; Neil was focused on the job in hand whilst Frank glared at him. Out of the corner of his eye, Neil saw the judges huddled together in a little group and then going to the announcer and whispering something. Funny, he thought, I wonder what is going on.

He soon found out as over the loudspeaker he heard the announcement, "First equal Neil Bartholomew and Frank Boyle".

Neil was furious and wasn't listening to their explanation. He wasn't quite sure what came over him as he rushed up to the fence judges and shouted, "Higher, put the jump up higher!"

But they just ignored him and looked on nonplussed. The judges called him over and explained that they'd stopped the competition on health and safety grounds, as the fence was getting very high, higher than had ever been jumped at the show before, so for the safety of both horse and rider, they'd called a draw. Neil wasn't pacified and stomped out of the arena, refusing to shake hands with the grinning Frank and throwing his rosette on the floor. The twins watched all his antics and were aghast. After picking up his rosette, they went after him and rounded on him.

"What are you doing acting like a spoilt brat? Who do you think you are, Harvey Smith?"

"Who," he replied crossly.

After some justified chastisement, he calmed down and, as requested, went and apologised to the judges and begrudgingly offered his hand to Frank, who just turned away, saying, "I'm not shaking hands with a sore and bad loser".

Neil had made an enemy out of the Boyles, not just for that day but probably for life.

When it came to leaving, the twins had already gone, leaving him to silently ride back on his own. Deep in his thoughts, he'd never had a rush of blood like that before he'd perhaps taken his own advice, of not letting anyone get the better of him, too far, and that the winning bug had taken hold of him, and he needed to take heed before it got him in more trouble.

He was soon back on talking terms with the twins, and after a few more days, they were back out riding around the countryside together with not a care in the world, and he was able to laugh at himself with the girls when his recent unsociable behaviour cropped up in the conversations.

At the next few shows, they all had plenty of success, especially Neil, who was becoming unbeatable, or as the twins put it, unbearable! His sister came to watch one show, and even she had to admit that he was good and was getting a lot more out of Simba than she ever did. The season was drawing to a close, and unsurprisingly they'd all qualified for the show jumping grand final, a class which Neil's mum Ann proudly informed him that she had won it twenty-five years ago

"Wow," said Neil, who was beginning to get a little bit cocky and self-assured, "was that in black and white?"

His mum just laughed and said, "Don't count your chickens, as you haven't won it yet!" and added cuttingly, "and you're not as funny as your dad".

As usual, the twins and Neil went together in their horsebox, and they arrived early so that they could walk the course and prepare themselves. As they strolled around, the twins exclaimed that they thought that the jumps were enormous, but Neil remained serenely calm and said that they were no problem and told them how he thought that they should tackle the difficult jumps. They'd seen the Boyles earlier, but they appeared to be keeping out of their sight, as they'd completely vanished. Frank was actually the defending champion, but since the arrival of Neil, his form had taken a dive for the worst, so a lot was riding on this class. When they went back to tack up, they led the horses out, and Neil stopped suddenly.

"He's lame; Simba's limping," he exclaimed.

The twins stopped what they were doing to come and inspect the sorry-looking horse. It was true; as Neil felt down his legs, he felt a swelling in one of his front legs.

"He wasn't like that this morning," he said sadly.

There was a broken piece of wooden pallet next to the horsebox, and as quick as a flash, Neil put two and two together, "I've been sabotaged, and I know who by".

The twins conceded that it looked suspicious but were quick to stop Neil from throwing unfounded suspicions around, so he left with having to withdraw from the class. On walking back discontentedly from the entries trailer, he passed the grinning Boyles.

"Buggers" he said to himself but didn't give them the satisfaction by showing them how angry and upset he was.

With Neil out of the reckoning, the Boyles were now favourites to win, and he heard Frank say, "The titles in the bag now".

However, Neil got the last laugh, as Tilly rode better than he'd ever seen her; she said afterwards that the pressure was off without Neil in the competition, to win the event, with her sister placed, and the Boyles both knocking a few fences down to finish unplaced. Neil was very pleased for the twins, didn't feel sorry for himself anymore, and was more concerned about his horse; Tilly was beaming as if she'd won the Horse of the Year show.

CHAPTER NINE

Schools Out

That was the end of the summer shows. Neil intended to go to some of the autumn indoor shows but had also agreed to do a bit of beating as the shooting season had started. Before this, the first day at sixth form college loomed largely. Neil had been cajoled into going to the local one by his dad, who had insisted that since he didn't want to go back to school to do his A levels, as it turned out, the school didn't really want him back after his poor O level results, then he'd have to do them somewhere else. Neil had finally agreed to give it a try but was lacking even a modicum of enthusiasm on the morning of his first day; he found it strange being dressed casually after the strict school uniform that he was used to. He'd enrolled in an English Literature A level course, which was at least something that he was interested in, and intended to enrol in a few more when he settled in. He didn't know anyone else that was going to the college as most of the local farmer's sons and daughters went to Agricultural colleges, of which there was a very famous one nearby, he'd once been there with his

53

family, for a charity event, and couldn't help but be impressed with the magnificent buildings, the facilities and the vast acreage surrounding it.

If he'd harboured intentions of going there, his dad soon extinguished them by saying, "All that they teach you here is how to drink gin and tonic and have a good time".

This increased Neil's interest, but sadly it was not to be, and where he was going couldn't be more different; in a suburb near the centre of town, Shakespeare Modern Sixth Form College was a grand title, but as soon as he arrived, he was sure that there was no way that it would live up to it. It was a modern building compared with the Agricultural College, built what looked like in great haste entirely out of concrete; Brutalism architecture he observed. He wasn't sure how he knew that and began wondering if he should perhaps be studying an architecture course instead. The building had a tired unloved look about it, where he presumed that having fun would be frowned upon; it instantly made him want to turn round and head home, back to the tranquillity of the stud farm. He could tell his dad that he couldn't find the place or that it had closed down, or it was full, but soon realised that these thoughts were unlike to get him anywhere, and he'd have to go ahead. He proceeded inside and expected a lot of noise, like at school, but all was quiet. He was directed to an office and resignedly filled in his enrolment form and was pointed in the direction of the lecture theatre by an elderly, rather overweight lady who looked as miserable as he felt. The large, tiered room was also quiet and relatively empty when he entered, and those who were there neither looked his way nor spoke or appeared remotely interested in his arrival, too busy studying their mobile phones. He guessed that the room would hold about 100 students and presumed that the course was undersubscribed, as there were only about fifteen there. He found somewhere to sit, not too near the front as he didn't want to appear too keen and waited and waited; the lecture should have started; ten minutes late, a scruffy man appeared, in his late sixties, with what looked like a CND badge pinned to one lapel on his jacket. He announced in a monotone voice that he was Dudley Cook, their lecturer.

"Bad luck, students" he said without a hint of irony.

Straight away, Neil took an instant dislike to him but didn't really know why. Dudley announced that he'd been lecturing for 30 years and mainly at this college and was ready for retirement as he was tired of lecturing and fed up with teaching. He told the disinterested students that all they had to do if they wanted to pass the course was turn up to every lecture, and he'd give them all a pass at the end of the year. They were then all asked to announce themselves with a brief description; most of the students appeared as bored as Dudley and muttered monosyllabic replies, hardly audible. Neil was surprised when a pale, thin sullen girl announced that she was Jan Cook, Dudley's daughter; nothing to be proud of, Neil thought.

When Neil spoke of his private school education and his home life on a stud farm, he was almost certain that he saw Dudley sneering, "Shouldn't you be at that posh college down the road?" he enquired in a derogatory tone, and after that, it gradually got worse.

It soon became apparent that Dudley was very fond of far-left politics and enjoyed talking about it at the expense of actually teaching the students anything worthwhile. Neil didn't really have any political leanings one way or the other but was finding what was like a Labour Party political broadcast tiresome.

He put his hand up and asked, "When are we starting English literature?"

"All in good time" came back the reply, but Dudley carried on as before. The rest of the class had put on headphones and were listening to music, well, the ones that weren't playing on their mobile phones.

Neil tried again, "I thought that this was English Lit, not boring politics," but he was wasting his time, Dudley was of the old school and had been lecturing for so long that he could do it in his sleep, and he almost did.

There had been a time, many years ago, when the students had listened intently to his tales of protesting, CND marches, Ban the Bomb and such things. His claim to fame was he once marched with a well-known duffle-coated party leader, but no one was interested any longer. At break time, Neil intended to speak to the other students to see what they thought, but most had wandered off for a smoke, of goodness knows what Neil thought. After the break, Dudley was getting into his rhythm and carried on as before.

An exasperated Neil shouted, "If I'd wanted to listen to the looney left, I'd have joined the Labour party!"

"They wouldn't have you!" came back the reply. It was getting a bit heated now, and even the other students perked up and listened.

"I'm going to make this year hell for you" continued Dudley with the conviction of someone who meant it.

"You're not!" Neil shouted back, "As I'm leaving, never to return," and grabbed his bag and strode out.

Dudley looked most unconcerned, and as he left, he heard him saying something about Greenham Common. Neil strode off towards the office but was stopped in his tracks as a hand roughly grabbed his shirt collar. He turned sharply to see Dudley's daughter Jan standing there in a threatening pose.

"Don't cause trouble for my dad," she said, "or else".

Or else what, Neil thought, but carried on towards the office and reached it without any other interruptions. Neil knocked on the door and was admitted and stated his grievances, but not unsurprisingly. He was met with indifference, "What do you expect? This isn't Oxford University".

Neil was getting exasperated, "I came to learn English Literature, not the history of the Labour party!"

This was met with stony silence, so Neil realised that he was beaten and couldn't carry on here.

"Are those the enrolment papers?" he said, pointing to a pile on the desk.

"Yes." He quickly rifled through them until he found his, ripped them up into many little pieces, screwed them up into a ball and lobbed it into a bin and left, never ever to return. He decided there and then that he wasn't cut out for further education and vowed not to try again, but he worried that his dad might not agree with his decision.

CHAPTER TEN

Country Boy

Surprisingly when he told his dad about the happenings at the local college and how he was never going back, he didn't disagree, and his mum just said, "I didn't think that place would suit you".

Now she tells me Neil thought. Unexpectedly the subject was dropped, which pleased Neil, though he was ever so slightly worried about his future. His dad suggested that he do what he'd done as a young man and go and get paid work experience at the same stud that he'd gone to. Neil stopped himself from making silly comments about how he thought that his dad had never been a young man. The one setback, or perhaps it wasn't, was the fact that the stud was on the other side of the world in Australia.

In the meantime, the shooting season was about to start. In the past, the gamekeeper Pete Wisdom, who was also a big follower of horse racing and spent a lot of his spare time at the races, used to call around at the house, talk shoot and race politics with Neil's dad and also scout for beaters. Neil was usually elsewhere lost in thought or deeply engrossed in a book or at his aunts in Yorkshire. He remembered that his sister Cynthia used to go and presumed that she'd enjoyed it, but as usual, he'd not asked her or shown any interest, thinking that trampling around in a muddy wet wood wouldn't be much fun. This year was going to be different as he was signed up for a few days, and he was really looking forward to it. His first day started wet and misty, but by the time he set off to meet the twins, the sun had appeared as if by magic, and he was hopeful that he was going to have an enjoyable time. He'd asked Steve previously if he could take Brock, as there was no way his dad would let him take his precious Labradors.

When asked, his dad said, "You'll ruin them; they're for picking up, not beating!"

How on earth was I going to ruin them, Neil thought, but he knew better than to argue with his dad. He told him that he was taking Brock, and he just sighed and shook his head, Neil, as usual, was hoping to prove him wrong, and on the first day, he did. There were about sixteen beaters consisting of local farmer's sons and daughters, gamekeepers — active and semi-retired, and some who were of the same clique; and also, some bored housewives with time to kill. On the first drive, Neil didn't really have a clue as to what he was meant to be doing, so he just copied the twins on either side of him and winged it.

He had Brock on a tatty baler band lead. "Can't you afford a proper lead?" the twins asked.

"No," shouted Neil, "I'm self-unemployed".

His private joke, but as usual, no one laughed. Brock seemed a little uncertain and nervous, not of the bangs but the shadows in the woods. The morning was uneventful and, as far as Neil could tell, had gone to plan. The beaters all sat down together for their sandwiches and supped mugs of tea brewed on a rusty old stove. The keepers, with their entourage listening to every word attentively, spoke of the morning, discussing such things as how the birds had flown, which drives they should do next, which Guns were shooting well, and laughing about those that weren't. The farmers were the quieter group, not easily stirred into any sign of emotion or enunciation, talking of straw prices and recent tractor theft and all things agricultural. The most interesting group, as far as Neil was concerned, was the housewives. They had all turned up in their shiny SUVs (Sports Utility Vehicles), which rarely saw any mud, expensively turned out in designer country ware, putting the farmers to shame. In fact, they were better dressed than some of the Guns. They had crazy uncontrollable dogs with fashionable names, mainly spaniels but a few Labradors; Neil had noticed that whatever misdemeanour their dogs performed, the keeper said nothing, but if someone else's dog did something wrong, they were instantly chastised.

Neil was slightly surprised to find that all the different factions got on well together, there might be some blue language and ribald humour, but they all mingled well together. He presumed that this was due to a shared love of the countryside; he couldn't really believe what his dad had told him that morning, that this way of life was threatened and could disappear before the next generation was old enough to partake.

They did another couple of drives in the afternoon, and again all went well, and collectively the Guns, beaters and gamekeepers all went home deeply satisfied and contented and perhaps a little tired, and Neil had earned his first wage packet, not a lot but as Steve said when he returned Brock, "It's better than a kick up the backside".

The next day was altogether different. Neil had been shamed by the twins over his baler band dog lead, so he had asked his dad if he could borrow one. His dad had flung him an old and worn one, and his parting remark was, "You could have bought one".

Neil replied incredulously, "What, go to a shop and spend money?" and left quickly before his dad could reply.

This was an important day as they were using the woods around the stud, and Neil's dad was shooting, which had made the keeper stressed and bad-tempered and jittery; Steve, the stud manager, never liked these days as all the mares and youngstock had to be brought in, as they couldn't risk the consequence of gunshot causing valuable equines to panic and bolt. It was another fine day and started similarly, the only difference being in the attitude of Neil's dog Brock, who'd appeared to have gained in confidence, pulling at his lead and barking.

"Shut that dog up!" shouted Pete on numerous occasions, but all to no avail as for whatever reason, Brock just got more and more excitable, especially when they got near a flushing point (where all the birds congregated).

Neil couldn't really see the problem as the barking was sending the birds in the right direction; well, sort of, though he had to concede that the constant noise was a little annoying. At lunchtime, the twins pulled his leg continuously.

"Can't you control that dog?"

"Shouldn't you get a muzzle for it?" Neil tried to point out that their dogs weren't much better behaved, but to no avail; as usual, they had the upper hand.

The final drive of the day was the wood above the Stud, where Neil had found Brock. They lined up and started waving their flags and attempting to drive the birds in the direction of the Guns. As they got near, there were a lot of birds flocking together in front of the beaters, and it all got too much for Brock, straining on his lead and barking uncontrollably.

Neil struggled to control him when suddenly the lead snapped, "Come back, Brock!" he shouted in vain, but Brock had gone, and birds were flying everywhere, but not necessarily in the right direction. When the Guns came into sight, Neil realised with a sense of foreboding that he was beating towards his dad, who was waving his gun around manically and with no success whatsoever. Brock reached his peg (where the Guns stand) and barked at his Labradors, Little and Large, and caused general mayhem and consternation. Neil quickly borrowed a lead and attached it to Brock's collar, but the damage was done; his dad had gone a strange purple colour and was issuing obscenities at anyone who dared to go near.

When he realised that Neil was to blame, he shouted, "Don't bring that useless mutt again".

His fellow Guns were laughing as their shooting hadn't been affected by the disturbance, and they'd had plenty of shots. Pete took Neil to one side and sternly said, "Don't let that happen again; otherwise, you won't be able to come anymore!" and he added with a smirk, "And your dad won't tip me as well as usual," before adding, "and he never tips that much".

Neil started walking back with the twins, who'd witnessed the whole sorry affair and were in a fit of giggles. When they'd finally stopped laughing, and Neil could get a word in, he asked them, "Who's the little lad who sat quietly in the corner at lunchtime, don't think I've seen him around before?"

"Oh, that's Tom Cooper junior," they replied.

"Why junior?"

"Because his dad's Tom Cooper senior, stupid."

Neil hadn't thought it was a silly question but let it rest and let them continue.

"Tom wants to be a jockey, and his dad is a trainer, who trains at Sunrise Farm, you know the place, just before you get to the Agricultural College".

Neil wasn't sure if he knew it or not but nodded anyway.

"We're off there this weekend," they continued, "to ride out the racehorses. Why don't you come along?"

Neil thought about this and warmed to the suggestion, thinking it was a good idea.

"Sounds great," he said.

The girls said they'd ask if he could go as well, and later that night, he got a text saying that it was all arranged, and he could go as Tom Cooper was short-staffed and he's heard what a good rider you are. Neil went home thinking that in a few days, he was going to sit on a racehorse for the very first time.

CHAPTER ELEVEN

House of the Rising Sun

Neil kept out of his dad's way for a day or so, as his mum had told him that she'd never seen his dad so angry, but when he thought it was safe to do so, he let it be known that he was going riding out at Tom Cooper's that weekend, his dad showed a lot of interest, and it appeared that the shooting debacle had been forgotten.

"Perhaps we'll make something of you yet, lad?" he said with a chuckle. He then went on to give Neil a highly detailed account of the recent history of the Cooper family.

Tom Cooper, senior, apparently had started life as a farmer, taking over from his dad, and became well known for breeding pedigree Charollais cattle, winning prizes at many of the local shows and even some of the bigger ones further afield. He'd always dabbled in horses and started training a few Point to Pointers that his wife usually rode. She was also an accomplished three-day event rider. The training Point to Pointers escalated until he took the big step of taking out a trainer's licence for both flat and jump horses. Then tragedy hit the family when his wife was killed in a car accident whilst taking the children to school; miraculously, the children survived the incident with hardly any physical scars, though what mental torment they had gone through, and probably still do, was unknown. The eldest lad, John, mainly ran the farm, though he helped out with the horses when needed and was a good little rider in his own right but preferred the slower pace and predictability of farm life. Tom junior had, unlike Neil, been riding horses since an early age and had ambitions of becoming a jockey, like many horse mad lads of his age. His dad, trying to keep him grounded, had hinted that few made it, but of course, this didn't deter him. Neil, on the other hand, had never thought about being a jockey, but now that riding thoroughbred racehorses was on the agenda, he was warming to the idea. The team was made up by neighbouring farmer's daughter Tracy Palin, who as well as acting as a housekeeper, cooking and cleaning, and doing the stables secretarial work, also rode out as well and could lend a hand to almost anything; in fact, she was indispensable. It was rumoured that she was keen on John, which Tom senior thought would be ideal as if they got together, they would have a full-time housekeeper and wouldn't have to pay her; wisely, he kept these thoughts to himself, and the fact that he missed a women's touch round the house, it hadn't been the same since his wife had died, not helped by the fact that none of the men was very good cooks and cleaning was something that other people did.

The day before he started at Sunrise farm, Neil accompanied his mum shopping in town, as he needed a back protector, or else he wouldn't be able to ride out at a licenced yard due to the strictness of health and safety rules nowadays. His mum told him how much safety had improved since her days. Her first hat, she told him, was so soft that you could bend it, and it offered little protection.

"Did you fall on your head a lot?" Neil cheekily enquired, "As that would explain a lot".

His mum ignored his attempt at humour, and they trudged into the equestrian shop. Neil remembered his last experience here when getting his legs badly pinched, whilst trying on jodhpurs, so he hung back, hoping to see a different sales assistant approach, but then he reassured himself that the same couldn't happen whilst trying on back protectors. However, the same smiling lady appeared with her long sharp-painted fingernails.

Instantly recognising them, she cheerily said, "Hello, how can I help you?"

"Back protector, please" Neil said.

His fears of pinched legs were soon assuaged, however, whilst checking the tightness of the back protector, she kept pinching his bottom, and he wasn't sure if it was accidental, as it happened with each fitting. However, he had to admit to himself that the experience wasn't too bad, in fact, quite enjoyable, but he kept this thought to himself.

On his first day, Neil set off to meet the twins and travel the short distance to Sunrise farm with a sense of anticipation and, surprisingly, without any nerves whatsoever. The weather was sunny again; in fact, some were saying that drought could be on the horizon. The Racing yard was down a very long winding track, in good condition, without any of the potholes usually found in the country and with manicured hedges on both sides and wooden posts and rail fences. The farm had a very impressive sign with both horses and cows featured, but with neither taking prominence, the stable yard was next to the impressive old farmhouse, and the farmyard was tucked behind, with a multitude of chickens darting between both yards, everything was immaculate giving the impression of a well-oiled machine. However, it wasn't today, as two members of the staff had recently been poached by a rival training establishment, so it was all hands on deck and one of the reasons why Neil's appearance was appreciated. The twins had told him that there were about twenty horses in training at present, the majority racing on the flat, a few jumpers, and one dual-purpose horse, and plenty of others, youngstock being broken, horses convalescing and a few old stars now enjoying a peaceful retirement.

The girls introduced Neil to Tom Cooper senior, who said that he'd heard that Neil was a good rider.

"Let's see if you can live up to your reputation, lad?"

He was given one of the older horses to ride, a grey horse who ran in staying races (long distance), named Grey Ambition, but apparently, his ambition, it appeared, had been not to win races, as he was regularly placed but rarely troubled the judge (rarely won). Neil found Grey Ambition a steady partner, the perfect horse for his first introduction into the heady world of horse racing. He did as he was bid and followed the others up to the gallops; they did a three-furlong stretch first at half speed, followed by a six-furlong uphill gallop at a little bit faster. Neil found it exhilarating and was pleased afterwards, over a quick cup of coffee in the untidy farmhouse, to hear that Tom senior had been happy with his performance, and it was arranged that they would all three come again on the following Monday, as Sunday was a rest day. The twins were their usual selves, laughing and poking fun at Neil.

"You've got the beginner's horse today, the seaside donkey; even our dad wouldn't fall off that!"

As the days turned into weeks and Neil began to not only outshine the twins but the wannabe jockey Tom junior, the jokes about his competence on horseback faded, though they still found plenty of other subjects to tease him on.

One of their favourites was his dress sense or lack of it, "Are you colour blind? Did you get dressed in the dark?"

He just laughed, as usual, thinking to himself that it was better to be noticed rather than ignored, and anyway, what was wrong with bright colours?

One day after the first string of horses had been out, Tom Senior took Neil to one side.

"Would you like a job here?" he said, "Stable lad to start with, but later on, I'm sure that we could get you a ride or two. We'd have to see how it goes".

Neil was amazed and really pleased that his hard work was about to be rewarded, so he accepted without a moment of thought. The twins, who were off to university soon but still intended to come home at the weekends and ride out, were genuinely pleased for him, though the teasing didn't stop.

"You'll have to watch your weight if you want to be a jockey," they joked.

Neil, who was only about eight stone soaking wet, couldn't imagine that weight would ever be a problem but smiled, nevertheless. It was agreed that Neil would be taken on for a trial period of a month to see how it went; he was warned that Tom junior was being primed to be the stables apprentice, so race riding opportunities would be few and far between, but Tom Senior promised that he'd try and get him a ride in an apprentice's race in a few months, and that was good enough for Neil.

He soon settled into the stable routine, though still not keen on the early morning starts, but at least now he had something to get out of bed for, and the riding more than made up for it. There was a great atmosphere in the yard, John Cooper was the complete opposite of his brother, a real outgoing character, and Tracy was an easy-going person, but as Neil said, she needed to be looking after the three Cooper men. It was great to see the twins when they turned up at the weekend, as they always brightened any situation; the only problem was Tom junior, a naturally quiet lad, but especially so when in Neil's company. He wondered if he should speak to him but decided to tackle his brother first.

John said, "Don't worry, as he doesn't say much anyway. He's been pretty quiet since the car crash, and none of us likes to talk about it".

Neil could understand that and decided to pursue the conversation no further, but John continued, "He's not a natural rider and has to work at it really hard, so I think that when someone like you with so much natural talent, with everything appearing to be so easy for you, well, to be honest, I think that he's jealous of you, I think that you've got more talent in your little finger than he has in his whole body, and he doesn't like it, would you?" he continued, "I think that he's petrified that you might take his coveted position as stable apprentice!"

Neil had never thought any of this and didn't know what to do about it, but just tried to be as friendly as possible with Tom junior, who he now realised thought of him not as a workmate but as a rival.

A few days later, whilst they were all tack cleaning, Tom senior walked in. Neil was cleaning a bridle but not doing a very good job, as he had froth and foam all over the place.

"You don't want to do it like that," he said, "do it like this," he demonstrated, using much less soap, "see, just like that," he said, handing the bridle back.

John and Sarah were giggling, but Tom junior remained quiet, but his demeanour was soon to change for the better, as Tom senior said, "I've picked a race for both of you at Lingfield, on the All Weather next Friday it's an apprentice handicap over a mile, you should both get in as there aren't many entries, are you both up for it?"

"Silly question," they said in unison, "of course we are".

For once, Tom junior was beaming and looked as happy as Neil felt. He could hardly believe that within a week, he would actually be a jockey.

CHAPTER TWELVE

Star Trekkin

For a change, it was raining on the morning of the race, and not just raining but raining hard, but as the race was on the all-weather track, the rain wouldn't make too much difference as the going was always standard. The two horses were loaded up into the horsebox, and Tom junior and senior, Neil and John and Tracy as grooms all climbed in, and they set off. The horse's Star Ship Enterprise and Captain Kirk, which happened to be full brothers, and both owned by the same owners, who had bred them and not unsurprisingly were Star Trek aficionados otherwise known as Trekkies. Tom senior spent most of the journey drilling into the lads that they should listen to all the instructions, especially about the course. There were thirteen runners in the race; an apprentice handicap, the hot favourite, was being ridden by Gilbert French-Saunders and owned by his father Oliver, who was a senior steward. He's an extremely well-bred horse, he'd told them, called Royal Appointment, that cost a lot of money at the sales and was expected to have been running in much better races than this one. Tom senior's instructions were to follow Gilbert during the race, as he's likely to be in the right place at the right time. When they arrived, Tom senior told them to meet him at the start at 12:30 pm, and then they would walk the track together; he and Tom junior, who looked as white as a sheet, went inside for a coffee whilst Neil decided to wander round the racecourse and get a feel for it, Passing the bookmakers he paid them little attention but chuckled to himself about a tale that Tom senior had told him of a Northern jockey who'd walked into the betting ring and placed a bet whilst still wearing his breeches and silks (colours), By the parade ring he bumped into the gamekeeper Pete Wisdom, who engaged him in deep conversation about his race and gave him a detailed analysis of all the horses and rival jockeys, he said much the same as Tom senior but in much greater detail, and eventually summed up by saying that in his estimation Neil had a great each-way chance with Tom junior and Gilbert French-Saunders mounts being the biggest dangers but added that he was backing Neil. As he made his escape, he looked at his watch, and the time 12:40 pm stared back at him, already 10 minutes late.

Knowing that Tom senior wouldn't wait, he rushed off to the start, but no one was there; they'd gone. No worries, he said to himself, I'll walk the course on my own, he could see Gilbert French-Saunders up ahead but decided against trying to catch him up as concentration would come easier without distractions, and concentration had never been one of his strong points. He planned to follow both Tom senior's and Pete's plan of action and follow the favourite and make his move near the finish to win cosily by a length; what could be easier? He got to the finish line, and there was still no sign of the Cooper family, and he noticed that there were two finishing posts.

Seeing a jockey there, he asked him, "Which finishing post do we use?"

"The first one," came back the reply, "the second one is for the sprint races".

"OK, thanks."

He looked at his watch again and realised that time had flown by, and the start of the race was getting close, and he really needed to be getting ready; He strode off to the jockey's changing room, where most of the jockeys were dressed and ready, he spotted Tom junior in a far corner and sat down next to him.

"Where have you been? Dad's not happy. Have you walked the course?"

This was more than Tom junior usually said to him in a full week.

"Yes, it's all done," Neil said, "did you listen to the steward's pre-race talk? I couldn't see you there?"

"Yes, I was at the back," Neil lied.

Tom junior was very talkative, and Neil realised that the old adage that quiet people become talkative and vice versa in times of stress was proving to be true.

All too quickly, it was time to go to the paddock and meet the owners and the trainer; the owners were brimming with excitement and anticipation.

"We've never had two runners in one race before," they said.

Neil was beginning to feel an added weight of expectation on his shoulders; the horse was proven, and the trainer had done all he could do, so it was down to him solely. Tom senior gave the final instructions. Good lucks were said, and suddenly Neil was on Starship Enterprise and off down to the start. He'd dreamt about this moment for a long time, and now it was happening.

"I'm a jockey," he said to himself and smiled.

There was no time for smugness, though; as they were about to line up, Tom senior's final piece of advice was at the forefront of his mind to keep away from the no-hopers, and there were quite a few of them. The flag went down, and they were off. Neil thought that it was just like an exercise gallop at home, apart from they were going a lot faster, and everything was happening a lot quicker.

Neil instinctively decided to disobey orders as, in his estimation, the front runners were setting too fast a pace, and wouldn't last to the finish, so he took a pull on the reins and settled in mid-division, and stayed there for the first half of the race, then very gradually and smoothly without upsetting the horse's rhythm, started to move forward passing one horse at a time until he had the leaders in his sights, Neil thought that they appeared to be tiring but couldn't be sure, Gilbert was about to take the lead with Tom junior poised just behind, from within the stands the owners were beginning to get excited, though like most weren't very good at reading a race. In the last furlong, Gilbert made his move and went for home with Tom junior chasing him, but flapping about in the saddle and unbalancing his horse, Neil, however, went past him with consummate ease and in his mind style and panache and went after Gilbert, who wasn't looking back and probably thought that he'd already got the race sown up, Neil had other ideas and drew level and gently eased about half a length in front just as the first winning post appeared, to win cosily, or so he thought! He couldn't understand why Gilbert and Tom junior surged past him as he was easing up and carried on to the second winning post and had an uncomfortable feeling in his stomach. All soon became clear, as first place was announced as number Three, which was Gilbert and Royal Appointment, with Tom junior second and Neil only third. He realised instantly that the second winning post was the correct one, and he cut a very dejected figure as he rode his horse back into the place reserved for third, where John met him and patted the horse and avoided his gaze until saying, "Dad's going to kill you!"

"More than likely," Neil replied, "you must have known it was the second winning post. Didn't you listen to the steward's talk?"

"I missed them but asked another jockey which winning post was being used, but it's ridiculous having two posts."

"The first post is for the sprint races; you're a fool!" With that, he took the horse away, and Neil was left to face the angry trainer.

Tom senior said gravely, "You should have won that race, and easily, luckily for you, the owners are just pleased to have two placed horses and probably haven't realised that you made an almighty cock up!"

Neil explained how he missed the steward's talk and asked another jockey which winning post was being used and had no reason not to believe him.

"Which jockey," enquired Tom senior.

"I don't know. He looked fairly old and had a weather-worn face and was wearing bright green silks and talked with a Scottish accent."

Tom senior shook his head, "I think I know who that will be; it'll be Angus Connolly. He's trouble. I wouldn't have him riding for me. You want to steer well clear of characters like that".

Neil said that he would, but little did he know how hard that was going to be in the coming months. Little was said on the journey home; though Tom junior kept scowling at him, it appeared that Tom senior had forgiven him when finally back at the stud, he cut a dejected and forlorn figure when he should have been in high spirits after what would have been his first win, he was determined to learn from his mistakes, when he next got a ride, but it would be a few more weeks before he got the chance to make amends.

CHAPTER THIRTEEN
Lady in Red

He had a little wait before his next chance. Neil had been surprised to see his sister Cynthia watching the gallops one morning and was even more surprised to find out that she had a share in a horse, a new recruit to the yard called Lady Calamity, recently purchased at the sales, where she had come from one of the bigger Newmarket yards, in fact, Henry Aske's stable, and he'd been a champion trainer for the last few years. She was a three-year-old filly, bred in the purple (well-bred), great things had been expected of her, and she'd been entered into a lot of the big races, but as often is the case, she didn't live up to the lofty expectations. She had a few races as a two-year-old but showed very little and not troubled the judge (she hadn't been placed). The larger stables often don't have the time needed to spend on problematic horses, so when next year's youngsters come in, they move some of the older ones out and send them to the sales. A change to a different yard often worked wonders, and that is what Tom senior was hoping for, Neil rode her on the gallops and reported that she was a cautious, nervous individual, but importantly, she had an engine and good paces.

"I think that she's lacking confidence," he told Tom senior, "she'll need handling with kid gloves".

Stable jockey Mark Williams, who'd ridden for the Tom Cooper senior for years and was a calm, dependable jockey, rode her in her first race for the yard, and she finished mid-division with Mark reporting that she was idling and wouldn't exert herself! Not very promising, Tom Senior thought. Next to ride her in her second race was Tom junior, who, as instructed, rode her very quietly and managed to make a bit of headway near the finish, but when he used his whip, she veered sharply away from it and lost her position and finished mid-division again.

Tom senior was getting a little disheartened now and wasn't sure what to do with her, so turned to Neil and said, "You're the horse whisperer. See what you can do with her".

Neil had never thought of himself as a horse whisperer but didn't argue and replied, "We just need to get her to relax and enjoy herself".

"That's easier said than done," Tom senior replied, "but I'll leave her in your capable hands".

By this stage, Tom junior had managed to win a race, and Neil was getting restless and really keen to break his duck and hoped that this horse represented a good chance of doing so. A comparatively easy race was found for her at Chelmsford Park over six furlongs and with only seven runners, of which none of them looked to be anything special. The bookmakers didn't share his enthusiasm, and he started at 20-1 in the betting. Neil met the exciting connections in the paddock, his sister he thought looked resplendent in a bright red coat.

Joking with her, he said, "How can a hard-up student afford a racehorse?"

"I've only got a small share," she replied, "she was a present from an ex-boyfriend. When we split up, I gave him his CDs back, but there was no way I was letting Lady Calamity go".

Neil hadn't realised just how enthusiastic she was, and with all the other syndicate members listening intently to everything said, not for the first time, he felt some pressure and pre-race nerves. Once the race started, as usual, these faded into the background as he gave the filly one hundred and ten per cent of his concentration. Straight away there was a problem, as he'd intended to slot into a mid-division position, and pounce late on when he hoped the leaders would be tiring, but there was no pace in the race as none of the other jockeys wanted to make it, so he made a split second decision and went to the front of the field where he reasoned that he could control the pace to suit his horse, hoping that the filly might enjoy herself out on her own unflustered by the other horses and not hemmed in, This turned out to be an inspired move, but perhaps more by luck than good judgement, as Lady Calamity relished the freedom and with Neil's urgings set a good pace striding out with purpose and gradually getting further and further ahead of the rest, until she'd slipped the field, with a furlong to go they were a good ten lengths clear and showing no signs of slowing down, Up in the higher echelons of the grandstand his sister and the other syndicate members were beginning to get very excited, and cheering their filly on, for most of them it was their first time in racehorse ownership, which made what appeared to be happening very special, Neil was oblivious to the cheering and general excitement and was just concentrating on winning the race. He'd watched many a race previously where a horse with an impressive lead ran out of energy near the line and was passed by the whole field, invariably finishing tailed off; he had no intention of letting that happen this time. He kept hold of the filly, hoping to keep a little in reserve for the final push to the line and risked a glance behind him and was pleased to see the rest of the field apparently toiling in his wake. His lead was now unassailable, and he galloped on to an impressive five-length victory, the distance diminishing near the line as the field vainly tried to close the gap. Neil's sister and the rest exploded in a communal feeling of joy and rushed down to welcome their horse back into the winner's enclosure, There was praise for the horse, trainer and lastly, the jockey, slapping him on the back and all talking together,

Tom senior had to leave to saddle a runner for the next race, but Neil swept along of the wave of enthusiasm, accepted the offer of a drink, as this was his only ride that day, Neil was beaming, he'd ridden his first winner, how could life get any better, when triumph turned into disaster as the announcer informed the listening crowd that number two had been disqualified and the second horse was pronounced the winner.

After frantically checking that he indeed was number two, all he could splutter out was, "There must be some mistake".

A moment later, all became clear as the announcer continued, "Number two Lady Calamity ridden by Neil Bartholomew is disqualified due to the jockey failing to weigh in".

The mood changed in a flash; Neil put his drink down, as his thirst had disappeared, and the owners looked aghast, as if not taking it in, some bookmakers had already paid out, and some were generously paying out on first past the post and the subsequently promoted horse. All Neil could think was how stupid he'd been; it was a schoolboy error and should have never happened. He'd thrown his first winner away and now his second one and was furious with himself, but this was nothing compared to the vitriolic abuse he received from his sister.

She tore into him, finishing with, "You'll never ride for us again. You're finished as a jockey!"

Even if she realised that her last few words were over the top, she showed no sign of retracting them. Neil was physically shaking when he trouped off to see Tom senior, whose other runner had run a stinker (run badly), which probably wouldn't improve his mood, Neil thought. On his way back to the weighing room, ironically, where he'd arranged to meet Tom senior, he bumped into Pete Wisdom.

"Great ride Neil."

"But I was disqualified."

"I know, but I got paid out, so I'm happy," he said, waving a wad of notes in front of Neil's face, with no sign of concern for Neil's plight. If only I could be happy, Neil thought.

Tom senior, in his usual calm manner, summed it up, "You rode a great race, using your initiative to set the pace, but I was worried when you got so far in front, but it worked out well, so we'll know how to ride her next time".

"With a different jockey," Neil miserably said, "I'll put Tom junior up, I expect".

Neil thought that he wasn't going to mention his mistake, but of course, he did.

"And let's hope that you never do anything as stupid as not weighing in again," before adding, "you've got a future as a jockey, probably more so than Tom junior, but if you don't get your act together very quickly then it just won't happen!"

CHAPTER FOURTEEN
The Bitterest Pill

It came as no surprise to Neil that the next race lined up for Lady Calamity came quite quickly before her handicap went up, and it was even less of a surprise that Tom junior was booked to ride her. Neil was expecting this, but it still hurt him deeply. She was going to be the yard's only runner on the day, and since John and Tracy had gone to market with some cattle, Neil was assigned to go to the races as a stable lad, which he thought was deliberate to make him think of what he'd done wrong, but he was determined to act with cheery good grace. The race was at Kempton this time, with only six runners. It was a similar race though not for apprentices, so it was open to all jockeys, which would make it a little harder to win.

Neil got her ready with Tom senior, with neither saying much though Neil made the comment, "Small field, so there shouldn't be any traffic problems". But only received a grunt in reply; he was pleased when it was time to lead her round the paddock, as out there he would be relatively speaking, on his own and left to his own thoughts; it should be me riding her, he said to himself.

She was shorter in the betting this time, generally around 12-1, so not really fancied, which surprised Neil after her last performance. Perhaps the last race was viewed as a fluke, he thought, but he realised that it wouldn't be quite as easy as the other jockeys wouldn't allow her to get such a soft lead. When the jockeys appeared, Neil got the shock of his life, as it wasn't Tom junior but Gilbert French-Saunders. Neil had never really spoken to him before and had built up a pre-conception of him being a spoilt little rich boy, only riding for something to do and probably not interested in speaking to a mere stable lad. He couldn't have been more wrong, as Gilbert turned out to be an engaging, friendly character with a strong will to go as far as he could in the sport. After explaining why, it was him riding as Tom junior had been taken sick.

"Probably a dodgy takeaway," he said.

Neil thought that this was unlikely and suspected an attack of nerves but held his counsel.

Gilbert went on to ask a lot of questions, "How do you advise that I ride her?"

Neil explained what had happened in her last race and was pleased when Gilbert said that he'd seen it and offered his commiserations for Neil not weighing in.

"It could happen to anyone," he kindly said.

Neil was really warming to him and thought that he could become a great ally in the jockey's ranks, that was, of course, if he ever got another ride. Neil explained that she had been lacking confidence, and making the pace seemed to suit her, so if he could keep her out of trouble and away from the other runners, then she could run a big race. In the paddocks, the owners, especially Cynthia, ignored him as they wished Gilbert good luck, and he then took her on to the course and let her go, and it was down to the jockey now. Neil could take no more part in the outcome and settled down nervously to watch the race on his own away from the other stable lads and lasses. The runners shot out of the stalls together and settled down to an even pace; Lady Calamity was fighting for her head and fly jumping, using energy that she would need later, let her stride on, Neil thought, but Gilbert didn't, tucking her in, behind the front three even though the pace hadn't quickened, This won't suit her Neil thought, "Let her go" he shouted to no one in particular, but there was nothing he could do but watch in agonised silence, two furlongs from the finish two runners set off together and Neil thought that Gilbert would go with them, but he didn't, and he was soon five length's adrift, in the final furlong the penny dropped and he set off in pursuit of the leaders and started to make ground, but too late or so Neil thought, it was looking like they would finish third, but the leaders who were having a good tussle at the front started to tire slightly and unbelievably Lady Calamity got up in the dying strides to win by a nose. Poor ride, good result, Neil muttered as he went to collect the horse and the jubilant jockey.

The owners were overjoyed, especially Cynthia, who pointedly said, "Now we've got a proper jockey; hope that you can ride her next time?" in a loud voice, which Neil knew was meant for his benefit, but he just treated it with the disdain it deserved.

Gilbert was pleased and told Neil that this had been only his third winner and gave him hope that he might yet make it as a jockey; he knew that some thought of him as a posh boy taking rides off proper jockeys, but he was determined to make it and was aiming to do well next season, his granddad had been runner up in the Champion Apprentice title, and he hoped to go one better.

"Good luck with that," Neil said, "I'll be lucky to get another ride, let alone become Champion Apprentice!"

On the way home with Tom senior, the race was discussed. Tom said that he was very pleased with the jockey and that the owners wanted to book him again.

"Well, he was lucky to win from that position," Neil said.

"Don't be a sore loser; a win is a win," came back the reply, and all that Tom junior, who was looking a lot better, could say rather unhelpfully was, "Well, at least he weighed in!"

Neil knew that he could have ridden the horse better and could have been on two winners by now, and looking forward to many more rides, if only he had weighed in! He also knew that time was running out to make his breakthrough as a jockey, and if it didn't happen soon, then it probably never would. For once, his dad was correct, he thought, that you must take your chances when you get them as they may not come round again.

CHAPTER FIFTEEN

Doin' It Right

Everything went quiet for Neil for a few weeks. The yard trained a few winners, but they were ridden mainly by Mark Williams and one with Tom junior on board. One morning, as Neil arrived, a horsebox drew up, and a small chestnut horse with a big white blaze was unloaded. Neil was informed that he was called Flash Harry and was owned by an ex-footballer called Jack Dawson, who'd got a reputation of being a bit of a difficult owner, as he kept moving his horses around and changing trainers.

"As often as most people change their underwear," Tom senior joked.

Apparently, he'd had some very expensive failures with the top trainers, whose training fees were at least twice what Tom Cooper senior charged, and after a run of disappointing results, a friend had recommended that he sent his horse to this small friendly yard, the horse he sent was well bred, but very small which had made him a relatively cheap horse to buy at the sales, Tom was his third trainer, and he was only a three year old.

Neil got allotted Flash Harry to ride, and the first time on the gallops, he came back and said, "He's all wrong; he wouldn't extend himself, just shuffled along, and seemed to dislike me getting on".

Tom senior took it all in, and the next day an elderly man appeared, instantly recognisable to everyone except Neil, as Will Sellers, the back man; he worked on Harry for about an hour each day for the next couple of days, always behind closed days, as that was the only way he'd do it, on the third day he came out of the stable and declared, "That's him done, he's fine now, everything is back in place, you'll notice an instant difference, he'll go and win for you now".

Neil rode him out the very next day on the gallops, and as soon as Harry realised that there was no pain, he was a different horse and flew up to the top of the gallops, faster than Neil had been before.

"He's a pocket rocket," he excitedly exclaimed on returning to the yard, and then slightly over the top, "he's the next Locksong".

"I'm surprised that you can remember that far back?" Tom senior joked.

"I've been reading some of my dad's old books," he replied in way of an explanation.

Jack Dawson was a frequent visitor to the yard, and Tom senior commented that he was a joy to train for, very enthusiastic, and he pays his bills, unlike some owners.

The first race for Flash Harry, for the yard, was pencilled in at Kempton in a week's time, and Neil just kept him ticking over until then. Mark Williams had been piling on the pounds recently, so as Harry was only small, it was deemed preferable to book one of the welterweight apprentices to ride. Unfortunately for Neil, it was Tom junior who was chosen; Neil thought that even with Tom on board, the horse was a certainty and would have put a bet on, but he wasn't sure if it was allowed. He thought that stable lads could bet but not jockeys, and he was both. Not wanting to risk getting in trouble, he kept his money in his pocket. He got the job of leading the horse round the paddock, so after letting Harry go and wishing Tom junior good luck through gritted teeth, he settled down to watch the race. Sadly, it didn't quite go to plan; Tom junior set off near the front, and when he came to make his move, some of the senior jockeys boxed him in, all legitimately, of course, and by the time he extracted himself it was too late, and he was a fast finishing, eye-catching third.

As Neil led him back in, he said to a forlorn Tom junior, "Don't worry as it wasn't your fault; it was those old jockeys boxing you in. Some of them are right tossers, especially that Connolly".

As he said that, not many people heard him, apart from Angus Connolly, who was riding the horse behind Harry, and he glared angrily at the back of Neil, burning holes in his jacket with his fiery eyes, figuratively speaking, but Neil was completely oblivious.

For Harry's next race, Jack Dawson had wanted a top jockey to be booked to ride him, but these weren't easy to come by for a small trainer like Tom senior, so he'd persuaded Jack to let Neil have a go with the proviso that if this didn't reap rewards, he'd try and get a top jockey for the next race. Neil was therefore booked and very excited but had a longer wait than expected, as the next intended race was abandoned due to waterlogging, so it was three weeks before he actually made it to another racecourse. Neil lined up on Flash Harry in a five-furlong maiden race at Wolverhampton, against ten other runners, with the favourite coming from the yard who'd trained Harry previously; the jockey riding it told Neil that Harry was useless, and he was wasting his time, though he used much more colourful language. Neil just smiled to himself and held his tongue and thought, we'll see about that. He set off near the front, keeping a little wide to avoid trouble, and as they came to the last furlong, he urged Harry on and set off for home, and in the last hundred yards, he suddenly realised baring accidents that he was going to win his first race, and extended his gallop and didn't see another horse, and he crossed the line two lengths in front, amongst the many joyous thoughts flooding through his mind, the main one was 'Don't forget to weigh IN'. Jack Dawson was over the moon, as it was his first winner in three years.

Neil said, "He'll come on after this, I think you'll have fun with this horse," and then rather cheekily, which caused Tom senior to scowl, "please don't change yards again, Mr Dawson".

He just smiled and said, "No chance," and handed Neil a package.

After he'd left, Tom senior told him off for acting too familiar with an owner after he weighed in and posed for photographs and changed; walking back to the horsebox, he opened the package to find it contained a monkey in notes (five hundred pounds).

"Is this OK?" he asked Tom senior.

"Yes, but don't flash it around."

"Shouldn't I share it with the rest of the lads from the stable?"

"No, you keep it. After all, you've earned it."

On the journey back, they talked about where they could race Flash Harry next. Tom had a plan; he'd give him a rest and bring him back in the spring and aim him for all the big handicaps over the summer.

Neil said, "I hope that I can keep the ride?"

Tom Senior said that he presumed so, but the final decision was down to the owner, who has the last say.

Neil was getting fed up with riding his old rickety bike to work in the early hours, usually in the pouring rain, so he decided to get his own wheels with his unexpected windfall. He fancied a Range Rover like his dad's but soon realised that his money would only buy him one wheel for a big vehicle like that. As for the insurance, well, it would have been cheaper to insure the Titanic, so he settled on a ten-year-old Suzuki Vitara, bright green, sold as a good runner, with one lady owner, though she was nowhere to be seen when he picked it up. The first time the twins saw it, they were in a fit of giggles.

"Neil, you've got yourself a hairdresser's car."

But Neil wasn't bothered what anyone said as he'd got his independence, and it wasn't long before the twins were accepting lifts in it. He soon found that having his own wheels was a great step forward, and he no longer arrived at work wet and bedraggled and totally fed up before the day had started, and the best thing about his car, or so he thought, was the cd music player, which enabled him to play his music, usually very loudly.

CHAPTER SIXTEEN

Spread Your Wings

Neil's very next ride was a winning one, and he was on his way to stardom in his words but nobody else's, and he was becoming ever so slightly overconfident, some might say cocky! Tom senior was doing his best to keep him grounded and faced a dilemma as he really had too many jockeys for a small yard, he couldn't get rid of his son, as he'd nurtured him since the car crash, and was hoping that he would come out of his shell now that he was riding winners, but sadly he was being overshadowed by Neil, with more and more owners requesting him, and some even preferring him over the established Mark Williams, so Neil might have to go, but that would be an unpopular move, and the dilemma kept Tom senior awake at night, and he had to admit that he didn't really know what to do, he had to admit that even though his son had done well, he had his limitations and would only at best become a journeyman, (average) jockey managing to ride a few winners each season, whereas with Neil, to use a well-known cliché the sky's the limit, and it was all happening very quickly.

The problem was slightly alleviated when Neil started getting outside rides for other trainers. The first one was for another small trainer, also with a farming background, called Sue Henry, she mainly used female jockeys, and Neil was curious as to why she'd chosen him. Tom senior recommended giving her a courtesy call before the race and offering to go to her yard and ride out the intended horse. When he did ring her, she said that riding the horse before the race wasn't necessary, as the horse was an easy, straightforward ride; she informed him that she'd picked him as she had been impressed with his recent race riding and said that his apprentice weight allowance would help but admitted that her main jockey Sarah had been banned for a few days, due to over-enthusiastic use of the whip. On the day of the race at Lingfield, Neil drove himself there for the first time in his shiny new to him Vitara, a hairdresser's car indeed, he thought as he drove along listening to his favourite ska music. It was a windy but warm day, but perfect for racing.

In the paddock, the girl leading Sunday Girl round introduced herself as Sarah and opened the conversation by saying, "Don't get too used to riding Sunday Girl as she's really my ride".

Neil looked at her and nodded. He thought that he recognised her but couldn't place her.

"Haven't I seen you somewhere before?"

"Yes," she replied with a smile, "you probably think that I look like that model in the car advert, don't you?"

He didn't but thought it better not to say so and just smiled. The trainer spoke very softly, and it was difficult to hear all that she said, but he got the gist of it. The horse was running well but only managing to get placed, but not winning, and she wasn't sure why as she thought that she had the ability to win. All too soon, she was wishing him good luck and legging him up, and a few minutes later, the stalls opened, and they were off. Straight away, Neil found himself struggling to keep up with the rest of the field, and embarrassingly he found himself in last place. He didn't get flustered and told himself to keep calm.

"Don't panic," he said silently, and in the second half of the race, as the pace slackened, he gradually started picking horses off and was going best of them all at the finish but only managing third place.

After dismounting, Sue sought his opinion. Neil said, "Sunday Girl struggled to keep up with the early pace but was flying at the finish. I suggest that you try a longer race."

Sue replied, "We were told that she had suspect stamina when we got her, but we've nothing to lose. What distance do you suggest?"

"I'd try another two furlongs at least, and if you want my services again?"

"OK, we'll try that, but I think that I'll have to use my usual jockey, Sarah. The owners prefer lady jockeys."

"I could grow my hair."

"You won't have to grow it much longer to look like a girl," she replied, smiling.

On his way home, Neil thought, so now I look like a girl and drive a hairdresser's car, though he was pleased that trainers were asking his opinion, which swelled his confidence. Confidence, however, wasn't a problem; it was overconfidence that was going to get him into a lot of trouble. He'd risen through the ranks with indecent haste; not that long ago, all that he'd ridden was an old rusty bike, and now he was riding expensive, highly tuned racehorses and holding his own with the senior well-established jockeys who had been on the racing circuit for many years, and some didn't take kindly to this young upstart muscling in and grabbing all the attention. He had the ambition to reach the top of the tree as quickly as possible, and so far, it all appeared to be going well, but appearances can be deceptive.

CHAPTER SEVENTEEN

Feeling Uneasy

Quite soon afterwards, and out of the blue, Neil got offered another outside ride, this time for a Newmarket yard run by Lez Allen. As Neil obviously didn't have an agent booking his rides, all offers came through Tom senior, and Neil could instantly tell that he wasn't happy about Neil riding for this yard but wouldn't say why. The racing community usually had everyone pulling together and helping each other, but Neil got the impression that Lez Allen was somewhat of an outsider. Tom senior was reluctant to talk about him but did say that he trained in a famous old yard, whose glory days had long since gone, Lez Allen's father-in-law Gerald Evans had been a good and successful trainer, but when Lez had married his daughter Celia, it had looked like things would carry on the same. He had a few successes early on, but it didn't last long, and when Celia left him, the yard slipped out of the limelight and became very secretive. He has moderate success with low-grade handicappers, but his last apprentice jockey met with an unfortunate accident. Tom senior had stopped talking abruptly and had refused to carry on, even when pressed, and rapidly changed the subject to inform Neil that his stable jockey was Angus Connolly, who just happened to be Neil's least favourite jockey. Tom senior suggested that Neil had probably been booked due to the weight allowance apprentice jockeys get, or perhaps they're hoping that you'll ride him badly to keep the horses handicap down before it goes up to an unwinnable level.

Neil did ring the trainer Lez Allen before the race but wished that he hadn't bothered as he was met with a very negative response as the trainer said, "You needn't come and ride the horse before the race".

"What about tactics and instructions?"

"Brian will tell you all you need to know on the day."

Before Neil could enquire who Brian was, the phone was slammed down. Neil was getting more and more uneasy about the race, but there was no way that he was going to back out at this late stage, especially as, on paper, it looked like another good chance of a winner.

When he arrived at Chelmsford, where the race was taking place, the first person he bumped into was Pete Wisdom.

"Hi Pete," he said, "can you point me in the direction of Lez Allen, please?"

"Doubt that he'll be here," he replied.

"That's the chap you want," he said, pointing in the direction of a small, stocky man leaning on the paddock rails smoking, "why are you riding for those bunch of crooks?"

Neil had already started walking away and didn't feel the need to reply, but privately he wondered the same thing, even though he had no reason to think that they might be dishonest. Brian turned out to be as talkative as his boss and just muttered, "Keep him covered up and don't hit the front too soon!"

He was riding a horse called Fagin, and he had a lot of good form, winning two out of his three last races. I wonder why they want me to ride him and not Angus Connolly, Neil said to himself. Fagin was led round by a miserable-looking stable lad, and the ability to speak appeared beyond him, and he didn't even look at Neil, there were no good luck messages, no owners in the paddock, and Neil was relieved when he was legged up onto the horse and left to his own thoughts. On the way to the start, Neil was pleased with the horses' paces, though he thought that he appeared a little jaded and lacklustre, as if he hadn't recovered fully from a very hard race or was losing interest in the racing game and getting a little stale, Neil couldn't quite put his finger on it. He was pleasantly surprised that when the stalls opened as Fagin seemed keen to race, the pace was very slow, so he struggled to keep him covered up, as his brief instructions had suggested, so he changed tactics and disobeyed orders and let

Fagin take the lead, where the horse merrily bowled along, blazing a trail, he soon had opened a lead of a couple of lengths, turning for home the pack were bearing down on him, Neil gave Fagin his head, and he kept on galloping and won by a fast diminishing length, Neil was a little concerned as walking back he seemed a little distressed and took a long time to recover, he intended to mention this to the connections, as thought that they should know.

If he was expecting the atmosphere to have improved, it didn't, and as he dismounted and patted the horse, the stable lad ignored him again, and Brian just said, "You disobeyed orders".

"I won, didn't I?" Neil sharply replied, "are the owners here, as I should go and speak to them?"

"No," Brian snapped, and that was that.

Neil was unsettled by the whole experience and sincerely hoped that he wouldn't be asked to ride for the yard again anytime soon. When he returned to Sunrise Farm, he discussed the day's events with Tom senior, who'd watched the race on the telly, he said "Great ride Neil, but I've got a strange feeling that you weren't expected to win the race, I'm afraid to say I think that's why you were booked, due to your inexperience, if they'd wanted to win the race, they'd have put Connolly on board, but that's just a feeling I've got".

"But why?" Neil asked, perplexed.

"Ah, that's just it," Tom senior replied, "I've absolutely no idea!"

Neil decided to just put it down to experience and try not to let it spoil his winning ride, but the day was going around in his mind, and he couldn't settle. He asked Tom senior again about the last apprentice at Lez Allen's yard, and he was a little more forthcoming this time.

"He crashed his car," he said, "but no one knew why as the weather was fine and the road was dry. I believe that he skidded off the road and hit a tree".

"So just a traffic accident then?"

"I can't remember the full story, but there was something suspicious about it, but I do know that he ended up with spinal injuries and will never ride again."

"What was his name?" Neil asked.

"Kevin Dee, he rode for us once but not very successfully as he wasn't strong enough, and the horse ran off with him."

"So he wouldn't have made it as a jockey?"

"Don't think so; he had a couple of winners but was never going far. I think he writes for the racing press now, but I don't know much about him."

This all got Neil thinking, it sounded far from being a normal accident, and he didn't want to end up in a similar fashion but thought that he was perhaps being over dramatic. He was beginning to realise that there were many layers to the racing game, to the sport of Kings and Queens, and that apparently not all of them were as honest as Tom Cooper senior.

CHAPTER EIGHTEEN
Money, Money, Money

Neil was pleased with how his career was progressing though the only thing troubling him was the continual and increasing animosity with Angus Connolly, and he was at a loss of what to do about it. He'd asked the other jockeys for help, but sadly, they didn't want to know and were no help. As a last resort, he discussed it with Tom senior, who said he thought that Connolly was a bitter, twisted jockey with a chip on his shoulder, his career had started really well after he won a few high-profile races and got himself noticed, but then it didn't actually go wrong, but even though he has been talked off as a potential future champion jockey, it never happened, the retainer with a big yard and riding top horses never happened, and he sank to the level he was at now, getting about 30–40 winners a season, which wasn't too bad, but nowhere near champion jockey level. Tom senior thought that perhaps he was jealous of an up-and-coming jockey like Neil who might actually achieve what he himself had never managed to do. Neil decided to try and get on with him or, at the very least, not antagonise him. Tom senior was also a worried man; he was pleased about how well Neil was doing but concerned about the effect it was having on his son, who had started well but now seemed to be lacking confidence and becoming more uncommunicative than ever, and, more importantly losing races that he should be winning, so much so that something would have to be done soon, but he kept putting the problem to the back of his mind unwilling to make any quick decisions. He was still wondering about letting Neil go, freeing up more rides for his son, but knew that his owners would be unhappy. He was also worried that if Neil went to another yard, then the owners might follow.

Tom had a runner at Salisbury early on in the new flat season, Flawed Ambition, which Neil had been booked to ride, mainly due to the owners requesting him. As soon as Neil arrived at the racecourse and went to the changing room, Angus Connolly winked at the other jockeys and said to no one in particular, "Here comes the long fellow," which those in the know will recognise as a nickname for the great Lester.

Neil thought that this was a compliment but soon realised otherwise when Connolly continued, "You wouldn't be good enough to clean the great man's shoes," then he looked round at the other jockeys and laughed. Some joined in, though it was uneasy laughter. Connolly was something of a bully in the changing room, so the rest tried to keep in with him.

Neil remained quiet, thinking it was better not to react. Flawed Ambition was a great big horse that took a lot of getting fit, and as this was her first race of the season, Neil wasn't expecting too much and was surprised when she was still in contention near the finish, but her lack of fitness found her out, and she faded to fourth. Next time she'll be spot on, Neil told Tom senior, who thought to himself that he'd put his son on next time and try and give him an easy winner. Angus Connolly had won the race and had opened a bottle of champagne given to him by the winning owners and was sharing it around the changing room.

Neil obviously wasn't offered any, with Connolly saying, "You're too young to drink. Go and get yourself a glass of water".

Laughter followed as Neil made a swift exit from the room. However, when he got home, his day changed for the better in a big way.

His Uncle Harry was there and was holding court with his family, including his sister Cynthia, who was just about speaking to him again. As Neil entered, Uncle Harry was telling the ensembled family members that he was cutting back on his bookmaking interests. He traded under the name Harry Bowen of Smart Racing, and either himself or a representative covered most of the race tracks and many meetings. He said that it was getting harder to make a living nowadays, especially on the flat. The family stared outside the window at the shiny new Jaguar parked, one of the latest models, but let him continue without comment. He carried on, saying that there was something funny going on, especially at the southern meetings, with some well-known gamblers seeming to have an edge in certain races, and he'd been losing substantial amounts, some days coming home with huge losses. With this in mind, he had sold some of his lucrative pitches (where the bookmakers stand at the races, nearer the punters, the more that they're worth, as they do more business).

He then leaned over to Neil and Cynthia with a smile on his face and said, "As I've got no kids of my own, I'd like you two to have this," and he handed them both a cheque.

They each looked at them and were shocked and left speechless as they'd both been given one hundred thousand pounds. They were both overwhelmed and overjoyed and thanked him profusely.

As he was leaving, he said, "Use it wisely".

Their dad said, "You can both pay me back the money you owe me".

"What money?" they both said.

"I think that he's joking," their mum said, "but it's hard to tell nowadays," Cynthia said that she'd pay her student loan off and put the rest towards a new car, and anything left would go into her house fund. Neil wasn't sure what to do with it. It was okay living at home, his mum was a good cook, and his dad was out a lot, but the idea of having a pad of his own suddenly sounded like a good idea. That very weekend he went looking at houses, and in less than a month, he had bought an ex-council semi-detached house, less than five miles away and nearer the stables, in a quiet little village. The twins joked when they heard where it was that it was a village for the old and retired, but he liked the tranquillity after the daily machinations at the racecourse. An additional bonus was that the next-door neighbours were a delightful, retired couple, Richard and Lilly Secombe, and what's more, Richard was a retired jumps jockey, so many evenings were spent sitting outside chewing the fat of the day over a can of beer and discussing the racing.

Richard was always telling Neil that he had it easy nowadays, and his favourite saying was, "In my days". Neil found it hard to believe that in Richard's days, the rails surrounding the racetrack were made of cast iron and sometimes with concrete posts.

"If you fell on them," he said and didn't need to finish the sentence.

Richard gave Neil little pointers about race riding. Some were very useful though some were a little outdated, but on the whole, he was very helpful, and if Neil did anything wrong in a race, he was soon told. Neil wasn't very good at cooking, and as the nearest takeaway was many miles away, Lilly Secombe used to take pity on him, and often when he returned tired after racing, he'd find that she'd left him a stew or something hot in a pot on his kitchen table. In fact, they swiftly became like grandparents to him, and he decided that buying a house was a really good move even though he seemed to have a lot of bills to pay, including a small mortgage. But whilst he was earning, he had plenty to cover his costs and was usually too tired to go out drinking in the evening and to spend any spare cash that he had, apart from the occasional night out with the twins, especially as he always started early in the morning. When race riding, he had to be very careful with his alcohol intake, as jockeys were now tested for it, and the last thing he wanted at this stage of his career was to be stood down for being over the stringent alcohol limit and as for drugs he'd heard rumours of a drugs problem among the racing community, but he hadn't any first-hand experience and had no intention of trying them.

CHAPTER NINETEEN

Getting Better

Neil continued to make progress, and his race riding got better and better, and conversely, Angus Connolly's dislike of him grew and grew. One day when back at the stud farm whilst collecting belongings for his new house, he told his mum about the problems he was having with Connolly and the ongoing feud. She surprised him by saying she had an idea about what it could all be about, but frustratingly she wouldn't explain why and just said that she would tell him sometime, leaving him intrigued and a little puzzled, but no amount of questioning would get any more out of her, though she did say that he was a bitter little man.

"Tell me something that I don't know," Neil had replied.

The next time he got the chance to speak to Richard Secombe, he asked him about Connolly and what he thought he should do. Richard had just suggested keeping out of his way but said that it was different in his day, as there were no cameras following the horses around during the races, and they could almost get away with murder.

"It was much harder in the good old days," he said.

"You mean in the eighteenth century," Neil cheekily replied.

Richard grimaced, and Neil smiled and said, "Only joking".

Richard told him about one jockey who gave him all sorts of trouble when he first started, so I pushed him through the wings of a jump, away from the stands unseen by the stewards. I made it look like an accident, obviously, but it got the message through to him, and after that day, we respected each other and actually became good friends.

"Well, I can't do that, can I?" Neil said.

Richard shook his head and agreed and said, "Connolly is a nasty vindictive little Scotsman and probably feels threatened by you, the new boy who is beginning to steal all the limelight".

Neil was lucky during the next week as his and Connolly's paths rarely passed as they were racing at different racecourses, so he put the problem to the back of his mind. Riding, as well as he was ensured that the winners kept on flowing and offers of rides from outside yards kept on increasing, he thought that he'd really broken through when he got offered a ride by the champion trainer, Henry Aske. It was only the yard's second string in the race, but even so, the horse Arab King was probably the best-bred horse that he'd ever sat on.

"My other runner will win," Henry had told him, "but you should get a good run from Arab King".

Henry turned out to be hundred per cent correct as his mount ran well, finishing third with the other stable runner romping home. Just for a moment, he started daydreaming about being a stable jockey for the champion trainer in the future but was in danger of returning to his dreamy childhood state.

The winners kept on coming, and for the first time, he was being spoken of as one of the up-and-coming jockeys who could win the champion apprentice's title. He was in third place, but there was still plenty of the season left to go. The runaway leader was Gilbert French-Saunders, which had surprised many; though Neil conceded that he'd improved a lot and had tidied up his riding style, he'd heard that he'd been having lessons from an old champion jockey, who'd obviously made big improvements. They had become good colleagues and firm friends, but since Neil was southern-based and Gilbert northern-based, their paths seldom crossed. Neil's riding was also improving, and he was getting very excited as Royal Ascot was fast approaching, and he was looking forward to the ride on Flash Harry and, hopefully, some other rides. Flash Harry was being aimed for the big sprint on the final day of the Royal meeting, his owner Jack Dawson had been dreaming of having a winner at the Royal meeting, especially since all his previous runners there had run badly and been a big disappointment, and Flash Harry appeared to have a good chance, a bit like Neil he'd started dreaming and one day he said that he was hoping for an invite to ride down the course in one of the Royal carriages, Neil and Tom senior had a good laugh about this after Jack had left, but then again you never know what might happen. Ascot was still a few weeks away, but like Cheltenham in the jumps season, it was all that anyone in the racing world was talking about, with virtually every trainer in the country hoping to have a runner there.

Tom senior was doing well, and a steady flow of new horses were arriving at Sunrise farm, so much so that he was thinking of building some extra stables and expanding his enterprise and possibly taking on more staff.

One new horse was very interesting, mainly due to his owner Don Grayson, who was a well-known pop star. Neil didn't like his style of music, calling it middle of the road, but obviously didn't say so, and when Don arrived to watch his horse on the gallops one day, with a car full of cd's of his latest album, which he handed out to all the staff, Neil had thanked him, he did think about selling it on eBay especially since it had been signed but instead decided to give it to his sister as a birthday present. His horse Careless Whisper had come to the yard with a reputation of being something of a tear away, so she'd been assigned to Neil to sort out. He'd started by doing a lot of roadwork with her, riding around the local lanes daily, and only when he thought that he'd settled her down did he start taking her up the gallops, but again on his own, as he was worried that other horses might excite her too much. This had all gone very well, and now he could ride work with the other horses, and she was as quiet as a lamb and, in Neil's words, "Ready for a race".

Tom senior had joked that Neil could set up as a problem horse fixer, but he'd replied that he'd rather be champion jockey first. Tom trying to keep him grounded, said, "You have to learn to walk before you can run".

Neil just smiled, but he wasn't really listening as ambition had got hold of him, and he was beginning to think, unwisely as it turned out, that he knew better than everyone else about most things, especially racehorses, when in reality, he had a lot to learn, as people who'd been in the racing industry all their lives were still learning.

CHAPTER TWENTY

Careless Whisper

It was to be Careless Whisper's first race in public. She was a big raw two-year-old and didn't initially seem keen on the racing game. Neil wasn't looking forward to the ride as she started playing up in the paddock and then fly bucking on the way down to the start and generally wouldn't settle. Neil was expecting trouble going into the stalls, and she unfortunately obliged by planting her feet and taking a long time to be cajoled in but surprisingly, once she was in, she calmed down and appeared settled. When they set off, she raced quite nicely; in fact, coming into the last furlong, she appeared to have an outside chance of victory. However, she started wobbling and veering about due to inexperience and weakness, and near the finish, she stumbled and lurched towards another runner, which just happened to be ridden by Angus Connolly, who instantly overacted and yanked his horse left, cannoning into another runner, who hit the rails causing its jockey to fall off. After the incident, both Neil and Connolly unsurprisingly finished unplaced. Walking back, Connolly was spitting feathers with what Neil thought was mock indignation.

He shouted at Neil, "You did that on purpose, Bartholomew".

By now, he'd dropped the nickname.

"You'll pay in the steward's room," Neil started saying, "there probably won't be a..." when the klaxon horn went, and the steward's enquiry was announced.

Neil felt like a schoolboy on entering the steward's room, and the feeling got worse as the stewards were all seated, and the jockeys remained standing and stood in a row. Connolly was in his element, seemingly enjoying himself dishing out wild accusations about Neil. Luckily the other jockey, who was none the worse for his spill, said that Connolly's horse had bumped his and that he had no idea what had caused that. The stewards replayed the race for all to watch and slowed it down where the incident occurred, and Neil had to admit that it looked bad.

He said, "Can we see the head on, please?" as he thought that would prove his innocence but was told to keep quiet and only talk when spoken to.

He definitely felt like he was back at school and was waiting for someone to say bend over, boy. The stewards asked him why he hadn't switched his whip into the other hand to correct the horse, which he had no answer to, and why hadn't he straightened his horse before making contact with

Connolly's. Neil tried to defend himself, saying that it was the horse's first race and that she was running very green and had stumbled, but even so, they never made contact with another horse. But they weren't listening, and it was all to no avail, and he got stood down for seven days (banned from race riding), which was bad enough, but it was even worse as it covered the whole of the Royal Ascot meeting, and he'd miss the ride on Flash Harry.

Tom senior was displeased not with the stewards but with Neil.

"You're becoming too hot-headed; you need to calm down and think about what you're doing. That incident could have been a lot worse!"

Neil tried to defend himself, "But I did nothing wrong. The filly stumbled but never made contact with another horse. Connolly just seized on the chance to get at me".

But Tom wouldn't listen. He was a stickler for obeying the rules and keeping out of trouble and said, "You're your own worst enemy, you think you know it all, but you don't!"

Neil had had a bad day and expected some support, but just snapped, "Watch the bloody race again," and left before it turned into a proper argument. The next day Neil was hoping that it had been forgotten, but it hadn't.

"Jack Dawson wants you to ride at Royal Ascot, and now due to your stupidity, you can't."

Tom senior said, "I don't want to upset him as if we're not careful he'll move his horse on again, and he's just promised to send me another one next season".

Neil was unhappy and said, "Well, I was really looking forward to riding Flash Harry at the Royal meeting". Neil thought that he was being punished for a crime that he hadn't committed, which in his eyes, made it a whole lot worse. Tom senior wasn't pacified and kept sniping at him all day, and he was really pleased when it was home time. Later in the evening, he sat in his garden with Richard, who had watched the race and was the first person who believed Neil's version of events, though he did point out that when she started weakening, Neil should have tried to hold her together and keep her running in a straight line which Neil thought was easier to say than do.

Royal Ascot started, and Neil had to sit out the whole meeting, and as Tom senior only had the one runner, Flash Harry, all week, after doing his jobs in the morning, Neil wasn't required until afternoon stables, so he was able to go home and watch the racing with his knowledgeable neighbour Richard.

On the day of the big race, Neil had gone to the stud farm to walk Brock, as he wasn't required by Tom senior, so on this day, he went to watch the race with Steve and Lynne. Unsurprisingly as he watched the Royal entourage progressing down the centre of the course, Jack Dawson wasn't amongst them, In the paddock Flash Harry looked spot on, and Neil expected him to run well, though he thought that the ground was perhaps a little firm, Tom junior had got the ride, and had appeared to listen when Neil had gone through tactics with him the day before. He looked a little apprehensive when he was legged up but didn't look as nervous as he had previously done; perhaps he's got his nerves under control, Neil thought. It was a big field with twenty-two runners, and Neil was expecting it to be a fast race due to the firm ground. Flash Harry broke well but never really got into the race, finishing nearer last than first. Both Neil and Steve commented that the ground hadn't suited Harry and that he hadn't been striding out as he did on the gallops at home. Neil texted the owner to say that he thought that it was the ground and that Tom junior had done nothing wrong.

The next morning Tom senior told him that Jack Dawson had taken it quite well but had insisted that he wanted Neil back on board for the next race, which he informed him would probably be at the York Ebor meeting. Something to look forward to, he thought; his Aunt Emily always went to this meeting, and she called it the Ascot of the North, so he thought that it would be nice for her to see him ride a winner.

The seven days suspension really dragged, and Neil was itching to be back in the saddle. One day before it ended, Tom senior asked him to take part in a local sponsored charity ride, which the yard always supported and sent a rider or two each year. Another new horse had just arrived from France called Le Moine Fou, and Tom senior suggested that Neil take it to assess it and see what its paces were like. Neil readily agreed but wouldn't have been quite as keen if he'd heard Tom senior telling his son that it had a bit of a reputation of being a tear away back in France and how riding it might make Neil realise that he didn't know it all and wasn't the finished article yet! This caused Tom junior to smile broadly for the first time in a long time.

CHAPTER TWENTY-ONE

Crazy Horses

Neil thought that Le Moine Fou was a funny name for a horse, but nobody seemed to know what it meant in English, or if they did, they weren't telling him. John and Tracy rode with him to the start of the ride, but when he asked John, he'd replied that he hadn't been the sharpest pencil at school and had detested French lessons. Neil's horse had sweated up on the way there, and he was beginning to get bad vibes as they rode to the start, where they met the twins, as the plan was for all five of them to ride together, and Neil had expected an enjoyable day away from the tensions and pressures of the racing world, and away from Angus Connolly. As soon as they started, the twins set off at a canter, suggesting that they try and finish the ride first, even though it wasn't a race, straight away Le Moine Fou reared up in the air striking out with his front legs, and then proceeded to reverse at an alarming speed into the undergrowth as the other four disappeared, and that was the last that Neil saw of them. His horse jig jogged, bucked, shied, stopped, started and gave

Neil the worst possible experience he'd ever had on horseback.

He began to think that he'd been set up as Tom senior had said, "You're the expert, so you can ride him", and he'd caught John smirking, so he presumed that he was trying to bring him down a peg or two, but it was too late now to think about that, as he had to try and survive the rest of the ride in one piece.

Tom senior had said that he could stop halfway if he liked, but when he got there, he didn't have a clue where he was, so he just carried on. Towards the finish, the horse actually began to quieten down, probably tired out like me, Neil thought. At the finish, everyone else had long since gone, so he set off riding back to the stables all on his own. The twins texted to enquire where he was, saying that they'd got home ages ago and were now in the bath. He'd texted back to say that he was on the way back but would rather be with them, but quickly added, "Rather be finished, not in the bath with you". But then again, he thought!

Neil finally got back as darkness was beginning to fall, and he dried the horse down before feeding him and leaving the deserted yard, thinking to himself that it was rather stupid to ride a horse for the first time ever in public before getting to know it. When he finally got home, he was cut and bruised and aching all over; before he jumped in the bath, he looked up the English for Le Moine

Fou and wasn't surprised to find that it translated as The Mad Monk, which explains a lot, he thought.

He was pleased that the next day was a Sunday and a day of rest for everyone, and it was the day of the local Country fair held on the village green in front of the local pub, the Hunters Arms, which he had been to many times before but was looking forward to it as, perhaps unwisely, he'd entered Brock in the dog agility class. He watched some of the earlier competitors and thought that the course looked easy enough, though he wasn't sure how Brock would behave as he'd never done it before. Well, his dog exceeded all of his expectations until that was it came to the tunnel section; Brock went in but didn't come out at the other end, no matter how much Neil called him, so as a last resort, Neil climbed in and preceded to scramble up the full length of the tunnel and out the other side with absolutely no sign of Brock, he climbed out and looked round but had to leave the ring as the next competitor was about to start, he spotted Pete Wisdom leaning on a post at the side of the ring.

"Pete," he said, "have you seen my dog?"

"Yes," he said, "he shot off in the direction of the fast food vans," and then added, "I see that you've got him fully trained now, ready for the beating season".

Neil left him chortling to himself and headed off in the direction of the fast food vans, expecting to find him eating discarded burgers and chips, but there was no sign of him. He went past the raffle tent where his dad was standing as he was organising the event this year, and Neil decided that whilst he was there, he might as well enter the raffle.

"Where's the main prize, the cake?" he asked.

"Oh, that's round the back, as the kids kept prodding it."

Neil said that he'd come back when they announced the winners and wandered off round the other sites and attractions, talking to a few locals, when suddenly he looked down, and Brock was there trotting obediently at his side as if he'd never been missing at all. Neil bent down to slip on his collar.

"Where've you been, old fellow? Did the tunnel remind you of the bad experience you'd had when I found you?" he looked down to pat the dog and gasped when seeing Brocks's extended belly. "Goodness," he said, "how many burgers and chips have you had?"

He walked back towards the raffle tent and almost bumped into Dudley and Jan Cook, who both scowled at him, but neither spoke, so Neil didn't either. He checked the winners' board, and as he expected, he'd won nothing. The cake he noticed had been won by the Colonel, known as Colonel Parachute by the locals, but Neil thought that couldn't be his real name, he could see the Colonel at the front, and he didn't look happy.

"Where's my blasted cake?" he was saying in a loud booming voice, but it turned out that the cake couldn't be found. He moved to the front as the Colonel was still remonstrating. He spoke to his mum, who told him that the cake had been put around the back but couldn't be found anywhere and that his dad was getting frantic. The Colonel, by now, who was always slightly red in the face, had gone a very dark rouge colour. His dad just stood looking uncomfortable and trying in vain to reassure the Colonel; Neil was beginning to enjoy this unexpected piece of local theatre when he suddenly had a thought, a missing cake and Brock with a huge stomach, surely the two couldn't be linked, could they, surely his dog hadn't eaten the cake, but the more he thought about it, the more he realised that he probably had!

He saw Jan Cook looking at him and pointing at his dog, so before anyone said anything, he quickly slunk off. He had arranged to meet the twins in the Hunter's arms but decided it wouldn't be a good idea to go in with an extremely fat dog when all the talk would be about a missing cake, so he returned Brock to Steve's, who luckily wasn't in but at the pub as well, so didn't have any explaining to do, and drove off to the relative safety and calm of his own house. Later on, he read a few online reports concerning the weekend events. The charity-sponsored ride had been a great success with a record turnout and record amount of money made, annoying Neil thought; it mentioned that the talented apprentice jockey had finished last. The country fair got a good review as well, though it did mention the cake debacle; though Neil laughed to himself when he read that Eric Bartholomew had replaced the missing cake with an expensive bottle of his own malt whiskey, that will make him wince, it's all for a good cause, Neil thought.

The next week when back at the stables, Neil told Tom senior about Le Moine Mou's behaviour and agreed to spend time with the horse and do his best to sort him out, promising perhaps rather optimistically, to have him ready for the racecourse in a few weeks. Meanwhile, the York Ebor meeting was approaching fast, and he was looking forward to riding Flash Harry. However, for a change, the sun blazed down endlessly and baked the ground, making it rock hard; racecourses were frantically watering their courses to try and maintain safe ground. The ground at York became firm, and Flash Harry became a doubtful runner. The owner Jack Dawson was very enthusiastic about running but was not a horseman and couldn't understand why they might not run. He was planning on entertaining a big party of friends and had hired a private suite; however, when Tom senior explained the dangers of running on firm ground and injuring the horse, causing leg problems and possibly curtailing the horse's career, he agreed to leave the decision in the trainer's hands. Sadly, the ground remained firm, and Flash Harry was declared a non-runner. Tom senior was getting worried as they were running out of options. However, Neil came up with a viable option.

"Why not aim for the Ayr Gold cup, as the ground is usually softer up there in Scotland?" he said. This was decided to be a good idea, though with his handicap being low, there was a worry that he might not get in and might be balloted out and end up in either the silver or bronze cup, just as competitive but for much less prize money, which they knew would displease Jack Dawson.

CHAPTER TWENTY-TWO

Accidents Will Happen

Tom senior had three runners at Ayr, and because of the long distance from their yard, they all travelled up the night before with John and Tracy, with Tom senior and the two jockeys coming up on the day of the races. The two full bothers Captain Kirk and Starship Enterprise, ridden respectively by Tom junior and Neil, were running in the race before the Ayr Gold Cup in which Flash Harry had just got in with a very low weight, giving him a great chance, or so Neil thought, even after his poor showing at Royal Ascot. Neil had to put Flash Harry out of his mind and concentrate on the race before, as each race was equally important for the different owners. He was legged up and followed Tom junior onto the course and cantered down to the start without talking, just going through the race in his head and formulating a plan. As the race got underway, Neil was behind with Tom junior ahead, sandwiched between a runner on his inside and one on his outer, who Neil recognised as his great rival and antagoniser Angus Connolly. He noticed him edging closer to Tom junior, and as they were nearly touching, he deftly and swiftly kicked his stirrup iron so that Tom's leg slipped out, and in a second, he lost his balance and fell off under all the hooves of the horses following and was kicked around like a rag doll, as the field thundered over him. Neil had managed to avoid the stricken jockey and tried in vain to look over his shoulder and check that he was okay, but he couldn't really see. He knew that the deliberate attack would be unseen by any of the steward's cameras as it happened between two horses. Neil had to switch his attention swiftly to the race; otherwise, it would soon be over; as the field reached the final furlong, he moved up on the outside of Connolly's mount, giving him plenty of room and drew level, the look on Connolly's face of shock, as he saw Neil confirmed his thoughts that the earlier manoeuvre had been intended for him, as both horses were in the same colours and similar number cloths 1 and 11, easy mistake to make Neil thought in the heat of the moment. Neil was thinking all this whilst easing past to win by a good length.

On the way back to the enclosures, he turned to Connolly and said, "I saw what you did," Connolly said nothing, so Neil continued, "you knocked Tom off".

"We just got too close and bumped briefly; he happens in the heat of a race," Connolly replied.

Neil wasn't easily shaken off. "You thought that it was me, and it was deliberate".

Connolly just smirked as he knew that Neil couldn't prove anything and wouldn't take it any further. By the time they had returned, Neil to the winner's place and Connolly to the also-ran's area, Neil could see the ambulance returning and was told that it was taking Tom junior to the local hospital, Tom senior was nowhere to be seen, and Neil got a text from him saying that he'd gone to the hospital to see how his son was, so Neil was left to speak to the winning owners and then help with Flash Harry and meet Jack Dawson in the paddock before the race. There were twenty-four runners, and he was quite confident but was careful not to raise Jack's hopes up too high in case things didn't go to plan. Jack's first concern was how Tom junior was, but Neil had no news for him, so they turned their attention to the race and the tactics. Neil planned to stay in the pack and try and keep out of trouble which might be easier said than done with the large field, then slowly weave his way through and get his head in front of the line.

"Sounds simple," said Jack.

"It is," said Neil, but more with bravado than confidence.

At the start, the runners took a lot of loading into the stalls, as some were being fractious and messing about; perhaps they could sense the occasion, Neil wondered. Then all of a sudden, the flag was raised, and the field thundered off. Neil got a good start and, as he predicted, was right in the middle of the pack, surrounded by the deafening sound of thundering hooves, and the pace was fast, and it wasn't until the last two furlongs that he was able to make any progress, and gradually move up the field as the front runners started to tire and fall back, he was able to weave his way through, with the sound of galloping hooves echoing in his head, and close to the finish he found his way blocked by a wall of horses, suddenly a narrow gap appeared on the inside, and he made a daring move and surged through and was in front as the finishing line appeared and won cosily in the end by a nose. He'd won his first big race, the biggest race the stable had ever won in a televised race. Before he could think of the magnitude of his success, a microphone was shoved in his face, and he was expected to do a coherent interview. He was hoping that the interviewer would be one of the attractive female presenters, but sadly it wasn't, but in his state of euphoria, he wasn't too bothered, he explained how he hadn't sat on a horse until about three years ago and the usual stuff about it being a team effort, and he thanked the owners and the trainer, who he explained wasn't there due to an accident in the previous race, he had wondered about seizing this opportunity and share his accusations about Connolly but thought better of it. Back in the winner's enclosure Jack Dawson as expected was all smiles and slapped Neil on the back so hard that he nearly tripped over.

"Where next?" he asked.

"You'll have to ask Tom senior," Neil replied, "just enjoy the moment and worry about future plans later".

Jack had every intention of doing so; after the winners' ceremony, where he joyfully held the big gold cup aloft, he headed off to the bar with his family and friends and ordered the biggest, most expensive bottle of champagne that they had, he could really celebrate as was staying the night in the adjoining hotel. Neil, however, had the long journey home to contend with, and he still didn't know how Tom junior was. A phone call soon after brought him back down to earth and took the gloss off his victory. Tom junior had smashed up one of his hips and faced a long time out of the saddle but apparently was in good spirits, buoyed up by the stable's success. Neil thought that if it was him, he'd be going mad and wanted to be fit again as soon as possible, and not for the first time, he questioned Tom junior's dedication to the sport but obviously kept all this to himself.

The next day's racing papers all featured Neil and Flash Harry, and there was a full-page article in the Sporting Life on his dramatic and quick rise through the ranks. However, what happened to Tom junior made it hard to celebrate, but when he next saw Tom senior, he was told to enjoy it while it lasted as he'd soon be yesterday's news. He also commented that it was a rather cheeky move on the inside, the senior jockeys won't like that, but quite frankly, he just wasn't bothered as he'd won the race, and surely that's all that matters. He told Tom senior that the incident where Tom junior came off had been no accident at all but could tell that Tom senior thought that he was mistaken. When back at home, he watched the race again with his neighbour Richard and even watching it in slow motion, there was no sign of Connolly doing anything wrong, and Neil could understand why there had been no steward's enquiry.

Richard believed what Neil told him and said that in the heat of the race, number one and number eleven would look very similar and could be easily mistaken, but you've got no proof of any misdemeanour and no real motive, he said, "Keep away from Connolly he's obviously got it in for you". Neil said that he always tried to, but it wasn't easy as wherever he looked, Connolly was there.

"He's a danger," Neil said, "he seems to enjoy trying to make my life a misery. It's as if it's his aim in life to thwart my progress".

Richard just shook his head and said, "Don't give in to him. He's just a bully".

Neil replied, "He needs warning off before something really serious happens". Prophetic words, as it would turn out, but it wouldn't be quite as Neil expected.

CHAPTER TWENTY-THREE

Dangerous

The atmosphere was frosty when Neil next went into the changing rooms, as the senior jockeys were far from pleased with this upstart young jockey taking liberties. Angus Connolly was particularly vociferous, saying, "You're not going to last long at this game if you don't show your elders the respect that they deserve". And for once, all the other jockeys were in agreement.

The headstrong Neil took no notice. In his mind, he was on an unstoppable upward curve, and his race-riding confidence had reached ridiculous levels, and inevitably he was heading for a fall. He appeared to have more time than the other jockeys at the business end of the race and nearly always made the right move. Then, slowly at first, things started to go wrong; firstly, in a race at an evening meeting at Salisbury, Neil had travelled well and had cruised behind Gilbert French-Saunders and thought that he was the only other runner going well enough to win the race, so Neil perhaps remembering his first gymkhana, where he'd been cheated out of his rosette, and had vowed to never let anyone get the better of him again, decided to make sure that he won the race, he drew level with Gilbert and boxed him in, and stayed there, Gilbert glared at him shouting, "Let me out, let me out, you bastard!"

Neil feigned not to hear him and just stayed there. Gilbert could have dropped back and switched round the outside, but there just wasn't enough time; fifty yards from the finish, Neil made his move easing past the two leaders and won cosily in the end, leaving Gilbert fuming in his wake. A winner is a winner, Neil thought, ignoring all the protestations behind him. Tom senior wasn't too pleased either.

"That looked ugly," he said.

"I won, didn't I?" Neil swiftly replied. He was on a wave and over brimming with confidence, which nothing could knock — well, not yet anyway. Gilbert apprehended him in the weighing room and gave him a mouthful of abuse, finishing by saying that Neil was a self-centred egotistic pratt! Neil just brushed all criticism aside, hoping that it would all die down in a day or two, but he was slightly perturbed as Gilbert was the only one in the weighing room that he'd really made a connection with and regarded him as a friend. Neil was now five winners ahead of his nearest rival, who just happened to be Gilbert, for the Champion Apprentice title, and was beginning to think that it was in the bag, though he should have thought about the old adage about counting your chickens.

He was beginning to become one of the strongest in a race finish and was making the other jockeys look slow and leaden; even seasoned commentators were beginning to take notice and comment on his coolness and strength at the finish. He, however, started taking unnecessary risks, nipping through gaps that weren't really there and squeezing through them, but as yet, he hadn't been subjected to the steward's wrath. The other jockeys continued muttering and complaining, especially Connolly, but there wasn't much they could do, as he was bending, not breaking the rules. Richard Secombe warned him to be careful, and Tom Senior told him to steer clear of controversy. This all went in one ear and out the other, and he carried on with his devil may care attitude. The very next week in a race, he found yet another tiny gap and shot through and grabbed a race which moments earlier Angus Connolly presumed was his for the taking.

On the way back, he grabbed Neil and said, "You shouldn't go up on the inside like that".

"I just did," Neil said, and then added, "you shouldn't leave a gap like that, should you," leaving Connolly fuming.

Later Tom senior, who was beginning to get exasperated with Neil, and would have perhaps dispensed with his services a long time ago, if it wasn't for Tom junior's injury, said, "In future, go round the outside, no more taking risks!"

What Neil didn't realise was that it was all going to go disastrously wrong, all of which could have been avoidable. In his next race, Neil did as he was bid and went all the way around the field, wasting valuable time and was beaten, finishing third in a race he thought he could have won, and what was worse, Tom senior told him that he'd thrown away a winning chance, which got Neil thinking, that he just couldn't do right for wrong.

The yard had a promising young horse, a well-bred two-year-old belonging to some loyal, long-standing owners, they'd had many horses before with moderate success, but this one was different. This homebred filly was called Galileo Girl by champion sire Galileo; she had actually been sold as a yearling, but the owners had a change of heart and bought her back a year later, but paid heavily for the experience, she had four white socks on her legs which Tom senior said was unlucky, but Neil couldn't see how body markings could affect ability. Her first race was at Warwick, a local track, and Neil was under strict instructions to look after the filly.

She had shown great promise on the gallops but was still very green, and Tom senior's parting instructions were, "Give her a gentle introduction but don't give her a hard time," before adding, "but win if you can". Schooling in public, Neil thought but said nothing.

As the race started, Galileo Girl travelled sweetly and, with her huge stride, was finding the racing game effortless. Neil kept her on the bridle and quietly kept creeping nearer and nearer to the leaders, his intention was to give her an easy race finish about fourth and give her an ideal introduction so that hopefully she would enjoy racing, but her huge stride meant that she was going so well that she was right behind the leaders with little effort, and he realised that he could win easily, with Tom senior's words replaying in his head, he decided to go right round the field, but suddenly a gap appeared between two runners and he instinctively went for it, a stride or two later he realised that the outside jockey was none over than Connolly, who swerved inwards to block the gap, Neil had to grab hold of the reins and try and stop going forward, but it was too late as Galileo Girl clipped heels and came crashing down, taking a heavy fall in the process, Neil was flung through the plastic rails and hit the turf at about the same time Galileo Girl's flailing body made heavy contact with the turf, and the ground around shook and resonated. Then all of a sudden, there was silence; the field had long since galloped into the distance. Neil tentatively sat up and watched with horror as a truck drew up and two men quickly erected a screen around the stricken horse. Next, he saw Tom senior appear breathing heavily after running down from the stands.

"Get up and go," he shouted, "we'll talk later".

"What about Galileo Girl? How is she?" Neil asked, concerned.

"Not your problem, now go before I really lose my temper."

"But we clipped heels; it wasn't my fault." But Tom had gone behind the screen, having dismissed Neil and showed all his concern to the horse. Neil tramped dejectedly back to the weighing room, not wishing to speak to anyone. The first person he saw was Pete Wisdom, who didn't say a word, just shook his head and tore up a betting slip deliberately in front of his face; then, by the weighing room steps, he met the two people that he'd rather not, the owners of Galileo Girl, understandably looking extremely concerned, this was their dream horse, which they'd spent years to achieve, and Neil could have thrown it all away with one silly move Luckily their eyes didn't meet, Neil wanted to say sorry but just hurried past quickly with his head down. When he came out of the weighing room, Tom senior was there waiting for him looking thunderous.

"How's the horse?" Neil said.

Tom senior ignored the question and said slowly, "I've been telling you to be careful for weeks, and you've completely disregarded all my advice, So I can't have you riding for me any longer; the owners won't stand for it, so I'll get all your belongings sent on to you, as from today your contract is terminated!" with that he was gone, luckily, as Neil would have stoked the fire as he intended to accuse him of overreacting. He was stunned and shattered and hadn't really taken it all in, he had great regard for Tom senior, who'd guided his fledgling career so expertly, and he thought of him more as a friend than a boss. He was really enjoying himself at the stables and had only wanted to do his best for them all; he'd quickly become part of the team and had hoped to stay there for many more years.

He drove home in silence. He couldn't even listen to his favourite Jamaican ska music. One thing was troubling him, and that was Galileo Girl. He needed to know what had become of her. After going home and showering and deliberately avoiding his neighbour Richard, he drove to Sunrise Farm, hoping that the horsebox would have returned by now. He parked a few fields away and wandered into the yard through the backway and walked across the farmyard. The stable yard was deserted when he reached it, and the only sound was of the horses contently munching their hay. He silently and, with a degree of trepidation, walked to the stable where Galileo Girl resided, and his heart lifted as she was there. Admittedly she looked a little sorry for herself, stood at the back of the stable and not touching her hay, but a brief glance told him that she was OK, and that was all he wanted to know. He then heard the farmhouse door open, and there were voices getting louder coming in his direction, so he slunk away, giving the yard one last furtive glance, hoping that this wouldn't be the last time he saw this place.

CHAPTER TWENTY-FOUR

Wuthering Heights

The next day was a Sunday, and there was no racing taking place in the locality, so Neil had time on his hands, and in his fragile state of mind, this wasn't a good thing. Neil rang Tom senior to apologise and explain what had happened. Tom senior had calmed down and listened without interruption to what Neil had to say. However, he said that the situation hadn't altered, and until Neil changed his ways, for his horses and his owner's sake, he couldn't have him back.

"A few months at the Racing school might do you some good," he said, but Neil had thought that was demeaning and below him. Tom senior admitted that Galileo Girl was ok, a little shaken. He said that he was planning a little race on the all-weather to check that all was ok, or he might just put her away until next season. She had shown enough; Tom said to justify an entry in the next season's one thousand guineas. With a different jockey, Neil thought.

"You do realise," Tom said, "that if she hadn't got up again, not only would I have lost the horse, and that would have been dreadful, but more than likely, the owners would have left the yard as well, and who knows what else. So I just hope that you realise how serious your actions could have been?"

Neil did or at least was beginning to, but he still felt a little bit badly done to and decided he'd have to ride with extreme care and safety in the future. Getting a ride was proving to be difficult, as he didn't have an agent, trainers would have to ring him directly, and the problem was that his phone just wasn't ringing. He was still five ahead for the apprentice jockey's title with only a week to go, but his usual overconfidence and swagger had disappeared, and he was a worried man. His nearest challenger was his friend, or was it foe now? Gilbert French-Saunders was flying, and with all his racing connections, he was getting plenty of rides and was eating away at Neil's lead and by mid-week, with only three days to go, he was only two behind. Neil was frantically ringing trainers who'd used him before and as he got more desperate, ringing trainers who'd never used him and even some who'd never heard of him, but it was as if he was tainted as no one wanted to use his services, apart from Sue Henry who he'd ridden for once before. She'd offered him a few days of work and one ride as her jockey and only employee, Sarah Howerd, was accompanying her boyfriend, whose horse he looked after was racing in France, so they decided to turn it into a few days' holidays. Neil jumped at the opportunity as not only was his lead in the title race all but gone, but he'd earned nothing, and he had his mortgage to pay for. It might only be a small mortgage, but it was a mortgage no less.

The very next day, he travelled down to Sue's yard and was very impressed with the stables, everything was immaculate, and the horses looked in excellent condition. Neil fitted in well with the laid-back attitude of Sue and helped with all the daily chores, but it was the riding out that he enjoyed most. He'd been given a bed in what Sue rather grandly called a Bothy adjoining the main house but was invited in for meals usually washed down with a fine bottle of red wine. On the second evening, Sue asked him if he'd like to watch the infamous race again, he didn't want to, but on reflection, he thought that it wouldn't do any harm.

Sue froze the action just before he made the dangerous manoeuvre and turned to him and said, "Now, if you could have a second chance, what would you do?"

"Well, obviously, I'd go round the other runners, but when that gap opened up, I just instinctively went for it; I couldn't stop myself."

"You had plenty of time to go round and would still have probably won, and the horse would have had a perfect introduction. What happened could have scarred such a young filly for life, or at the very least sour her." Neil had to agree, but Sue softened her message by adding, "You've got more talent already than most jockeys achieve in a lifetime of racing, don't ruin your career before it's even started!"

That night Neil struggled to sleep with recent events going over in his mind and especially Sue's words of wisdom. He was determined to improve but, more importantly, ride safely. He'd learnt his lesson, though; hopefully, it wasn't too late. The last day before Sarah returned, Sue booked him for a race on Sunday Girl, the horse that he'd ridden before, at Chester, a unique round course which he'd never been to before. He walked the course with Sue and was amazed at how tight it was and how it was continuously on the turn. He turned to Sue and said, "Some horses won't like this. It'll unbalance them, but I think that Sunday Girl will handle it fine". Sue led the horse round herself and legged Neil up and wished him good luck.

It was only a small field, so Neil wasn't expecting any problems, especially since Angus Connolly wasn't riding in this race. As the race started, he settled near the rear as the front runners blazed a trail; Sunday Girl settled well and, more importantly, coped well with the turns, so he just let her stride on and kept on the outside away from the other runners, he gradually got into the race and was able to keep galloping and win by a very easy three lengths. Sue was pleased and said, "We'll make a jockey out of you yet".

The next day, as he was leaving the yard, Sarah Howerd returned and jokingly said, "Pinching my rides again, I see?" And she added with a smile, "And you nearly rode as well as I do".

"Whilst the cat's away," Neil replied.

"Well, Sue usually only uses lady jockeys, so if you want to ride for her again and win this title, I think you might have to resort to a sex change."

They both laughed, Neil could see why she received a lot of male attention as she was a very vivacious girl, but he still couldn't place where he'd seen her before and was beginning to think that he had imagined it.

Neil received no more offers of rides, and as he'd feared Gilbert had drawn level, with only one day to go, he had thought of asking Gilbert to do the honourable thing and stop riding and call it a draw and share the title, he remembered it happening many years ago, but thought better of doing so, as those days of chivalry were long gone. Whilst checking entries for the last day, he was horrified to see, in a cruel twist of fate, that Gilbert had been booked by Tom senior to ride his sister's horse Lady Calamity in the final race on the card. That should be my ride, Neil thought but was determined not to get bitter about it. Lady Calamity had had a break and looked very fresh and well in the paddock as Neil watched it on TV and sat with his neighbour Richard.

"She looks ready to run a big race," Richard said, which was the last thing Neil wanted to hear, but he had a feeling that he knew what was going to happen, Lady Calamity was 5-1 in the betting, and long before the finish Neil knew his fate as she won by half a length and Neil had lost the apprentice title. Straight away, he texted both his sister and Gilbert to congratulate them but received no replies from either of them, but he felt better for doing so. Down in the dumps didn't describe how he felt, and that night he sat down feeling numb and for the first time in a long time, he felt tears welling up, and he went to bed feeling as miserable as he used to do at boarding school all those years ago. He wasn't down for long and the next day he rose early and walked to the local shop to buy the Sporting Life, not to read about the success of Gilbert French-Saunders, but he couldn't help glancing at it, and was annoyed that he hardly got a mention, but to read the jobs vacant section and one advert caught his eye, it was for a apprentice's job for Arthur Manning in Yorkshire, that sounds interesting he thought and I'm sure that the yard is near where Aunt Emily lives, so I wouldn't mind working there, as there was no phone number to ring or contact details, Neil decided that it might be a good idea to just turn up and apply in person, No time like the present he thought, so the very next day after a long tedious journey he arrived at his Aunt's cottage unannounced and burst into her living room full of enthusiasm and found that he'd interrupted a WI meeting in full swing, the ladies all stared at him and his Aunt quickly ushered him out of the room and he swiftly left with many eyes staring at him feeling like he'd interrupted a meeting of Churchill's war cabinet, such was the apparent seriousness of it, he went into the kitchen with instructions to make himself a cup of tea and was told that the meeting would soon be over . Luckily, they soon all dispersed except one called Kathleen, who his Aunt was going to take home, and she said that she'd take him as well and drop him off at the racing yard as he'd never find it on his own. She was spot on with that assumption, Neil thought as she drove through Middleham and climbed higher and higher up narrow lanes twisting and turning until they were nearly at the end of civilisation.

"Where are we going?" Neil asked, "Wuthering Heights?"

"Somewhere very similar," his aunt replied.

They finally arrived, and she dropped him off, saying that she would be back in an hour or so after having a cup of tea with Kathleen. Neil surveyed the scenery. It was a rambling old stable, very imposing but had seen better days. He presumed that he was at the right place as there were horses everywhere poking their heads out of new and old stables, cow byres and some in an impressive new American barn and plenty dotted about in the fields enclosed with ancient dry stone walls. He was a little apprehensive now as his aunt had warned him that Arthur Manning was a real character and one not to suffer fools gladly. He was directed to a newish barn complex and found the

LESTER BOYD

trainer sitting on a straw bale with a half-empty bottle of whiskey next to him and brandishing an antique shotgun.

He said as a way of introduction, "I'm shooting vermin. How can I help you, lad? Are you interested in a share in a hoss? I've plenty here that will interest you; how much are you wanting to spend?"

"Um, I'm not here to spend money," Neil said and got a disbelieving stare from Arthur, "I'm Neil Bartholomew".

"Nah, never heard of you, but I've got the perfect hoss for you. It's only being syndicated in six shares, so you'll feel like a real owner; anyway, sit down, and I'll pour you a glass of grog."

Neil sat down, realising that this was probably going to be a fruitless journey. The shotgun suddenly went off, making him nearly jump out of his skin.

"Got the bogger," Arthur said excitedly as he reloaded. It's lucky that there's no horses in here, Neil thought, or the noise would have caused a stampede.

Arthur continued talking, "If you don't want a share in a hoss, how about an Aberdeen Angus heifer'? I've got some good beasts for sale down at the farm".

"No, thank you," Neil said politely, "I haven't come to buy anything," he took a gulp of the strong whiskey, "I've come about the job".

152

"What job, lad?" Arthur said, appearing puzzled as he swung dangerously close to Neil and fired again. "Dam, it missed this time".

"The job for stable apprentice," Neil said, hoping to get out of here as soon as possible and still in one piece.

"There is no job," Arthur said. "That was filled ages ago; someone should have taken the advert out of the paper, I suppose".

Neil looked crestfallen and took a huge gulp out of the already topped-up mug of fiery orange liquid.

"Never mind, lad," Arthur said, slapping him on the back, "I'll show you round the yard, and I'm sure that we'll find a hoss to suit your pocket". Neil was beginning to think that this eccentric Yorkshireman was like Arkwright in Open All Hours and that he'd eventually end up selling him something. Thankfully he put his gun down, and they set off around the yard, and Neil soon realised that he was no fool as he came alive and had encyclopedic knowledge about every horse in the yard, its breeding, its ideal distance, the problems they'd had, the races they'd won or would be doing soon.

"I'd put a penny or two on this one," he said, stroking a tall grey horse, "she'll win at Carlisle next week". Neil found his wealth and depth of knowledge fascinating and realised that he was in the presence of a true and proper horseman.

As he was leaving the yard, Arthur leaned in closer and said, "Don't worry, lad, you'll make a good jockey; you just need your rough edges smoothing off. I'd have straightened you out if you'd come here." And with that, he winked and was gone, and Neil realised that he'd known who he was all along and thought that it would have been interesting to work there. As he was leaving, he glanced at a photo stuck on a door of what he presumed was the team of stable staff, and right in the centre stage was the blonde girl that he'd seen at Catterick Races. "So this is where she works," he thought to himself.

A stable lad came past, and he asked, "Is she around? Can I speak to her?"

The lad looked at who he was pointing at and said, "Nah, she left, went down south, I think," and walked off. Neil returned to the entrance feeling slightly light-headed, which always seemed to happen when he came to Yorkshire, and thankfully, his aunt was waiting for him.

"Any good?" she asked.

"Sadly not," he replied, "but I've seen some great hosses!"

He had an enjoyable meal at his aunt's and stayed overnight before returning home the following day. He was getting desperate to find a job now and decided that he'd have to take whatever was offered if indeed anything was, and one offer sounded too good to be true: 'Stable lad and apprentice jockey wanted for famous Newmarket yard, apply Bleak house racing'. Sounds interesting, he thought, so he instantly rang it and spoke briefly to someone called Brian, and it was arranged for him to start the following week on trial. Something funny, he thought as I must have been the only applicant, he looked up Bleak House, and his heart sank as it was Lez Allen's yard, the yard he'd won for when he was convinced he wasn't meant to, and Brian must be the miserable head lad. It was all making sense now. He wondered about backing out but reasoned that it couldn't be that bad, could it?

CHAPTER TWENTY-FIVE

New Beginnings

It was with a distinct lack of enthusiasm that Neil portrayed as he arrived at Bleak House, Lez Allen's horse training stables. The name itself was a bad omen, he'd read that it had once been one of the leading stables in the country, but on arrival, he realised that those days must have been a long time ago. The entrance and the trainer's house looked grand, but on closer inspection, he noted that the stone pillars supporting the entrance gates were covered in grim, and one was leaning at an alarming angle. The gates themselves had peeling paint and were beginning to rot. He expected to find a busy, bustling yard, but as he went in, all was quiet, he looked down the rows of horses which were all looking a bit miserable and uneasy, and as he walked past them, their ears went back. It was all so different to the bright faces that used to greet him at Sunrise farm. The yard stretched down two parallel sides with a side yard round a corner; at the bottom of the main yard was a big locked shiny new metal gate, and Neil was instantly curious, but before he had time to investigate, there was a rough tap on his shoulder, and he turned round to see Brian standing there, he'd appeared silently from whence Neil knew not.

"Bartholomew, I presume?" he gruffly said.

"Yep, that's me," Neil replied, trying to sound enthusiastic but sadly failing.

"Right, I'll show you where you're staying; follow me."

Neil was hoping for some modern stable lad accommodation, but sadly this was not to be. As they walked along, the yard was pointed out to him; when he asked what was behind the shiny steel doors, he was informed that it was the extension yard not yet finished.

"So why the steel gates?" Neil enquired innocently.

Brian stopped walking and turned and rounded on Neil, "If you want to get on here, you'll have to stop asking questions and just do as you're told". The main accommodation was pointed out at the top of the yard near the road, but they walked past this round a corner where a dilapidated old mobile home stood surrounded by muddy puddles, next to where the staff parked and amongst the remains of some very old wooden stables, by the looks of them, unused for many years.

Neil looked downcast when he saw it, but Brian snapped, "It'll do for you, especially as I don't expect that you'll be staying very long. No one ever does. Be ready for work at 4 o'clock," and he left Neil to investigate his new home alone. He went inside, and as expected, the caravan smelt damp and unlived in, and he wondered when it was last used. The windows all appeared to be intact but were caked in grime that you could hardly see out of them. The roof didn't appear to have any damp patches, so he presumed that it was watertight, which was a relief, though it was full of dents as if someone had walked across it. The caravan had two doors, one with a lock which amazingly worked and the other with the lock hanging off and had been propped shut with an old wooden chair. His first job, he decided, would be to buy some bolts and make the caravan secure, not that he'd have anything worth pinching, but he didn't want anyone coming in at night and turfing him out of bed as he'd heard tales of what could happen to new lads. On the plus side, there was running water and electricity from a frayed electric cable leading from the main yard that looked like a fire hazard waiting to happen; the bedding was damp, so he turned on an old heater to try and make the place vaguely habitable. He opened the fridge door and quickly closed it as it looked like it belonged to a mad scientist who had been growing some weird cultures in it. On the wall, there was a lopsided photo that caught Neil's eye, he looked closely at it, and it featured a smiling Lez Allen with a young jockey, who he presumed could be the last apprentice, Kevin Dee, but couldn't be sure.

As requested, he went back to the stables at the time requested and wandered around looking for Brian. He peered into the first stable he came to and said hello to a girl with her back to him. As she turned around, he got the shock of his life as it was the stable girl he'd seen at Middleham and Catterick races, though her vibrant attitude had been replaced, and like the horses, she looked thoroughly miserable.

Neil said, "Hello again".

She looked quizzically at him as obviously didn't recognise him, and why would she, he had just been a face in the crowd, she introduced herself as Dawn, she said that her dad trained in the North and that he was sending her to various stables to gain experience before she eventually took over from him.

He was getting her full life story, as she seemed pleased to have someone to talk to and carried on, "My dad suffers from gout, and struggles some days, and keeps saying that training is a young person's game nowadays, which is ironic as the last yard I worked at was for an eccentric octogenarian, who acted like someone half his age and compared with this horrible place, was a pleasure to work there".

"Arthur Manning's yard," Neil said.

She looked shocked and a little concerned, "How do you know that? Are you a stalker?"

Neil was about to reply, but Brian put his head around the stable door and shouted at Neil, " This isn't the women's institute; you're not here to enjoy yourself." He took Neil to where his two horses were, pointed where the bedding was and the forage, and said, "Come to the tack room when you've finished here".

He was going to ask where the tack room was, but Brian had gone again, he went to stroke his first horse, but it appeared unresponsive and listless. He didn't even know its name but thought that he'd be able to get its confidence after a few weeks of tender loving care. When he'd finished, he went back to find Dawn to ask where the tack room was.

"Come with me," she said, "I'll show you, and you can meet the team, but I warn you, there's some rum buggers working here". Neil followed her and apprehensively traipsed into the room. Sat down in a corner in a plume of smoke were the twins Frank and Derek Boyle, who'd been his old adversaries from his show jumping days. It suddenly all clicked as he'd thought that he'd seen them at various racecourses recently darting furtively about.

They sneered at him in unison, "It's boy wonder, what the hell are you doing here?" he was beginning to wonder the same thing.

"I'm the new apprentice he said," but they just winked at each other and laughed. To make matters worse, the next person to walk in just stared at Neil and said, "My dad hates you," before grabbing a headcollar and walking straight out.

"Who's that?" Neil asked.

"Jason Connolly," came back the reply.

Oh god, Neil thought, it's blasted Angus Connolly's son; who's going to walk in next Ronnie Biggs? He didn't have long to wait as a lanky, thin girl brushed past him who he instantly recognised as Jan Cook, Dudley, the lecturer's daughter. She sat next to the Boyle twins, who handed her a cigarette and laughed with them but studiously ignored Neil.

Dawn had already left, so he decided to make his exit, but as he was leaving, the Boyles shouted, "We'll take you for a drink tonight, be ready at 8 o'clock''.

He couldn't believe his ears; he hoped that perhaps things were going to be OK, and they were going to let bygones be bygones, and he decided to give it a go. Perhaps working here wasn't going to be too bad after all. What he didn't know was that they had a little surprise awaiting him before then.

CHAPTER TWENTY-SIX
You're Not Welcome Here

Neil went back to the caravan reluctantly and cursed the twist in fate that caused him to end up here. He went to the local chippie and got himself some fish and chips and a can of fizzy pop and returned, laid them out on the faded Formica table and was just about to start eating when both caravan doors burst open, and he was grabbed from behind, and many hands stripped off all his clothes, and he was hoisted up in the air and paraded around the yard accompanied by a lot of shouting and jeering, he quickly realised that this was his initiation ceremony, he'd heard that they used to happen a lot in the past, and usually involved been stripped and covered in hoof oil and sometimes dunked in a freezing cold water trough, that part he certainly wasn't looking forward too. The mob took him as far as the main house, where a hatch was opened, and he was covered in what appeared to be a greasy, oily substance, and unceremoniously thrown in and slid down what he realised was a heap of coal, as he was in the coal bunker, the hatch was slammed shut and he heard voices saying, "We'll leave him there for an hour and then let him out in time to go to the pub".

Well, if this is the extent of the initiation, I've got away lightly, he thought as he sat shivering, imagining that he was black from head to foot, but it was hard to tell in the pitch dark. As his eyes grew accustomed to the lack of light, he could just make out a door at the end of the chamber, he managed to unbolt it and moved through to the next room and was met by a hot blast of air, which was appreciated as he was beginning to shiver uncontrollably, and in the corner, he noticed a big boiler, he went and stood near it and got some instant relief as the warm air surged through his body. He found an old hessian sack and wrapped it around himself and imagined that he looked vaguely ridiculous. This shouldn't happen to an up-and-coming jockey, he thought, but then he wondered if he still could be classed as such. He moved further on and round a corner and came face to face with a big blue shiny door, which he tried but it was locked, he looked to the right and saw a flight of worn pitted steps leading to yet another door which he presumed led to the house above, whilst he was stood looking at the door he saw the handle turning so he quickly slunk off to hide in the shadows as someone came down and unlocked the blue door and went in, he could see light emanating out and hear voices, presuming that someone was on the phone, and could hear a few words but not sentences, and all he heard clearly was, "Will not win".

He decided that this might be his chance to get out through the house, so he silently started ascending the steps. As he got to the top, he tried the door, but it was locked, and what was worse, the blue door slammed below, and someone was coming back up. Panicking slightly, he looked left to see a bare wall; he looked right, and he could see a narrow gap in the wall. He quickly jumped through and found himself in a very small empty chamber with just enough room to sit down. At eye level, an icy blast hit him in the face, meaning that it connected to the outside world. After sitting for a few minutes in complete silence, he decided to return back to the coal bunker, so he retraced his steps and found the hatch was now open, so he climbed out and treading carefully with his bare feet, he went back to his miserable caravan, after collecting his clothes which were strewn around the yard. He looked at his plate of congealed cold fish and chips and his can of flat fizzy pop, and his appetite and thirst vanished. He caught a glimpse of himself in the cracked mirror and didn't recognise the black and bruised apparition that stared back at him. The last thing he wanted to do now was to go for a drink, but he knew that there wouldn't be an opt-out option, so he went into what could be loosely termed as a bathroom and felt sure that there was a rat looking up at him through the shower plug hole, he peered closer, and if there had been anything there it had now gone, he had already turned the boiler on, and surprisingly the water was actually warm, and he managed to actually get himself clean, and when his new workmates burst back into the caravan, he actually looked human again, though not particularly looking forward to the evening out, but thought that if they're buying the drinks, then they can't be that bad. Three of them turned up, Frank, Derek Boyle and Jason Connolly; sadly, no Dawn.

He asked, "Where's Brian?"

"None of your business," came the reply.

Good start, Neil thought. The pub turned out to be within walking distance, was packed with stable lads and was very busy. Neil had realised a long time ago that stable lads were very thirsty people and could put a lot of drink away. He was disappointed as it looked more like a backstreet city boozer than a quaint country pub, but it served beer, and that was all that mattered.

The three of them mainly ignored Neil, and he was surprised that he was expected to buy the first round, "I thought that you lot were buying," he said.

"We'll buy the next round." But he doubted it. He saw Jason talking to the landlord and heard him call him Uncle. He looked above the bar and read, Sean Connolly licenced purveyor of beers and spirits, I bet he's Angus Connolly's brother, just my luck, can it get any worse and of course it did, he ended up buying the first three rounds, all part of his initiation he was told, by then he'd had enough of their course degrading conversation, mainly about what they'd do to the girls sat in the bar, in your dreams Neil thought, he excused himself saying that he was off for a Jimmy Riddle with no intention of returning. He wandered off and was amazed to see the jockey Sarah Howerd sat on her own, looking as attractive as ever.

He sidled up towards her and said, "What are you doing in a dive like this?"

"We usually go to the new wine bar at the other end of town, but I was hoping to meet my sister. She works with those tossers at the bar," she said, pointing at Neil's so-called workmates, and suddenly it all clicked together. She must be Dawn's sister; that's why she had appeared familiar when he first saw her.

"You're Dawn's sister," he said.

"And you must be the new lad then?" she said, "Dawn said that he was dishy".

"Dishy," Neil repeated, "has she swallowed a Jane Austen novel?"

Smiling, she said that she was there with her boyfriend, who works at Henry Aske's yard, "He's up at the bar buying the drinks".

"Lucky lad," Neil said.

"Do you mean lucky coz of where he works, or because he's got me as a girlfriend?"

"Both," Neil said quick as a flash.

Sarah said, "Dawn hates it at Bleak House. She says something funny is going on, and she's

166

looking for somewhere else to go, she says she doesn't feel safe, and at night her bedroom door rattles when the drunks return from the pub''.

Before she could say anymore, her boyfriend returned, shaking his head, saying those idiots from Allen's yard split his first round and refused to pay for a replacement. After a quick introduction, Neil said that he'd tell Dawn that he'd seen her sister and made his escape before he got roped into buying yet another round, as he'd long ago realised that they had no intention of buying him any drinks.

When he got back to the yard, all was quiet, but he thought that he could see light emitting from behind the steel door at the bottom of the yard and wondered to himself what could be going on down there at this time of night but was too tired to go and investigate. He could see that the curtains were tightly pulled closed in Dawn's bedroom, probably fast asleep, so he abandoned all thoughts of going to see her. He resignedly entered the dingy caravan, turned the lights on and looked round, and sighed. Is this my life now? He locked the door and put a plank across the other one and tied it with string so that no one would be able to get in, as he wouldn't put it past the drunks on returning from the pub, turfing him out of his bed. Surprisingly even though the bed was a bit lumpy and had no springs, just a solid plank of wood as the base, he slept really well and didn't wake until morning, and noticed a broken branch wedged in the door, where obviously someone had tried to get in, first spare time I get, I'll go and buy some bolts for the door he thought, but in the back of his mind, he wished that he was still working at Tom Coopers and wondered if he'd ever be able to go back there?

CHAPTER TWENTY-SEVEN

My Girl

Neil was feeling a little delicate the next morning, especially as it was an early start, and the Boyles, Connolly and Cougan made him feel worse as any pretence of goodwill was long gone as they spent every opportunity to be as nasty as they could be to him and to Dawn as well. They both kept out of their way as much as possible and went to the safe haven that was the tack room where the gang of Four, as Dawn had named them, rarely entered as somehow, they'd got the two silent foreign grooms to clean all their tack for them, using either bribery or violence of which one Neil had no idea. Dawn was very quiet when out in the yard, but in the tack room, she relaxed and talked freely with Neil.

He told her about the initiation ceremony and was appalled to hear that the same had happened to her, "I was the lucky one, I suppose," she said, "as I was allowed to keep my bra and knickers on, but that didn't stop their wandering hands". She visibly shuddered at the memory.

"You should complain," Neil said.

"To who? No one would listen here; they'd just laugh," she replied.

Neil could tell that he was raking up bad memories, so he moved on to brighter topics, "You never told me that you had a sister who is a jockey?"

"You never asked," came back the reply. Neil went on to say that he met her at the pub last night with her boyfriend, hoping to see you.

"I've been there once," Dawn replied, "and that was one time too many".

The only other times the two of them managed to snatch a line or two of conversation were at the races or riding up to the gallops. Neil was surprised at what a joy some of the horses were to ride out, especially at their faster pace. He was impressed at just how good they appeared to be, especially in relation to their lowly handicap ratings.

He'd asked Dawn about this, and she had just looked round nervously and said, "Just don't ask questions like that, or you'll regret it!" but Neil wasn't satisfied, the yard seemed to be shrouded in secrecy, and he had no idea why?

One night he couldn't find his phone, so he wandered back to the tack room, thinking that it might be there. As he approached, the yard was in the dark, and all was quiet, just the reassuring sound of horses munching their hay, but then he thought that he could hear a sound coming from the bottom of the yard behind the steel gate. He silently crept down to listen, there was definitely something going on as he could hear voices and a strange mechanical whirring sound, but he decided not to hang around as he had the distinct feeling that if he was found lurking around, the situation would become dire for him, so he slunk back to the detested caravan and started reading a Dick Francis novel which put even more ideas of what could be happening into his head. In the morning, he told Dawn what he'd heard; admittedly, he didn't have much to tell her, but she looked alarmed and said, "I don't like what's going on here and don't want to know".

"Aren't you just a little curious, Dawn?" Neil asked.

"No, I hate being here and just want to find another job as soon as possible."

Nothing of interest or intrigue happened for the next few days, and life was just about bearable, especially when the gang of four weren't about. That evening, Neil suggested to Dawn that they go out for a drink.

"Nah," she said, "I don't like the local, and you know who'll be there?"

"No, not there," Neil said, "but the new wine bar at the other side of town, it's called The Bike Shed. I've heard that they serve some great craft beers".

"But I don't like beer," she replied.

"Don't worry, as they'll have all the normal drinks as well."

He was pleasantly surprised when Dawn agreed, and they walked there in a relaxed mood. It was very busy but a lot more refined than the

Printer's Arms, the pub he'd gone to on his initiation night. Neil spotted a group of lads from Henry Aske's yard arriving, including Dawn's sister Sarah's boyfriend, who, as he walked past, said, "Hello, are you two courting?" They both shook their heads.

"No, it's not a date," Neil said, "it's just a quiet drink".

"If you say so," the lad replied, winking at Dawn.

Neil got himself a pint of Drunken Duck porter, "A really nice pint. It's brewed somewhere up north near where my aunt lives".

"Fascinating," Dawn said, supping her Jager bomb.

"What is that you're drinking?" Neil said, sipping a bit and pulling a face.

"It's Jagermeister and Red Bull; it gives me energy," she giggled.

They had a great evening and probably drank more than they intended, and the conversation flowed without any periods of silence. Neil asked her if she'd ever fancied being a jockey like her sister Sarah.

"No, not really; my heart is in training. I want to take over from my dad when he eventually retires. I just hope that he doesn't go on into his eighties like that trainer I worked for in Yorkshire."

"Well, if you need a good jockey when you start, you'll only have to ask."

"Why?" she replied, "do you know of one?" They laughed before she continued, "I'm meant to be out in the racing industry learning as much as possible, but I'm learning sod all here!"

Mention of the yard brought them back to reality, and they both went quiet, deeply entrenched in their inner thoughts until Neil shook them out of the dark reverie by going up to the bar and buying another round. The bell for last orders rang all too soon, and they left laughing and joking. As the cold air hit them, Neil looked at the wine bar sign glowing in its brash neon lights and, on impulse, said, "Do you fancy a snog behind the Bike Shed?"

Before he knew what was happening, she was all over him, kissing him with urgency; she relaxed as all her recent troubles were released. Neil kissed her back, and they had a passionate few moments, with Neil thinking that he'd have to buy her Jagerbombs again. As they walked back hand in hand, they heard a shout from the other side of the street and got a thumbs up from her sister's boyfriend.

"He'll tell Sarah now," Dawn said.

"Does that matter?" Neil replied.

"I don't suppose so. We're only holding hands; it's not as if...." and she drifted off, not finishing her sentence.

When they got back, Neil said, "Do you want to come into my luxurious accommodation?" He was surprised when she agreed, but as soon as they were in, the romantic moment started to fade.

Firstly, it was freezing; Neil put the one bar electric fire on, but it made little difference, Neil busied himself around the caravan trying to create a romantic atmosphere, but she wasn't helping.

"What's that smell?" she said.

"Oh, that's just damp, nothing to worry about," he lit some candles and balanced them on the window sills and turned the lights off, "you look really attractive in the candlelight," he said.

"That's coz you can't see me properly," she replied.

This wasn't going quite as he'd planned or hoped, he walked over towards her, stubbing his toe on the fire, but just about managing to suppress a scream, he took his shirt off as she peeled her t-shirt off to reveal a rather tatty red bra underneath, reading his thoughts she said, "All my good clothes are back at home, I didn't risk bringing anything smart down here, as I thought that it would go missing".

Neil sat next to her on the bed, noticing that the cold had caused goose pimples to appear on her white skin. He moved closer to her and leaned in to kiss her when suddenly the caravan started rocking, and they heard shouts outside. Oh no, Neil thought the gang of four were back from the pub, and in that instant, the moment vanished. As the caravan rocked, the candles fell off the windowsills, and Neil grabbed them to put them out and managed to burn his hand. He then went and sat next to the now fully clothed Dawn.

"Stay quiet, and they'll soon get bored and leave." So they sat side by side, not looking at each other, and a few moments later, the rocking stopped, and all was quiet, and they presumed that the gang of four had gone.

"I want to go back to my room," Dawn said.

"OK," Neil said, "I'll escort you, they could be still lurking about, and I don't trust them, tanked up".

"I don't trust them stone-cold sober," She replied.

As all was still and silent as they quietly exited the caravan, "We'll go the long way round, through the old wooden yard," Neil said, "as I doubt that they'll be hanging around down there?"

They walked slowly, following the light from his phone, and went round the back and started coming up the other side. Neil suddenly stopped and listened.

"Can you hear that? It's that mechanical sound again."

They were level with the mysterious buildings behind the steel doors, but Dawn wasn't interested, "Come on, Sherlock, I'm frozen and just want to get into my bed".

So reluctantly, Neil allowed himself to be dragged away, and they entered the yard via the little gate below the main house and crossed the yard unhindered and entered the stable lad's accommodation. They quickly walked up the stairs and along the corridor until they reached Dawn's room. She quickly unlocked the door, said good night, rushed inside and locked it before Neil had the chance to ask if she wanted him to come in and check that no one was there. Charming, he thought and turned to retrace his steps when he heard sounds coming up the stairs. He realised that it was the Boyles returning to their rooms on the floor above. He didn't fancy a confrontation, so he quickly ducked into the communal bathroom as they walked past and heard some derogatory talk about himself.

"I wonder if Neil really has pulled tonight?" Derek said.

"Don't be daft," Frank replied, "There's more chance of him riding a Donkey Derby winner". This was followed by laughter as they slowly disappeared and their chat receded. Donkey Derby indeed Neil thought I'll show them. He started back, but a noise below in the yard stopped him in his tracks. He'd heard a loud banging which sounded like the closing of the big steel door, so he rushed downstairs to get a closer look. As he went back into the yard, he could see a light flashing at the other side, and it soon registered to him that someone was walking a horse along from behind the steel doors, but what on earth could they have been doing at this time of night, he thought. They went round the corner, obviously putting the horse back into its stable, but which horse he didn't know. He was pondering all this when the light reappeared and headed his way, so he quickly hid in the tack room, in the shadows, the light suddenly came on, and a headcollar was flung on the floor, and the light disappeared, he'd seen enough to know that it was Brian Cougan, and a few moments later he heard a slight slam as his house door was closed. Thinking that the coast was clear, he went to the door and turned the handle but was dismayed to find that it had been locked, so he had no option other than to bed down for the night, which he did, and it turned out to quite comfortable, better than the beastly caravan. He dreamt about his night out with Dawn and the mysterious incident behind the steel door but could think of no reason why a horse would be taken down there at this time of night; it was a mystery that he intended to one day solve. The next day was back to normal.

Dawn just said, "Great pub, we must do it again sometime".

He enjoyed his days at the races leading the horses round, but not when the jockey was Angus Connolly. On one such day, Neil was leading round Lastthrowofthedice, and Angus Connolly was the jockey. He looked down at him and said, "Best job for you; you're finished as a jockey".

Neil had a long time ago decided it was best not to react and just ignore him, and just take what he said until he got bored, which didn't seem to be happening any time soon, and some of his comments hit home. The horse won easily, and Neil was tempted to say to Connolly that his aunt could have ridden this one to victory but resisted the temptation and just smiled through gritted teeth. Back at the stables, he told Dawn all about his day and his hatred for Connolly and mentioned the night before, not noticing that the foreign grooms were silently sitting in the shadows cleaning tack. He later saw them talking to the gang of four and pointing in his direction. They'd obviously been listening to all that had been said and reported it straight back to his antagonists, and he realised in the future he'd have to be careful what he said when the foreign grooms were around.

He was beginning to wonder if he'd ever get a ride at this dreadful place when a few days later, Brian said to him, "You're riding Last throw of the dice tomorrow". Neil couldn't believe it; it was his first ride in weeks. He asked why he'd been chosen.

"Your weight allowance will help," came the reply.

Neil was actually very excited and couldn't really sleep the night before and was feeling a sensation akin to the one he had on his very first ride. He'd ridden the horse on the gallops, and it was a flying machine, usually very keen and eager. The race was a lowly affair at Bath. He drove himself there as he didn't fancy the journey there and back with the Bleak House Staff, Jan Cook was leading the horse up, and he knew that she would be a laugh a minute, not. It was a longer journey that he expected, and he arrived a little late and flustered. The first person he saw on arrival was Pete Wisdom.

"Do you go to every meeting?" he asked.

"I'm actually down on holiday with the wife, she's gone shopping in the town, and the money that I've got on you should pay for the holiday." His overbrimming optimism made Neil feel a little uneasy and slightly queasy, but he consoled himself with the thought that there wasn't much to beat in the race.

As soon as he saw the horse in the paddock, alarm bells started ringing as the horse looked somehow different, but he wasn't sure why. Lez Allen was showboating with the owners in the paddock and completely ignored him and gave him no instructions, just saying that Brian would have told him what to do, but he hadn't. Luckily Neil had done his homework and watched the horse's previous races, and looked at his form, so he knew that the horse needed holding up and gradually being brought into the race. As soon as he got on the horse, his heart sank as he lacked his usual enthusiasm, or at least what he'd shown on the gallops, and just cantered slowly to the start. When the race started, the horse lumbered listlessly into action, and despite Neil's frantic urgings, he failed to spark and didn't really get into the race finishing a distant and disappointing fourth. This was the first time that Neil had been on a beaten favourite, and he didn't like the experience. The horse's odds had drifted near the start, so someone knew that he wasn't going to run well, Neil thought. He knew that the horse should have won and easily, but there was nothing that he could do about it. He intended to tell the trainer all this, but he was nowhere to be seen.

Jan Cook, who rarely spoke to him, just said, "Looks like we'd better get Angus back on board next time". That hurt Neil and worse was to come as on the way back to his car Pete Wisdom marched up to him and eyeballed him. He definitely wasn't in the mood for pleasantries and laid into Neil, who didn't really get a chance to defend himself. Pete said that he'd invested heavily on the horse and was far from happy and finished his invective with the cutting remark, "You'd better stick to riding clothes horses in future. You'd probably get one of those to go faster than you managed today," before storming off, muttering about useless jockeys being the bane of his life.

Neil thought that this was unfair and rich coming from a man who'd probably fall off if he tried to ride a bike, but he reasoned that being a jockey, he'd have to put up with a lot of flak from disgruntled punters. So what had started looking like an enjoyable day ended up being the opposite, and it was a long journey home as he self-analysed the race in great detail in silence, as he had no appetite for his usual cheery music. When he got back, Dawn was also a little distant, which made matters worse as she was the only friend he had here, so he went to bed in his dingy caravan, thoroughly miserable, hoping that tomorrow would be a better day. He had always thought of himself as an optimist, but even he was struggling to look on the bright side at present.

CHAPTER TWENTY-EIGHT

My Evil Twin

One night as Neil was trudging discontentedly through the mud and puddles back to his caravan, he got what he thought was a welcome surprise as a car drew up, which he instantly recognised as belonging to his great friends, the Milligan twins Tilly and Dilly. He hadn't seen them recently and had only been in contact via a few and far between texts. He wrongly presumed that they'd come to see him but thought that it was a long way to travel on an off chance.

They got out of the car with their usual vibrant burst of energy, and Neil noticed that they were dressed up to the nines, "You're all glammed up," he said.

"We're off on a date," they replied.

"I don't remember...." Neil started saying but was swiftly interrupted.

"No, not with you stupid, but with the Boyle twins." Neil was shocked and couldn't hide it. "What, with the evil twins, you're joking?"

"No," they replied indignantly. "Don't you know that twins always go out with twins?"

Neil had never heard this before and said, "But surely not them; you know what they're like".

"Well, we've seen them at the races when we've been helping out Tom Cooper. He's very short-staffed, you know." This was a dig at Neil, but he ignored it as they continued, "They seem to have changed, and anyway, no one else asked us out".

"Changed," said Neil, "Changed for the worse, more like". They just pulled faces at him. "Well, be careful," he said.

"You sound like our mum. Next, you'll be asking us if we've got clean knickers on."

"No," Neil replied. "They shouldn't be seeing your underwear." They just giggled as the Boyles arrived and greeted the girls and ignored Neil, and then they were all gone, leaving Neil bewildered, and though he didn't like to admit it, a little jealous, he carried on towards his caravan disconsolate and dragging his feet feeling a little puzzled, when he first met the Boyles, the twins had told him that they were okay once you got to know them, he began to wonder if something had been going on for a long time. The next few days went by without incident, but even though he was curious, there was no way that he was going to ask the Boyles about their love life. He confided in Dawn in one of their daily tack room chats, and she said that she couldn't understand it as the Boyles made her skin crawl, but she said some girls are attracted to the wrong sort, to the bad lads. Neil watched the Boyles from a distance, trying to see if there was any change in their attitude or if he could overhear a conversation, but nothing came to light, so he put it to the back of his mind and almost forgot about it, that was until he went back home one weekend. As he neared home, he came across the Cooper racehorse string as they returned from the gallops with the twins leading. As he drove level, he slowed down to catch a few words with them.

"How are you doing?" he asked.

"Fine." They both replied, but they didn't really sound fine.

"How was twin on twin action?" he cheekily asked.

"Oh, them," they replied, "we sacked them; they were no good to man nor beast, they're just drunken yobs with no social graces and actually very boring". They then added with a smirk, "And they've got tiny little wieners," and this was followed by rude gestures, which started the whole string laughing.

Neil was shocked but quickly regained his composure, "I hope that you didn't belittle their manhood in front of them, or they'd have gone mental. I warned you that they're dangerous".

"Of course not. We're not stupid, we just stopped returning their calls, and they soon gave up, but don't you dare say anything to them." Neil assured them that he wouldn't and carried on his way. He'd have loved the chance to goad the Boyles but knew if he did, then things would turn ugly very quickly. Next chat time in the tack room, he told

Dawn all about the twins in hushed voices, but they obviously hadn't been careful enough as unbeknown to them the foreign grooms had been lurking in the shadows, and at the first opportunity, they repeated all that they'd heard to the Boyles, Neil didn't have to wait too long for their reaction, as when he came back for afternoon stables, he was grabbed from behind by Derek who without speaking apart from muttering a few obscenities and before Neil knew what was going on, had punched him in the stomach, leaving him bent double badly winded.

Frank suddenly appeared, shouting, "Leave him; he's not worth it. We've got bigger fish to fry. No one ridicules us". Frank grabbed his brother and roughly pulled him off, and they left Neil as the pain subsided. A few moments later, he heard their car starting up and heard the engine revving up, and then they were gone in a sea of scattering gravel and petrol fumes, and he had no idea where they were going. A day or two later, at the races, he bumped into John Cooper from Sunrise farm, who asked him if he'd heard about the car crash Tilly and Dilly Milligan had had.

"No," he replied, shocked, "what happened?"

"No one really knows," he replied, "apparently their car left the road, and they hit a tree. It appears that they'd had a collision with a stolen car which was found burnt out a mile or two away from the incident".

"How are they?" Neil asked, very concerned.

"They're okay, I believe. Badly shaken and with a few broken bones, but they won't talk about it."

Neil tried texting the twins numerous times but got no reply, so as a last resort, he rang their home landline and spoke to their mother, who informed him that they were back home convalescing and would be okay once their broken bones had healed and their concussion had gone, she did admit that she was a little worried as they were very quiet which was unusual for them, she told him that they wouldn't really talk about the incident, and strangely they were blaming him for the so-called accident. Neil assured her that he was in no way responsible for it, and he was pleased that she seemed to believe him. He asked her to pass on his good wishes and hoped that they had a speedy recovery, but since they weren't speaking to him, there was little else that he could do except ponder on what had happened and worry about them. He couldn't get it out of his head, and it started to affect his sleep, with his mind going into overdrive and coming up with various scenarios, and he was beginning to think that the Boyles were somehow involved, but he said to himself, surely even they wouldn't have caused the accident, but he just didn't know, but he grew more and more determined to find another job and get away from the Boyles, he certainly wouldn't miss anything about Bleak

House, especially the blasted caravan. Whilst all this was occupying his mind, he got a very welcome distraction when he was booked to ride three runners for the yard on the very next day.

CHAPTER TWENTY-NINE
Disappointment

Neil couldn't really understand why he'd been booked to ride three Bleak House runners but wasn't complaining though he did have a slightly uneasy feeling. Of the three runners, he knew the first one he was to ride Captain Confusion very well as he regularly rode him out on the gallops, so he knew his character inside out and had found him to be a very calm and placid horse, his second ride Cracked Eggs was a completely different character and was more of a handful as Dawn had reported back to him as he was one of her rides, and his third ride Jam Butty had been claimed recently, (claiming races occur where every runner can be bought for an advertised price in a claiming race), from another yard and so little was known about her, they all, however, had good chances of winning and Neil had gone to bed with a spring in his step for a change and in a happy mood and had dreamt of riding his first treble. In the misty damp reality of the next morning, the dreams of the night before seemed unrealistic, and his confidence was ebbing away, but he was still hoping for a good day. The racing was taking place at Nottingham racecourse, one that he hadn't been to before. As was becoming the norm, he drove himself to the races with the rhythmic beat of his loud, cheery music keeping his spirits high and keeping his misgivings at bay. Captain Confusion was led around the paddock by one of the silent foreign grooms, Neil didn't even bother trying to speak to him as he knew that there would be no response, and as expected, there were no instructions given to him by Lez Allen, who just ignored him as if he wasn't there, Neil was getting used to this stony silence, and in this case, he wasn't too concerned as he knew how to ride this horse from his experiences on the gallops. As the race started, he tried to keep him near the leaders, but this was taking more effort than he expected, and when he kicked for home, the horse found very little, and he was very lucky to finish a distant third, and he'd expected so much more, and on all known form he should have run so much better.

Nothing was said as he unsaddled, as he was met with a gloomy silence. He had some spare time before his next race, so he sat in the changing room reading the Sporting Life and studying the form, his phone ringing awoke him from his reverie, and he was pleased to hear trainer Sue Henry on the other end asking him if he was available to step in and replace Sarah Howerd on Sunday Girl in the last race of the day, as Sarah had called off at the last minute due to a mystery illness, Neil of course readily accepted and was sure that at least one of his horses would be running as expected. It was now time for his second ride on Cracked Eggs, and he went out to the paddock filled with apprehension. As he got on the horse, he realised that the horse was a lot quieter than expected, and again he had to work hard to keep the horse competitive, and as in the last race, he came to the last furlong with a chance only to fade into the third position again, on the walk back in the horse appeared really tired more like as if he'd just run in the Grand National, Neil was by now getting a bit annoyed, it was obvious to him that something was going on with these horses as he was beginning to be convinced that they were being stopped somehow and what really worried him was that it looked bad and could have implications for him as it looked like he wasn't trying.

Sure enough, as he went out for his third ride, Pete Wisdom leaned over the rails and said, "You could make it a bit less obvious that you're not trying. I hope that they're paying you plenty to lose races?"

Neil just gritted his teeth and ignored the accusations, knowing that he'd be wasting his time trying to defend himself he just hoped that not too many people were listening. Consequently, he certainly wasn't looking forward to his third ride for Bleak House on Jam Butty, and sure enough, it was almost an action reply to the first two races. She, like the other two horses, appeared, if anything, a little tired and again, he came to the closing stages with a winning chance only to struggle to even get a place and just hung on to fourth place, no one spoke to him, and the trainer was nowhere to be seen. Neil's mood was as black as could be possible when he entered the paddock to ride the Sue Henry trained Sunday Girl, but on seeing the friendly face of Sue, who was leading the horse around herself, he tried to brighten himself up.

She smiled at him, and as she was legging him up, she said, "You want to get away from that yard as soon as possible before they bring you down. Look what happened to their last apprentice?" What really did happen to him, Neil wondered as Sue continued, "But please forget them for the next few minutes and concentrate on my horse".

This he managed to do admirably and had a lovely ride which reinvigorated his spirits, and what was an added bonus was the horse that he beat into second was a Bleak House runner ridden by none other than Angus Connolly.

Sue was very pleased as, for a small yard, winners were few and far between. She said to him, "You rode that really well," and then with a smirk on her face, "almost as well as Sarah".

So Neil went home with his faith in the racing game somewhat restored. When he got back to the yard, he was determined not to let sleeping dogs lie and demand answers. No sooner had he parked his car than he was straight round to Brian's cottage and banged on the door.

Brian came out and listened to what he had to say with indifference and replied, "A bad workman blames his tools," and pushed Neil back and slammed the door shut with a ferocity that rattled the glass panels.

Incensed, Neil marched down to the steel doors and banged on them violently, but as expected, they were locked, and as he started calming down, he came away, deciding to save it for the next morning. As he walked past Brian's abode, he overheard snatches of a conversation catching a few words, something about someone being trouble, and they'd outstayed their usefulness, and they needed to get rid, but he wasn't sure if it was him who was being discussed. Deeply troubled, he headed back towards his caravan, and he could see Dawn staring down at him from her room, looking worried, but luckily there was no sign of the Boyles or Jason Connolly, probably still at the pub, Neil thought. Sleep was hard to achieve, and he tossed and turned all night with many wild thoughts going through his mind over and over again. He woke up bleary-eyed, still tired and suffering with black humour. He did his three horses in the morning without getting the usual satisfaction, with the horses playing up almost as if they could tell he was suffering mentally. He didn't manage to speak to Dawn on the gallops and was hoping to see her in the tack room, but she wasn't there as she had gone early with a horse to a distant racecourse. No one spoke to him until after evening stables when Brian came up to him to tell him that he was riding Money Tree the next day at an evening meeting at Warwick. The horse was a prolific winner and had won her last three races, so she was on a four-timer, with Angus Connolly riding her to each of her last three wins. Neil couldn't understand why he'd been asked to ride him and was deeply suspicious, it did cross his mind to say that he wouldn't ride it and just pack his bags and leave there and then, but his professional pride wouldn't let him and he intended to give the horse the best possible ride he could, but dark foreboding thoughts kept resurfacing in his mind, and he had another bad night tossing and turning, the lack of sleep was beginning to affect him, but all he could do was optimistically hope that tomorrow would be a better day, and with that thought, he snatched an hours sleep and dreamt about a Bleak House horse actually running as expected and perhaps even winning.

CHAPTER THIRTY

Things a Get From Bad to Worse

Money Tree looked the part in the paddock and was vying for favouritism with a runner from the champion trainer Henry Aske's yard. These two had met in their previous race, with Money Tree winning by a short head, when ridden by Angus Connolly, Neil was hoping to banish his demons and ride a winner for the Bleak House yard, then he'd decided he could hand in his notice in a blaze of glory, but he hadn't put any thought as to what he might do after that.

One of the racing channels was televising a select number of evening meetings, and this one at Warwick just happened to be one of them, which added a little bit more tension to the proceedings. When Neil entered the paddock, he spotted Lez Allen being interviewed by a racing presenter, and he appeared to be all smiles; they don't know the real Lez Allen, he thought to himself. When the trainer finally entered the paddock as expected, he completely ignored Neil, and as usual, the foreign groom leading the horse round was silent. The head lad Brian was nowhere to be seen either. Luckily, as usual, Neil had done his homework and had worked out a plan. He wanted to make a good start and try and settle just behind the leaders and leave making his move until the last possible moment, which he knew was the critical and difficult part, and then hopefully get Money Tree's head in front. The horse had never won at this distance, and in Neil's opinion, the extra two furlongs were a worry, so he needed to conserve as much of the horse's energy as possible. Like the recent runners, the horse didn't seem particularly fresh on cantering down to the start but trying to reassure himself, Neil put this down to all the races that the horse had had recently in quick succession of each other. As had happened previously with the other runners, his mount drifted in the betting just before the off and started at 5-1 second favourite. The race started as he expected, and he was able to maintain a good position though it took more effort than expected. With two furlongs to go, the favourite was just in front of him, and soon after, it set off for home. Neil, as he'd planned, was keeping hold of his horse, intending to leave it until the last possible moment before trying to overtake the front runner and take the lead, worryingly though he had to work a lot harder than he expected to just maintain his position, so was further back than was ideal and when he tried to reduce the deficit, as had happened previously the horse found nothing and he finished a good ten lengths behind the easy winner, Money Tree had beaten this horse in their recent last meeting, so Neil wanted to know what was different and the only reason he could come up with was foul play.

Neil's face was as black as thunder and heavily creased with all the frowning as he returned, and his demeanour got worse when Pete Wisdom walked alongside him and shouted at him, "Another great effort at stopping a horse Neil, luckily I backed the winner". Neil had had enough, and when he got off the horse, he turned to Lez Allen in full view of the TV cameras.

"You'll have to find yourself another jockey; I'm finished with this place. I'm off to the stewards to tell them what you and your motley group of criminals have been up to."

"And what exactly do you think I'm up to? You're the one who's been constantly disobeying orders and losing races that you should really have been winning. That's four you've stopped now, so you'll never ride for us again!"

This wasn't going well, and Neil didn't want a public slanging match, especially as the TV cameras were everywhere, so he decided to go and find the stewards and put in an official complaint, As he'd never been to Warwick before it took him a long time to find their room and when he did to his horror he found that Lez Allen had beaten him to it and was already there, and listening outside the door he could hear that he was already in full flow, it was almost as if he was expecting this and had prepared for it. He listened to hear himself being described as being completely bent and how he'd thrown four races for Allen that any other competent jockey would have won easily. Lez Allen was putting on a good performance, and Neil was beginning to wonder if he'd been an actor in the past. He was painting a terrible picture of Neil, saying that no other trainer would take him on, and he'd given him a chance, and this is how he'd been repaid. Neil was beginning to think that all that he could hope for was that the stewards wouldn't be taken in by all the rubbish that Allen was spewing, but they were, he could understand why, as Allen was an established trainer with an unblemished record and if Neil was honest, he was just a nobody. He was called into the dark room with a strong aroma of alcohol. He was made to stand and asked to respond as the allegations against him were read out.

"Well, firstly, I'd like to congratulate Mr Allen on his Oscar-winning performance of complete fiction." This was not a good start as they didn't seem to appreciate a cocksure little jockey getting above himself.

"Cut out the theatrics," he was told, "and answer the questions".

The head steward then started quizzing him, "Did you, as Mr Allen said, disobey orders?"

"No," Neil replied, "As I never get any orders or any instructions whatsoever".

"Did you stop the horse in question, Money Tree?"

"No, I've never stopped a horse, and I never will." Allen laughed out loud as he said this.

They continued questioning for a little longer but didn't seem at all impressed with his replies. They then replayed the race on a big screen at the front of the room that showed the race from many different angles, and Neil had to admit to himself that it looked bad; feeling worried, he blurted out, "You need to dope test this horse".

"Don't tell us how to do our job."

But he hadn't stopped yet, "And check out Bleak House Stables; there's something not right there".

"We won't tell you again to hold your tongue, and for the record, Mr Allen has a clean record. His stable has never failed a drug test, and his yard will have been checked, as do all yards with horses in training. Mr Allen has never been in trouble with the racing authorities."

With that, they dismissed Neil and told him to wait outside whilst they discussed the contentious events. After about half an hour, he was still standing there and was beginning to think that he should just wander off, and he also couldn't understand why Allen was still in there when he was summoned back in to be informed that the case was being sent to headquarters and that he'd have to report to Portman Square tomorrow at 11 o'clock, and that was it, he was ushered out, and he could hear laughter going on, so he knew who's side the stewards were on. Surely they're not involved as well, but he dismissed that thought, but one thing that he was sure about was that someone somewhere would have made a lot of money out of Money Tree not winning; it certainly was magic for those involved.

CHAPTER THIRTY-ONE
Al Capone

Where's Portman Square, Neil wondered, and where am I going to stay tonight? He decided that there was no way that he was going back to sleep in the caravan, not even for one more minute. He, however, went back intending to collect his meagre belongings. He parked a hundred yards away, unseen from the yard and tentatively approached it. When he got near, he noticed that the lights were on, and he could see figures inside darting around, rifling through his belongings and ransacking it, he presumed. He watched for a little while longer as the night was drawing in and his vision became obscured by the dark. He was getting cold and bored when he noticed the lights going off, so he moved closer and it appeared that the caravan was empty, so he sneaked up to it, and all was quiet though the door was swinging backwards and forwards in the slight breeze, he silently went in realising that if they came back, he was trapped, he grabbed his sleeping bag, which he'd been using for ease, and quickly filled it with as much of his belongings that he could find, there hadn't been much here to start with, and some items had been taken, so he was in and out very quickly, he looked back as he said a silent good riddance to the caravan and the whole Bleak House experience, and he slipped away back to his car, thinking and worrying about Dawn who was still working there, and he wondered how they'd treat her knowing how friendly with him she was. He texted her, and she quickly replied, saying that she was fine but keeping her head down but now that he was gone, she was going to hand her notice in. he told her about his impending Jockey Club meeting, and she advised that he went looking smart, in a suit. A suit, he thought. The only one that I've got is my birthday suit, and I don't think that that would go down well.

It was getting late now, and he couldn't be bothered to drive to his home or the family stud, so when he was a good distance away from Bleak House, he pulled into a litter-strewn deserted layby and cut the engine and settled down for hopefully a few hours sleep which was a struggle as inside his car it was a lot colder than he expected and time dragged, he'd just managed to drift off when he was rudely awakened by a blaring horn and woke up to see bright lights, and for a brief frightening second he thought it might be the Boyles paying him a night visit, but it turned out to be a dirty great big tractor which parked right next to him and a ruddy faced farmer jumped out of the cab and started knocking on his window, and it soon became clear that he was blocking access to the farmer's field as in daylight he could see a gateway, apologising he swiftly moved off and headed off to find a garage to fill up with fuel and buy a sandwich for breakfast and freshen up in the Gents toilet. He was running late by now, so he dashed into a charity shop and picked the first suit that vaguely fitted him. The fact that it was pinstriped didn't bother him. He arrived at the meeting slightly late, and a little flustered, and his suit made him look like a cross between Al Capone and Walker, the spiv from Dad's Army. The meeting had already started, and he knew that his late arrival gave a bad impression. The stewards were all extremely smartly dressed in regulation tweed and immaculately turned out, so the comparison with Neil's appearance was highly noticeable, especially since he'd forgotten to clean his shoes. This was a bad start, he thought, and it went downhill from there.

The senior steward of the meeting was Gilbert French-Saunders's father, Oliver, who glared at Neil as soon as he entered the room. It was explained to Neil that he was being investigated for bringing racing into disrepute by affecting race results by stopping horses running to their true merit.

Neil told them that he'd never had and never would stop a horse and said rather exasperated, "I've already told the local stewards at Warwick all this". He then said that they should be investigating the bent trainer, Allen, and his motley band of corrupt stable lads.

He was told in no uncertain terms that it was him who was being investigated and nobody else. He was then asked why he had links to a bookmaker known as Harry Bowen of Smart Racing and why he had received substantial sums of money from him. Oliver French-Saunders looked at him with a smirk, and Neil was convinced that he'd taken an instant dislike to him, perhaps due to the incident on the racecourse when he'd blocked his son and made him look stupid, but surely he shouldn't let personal vendettas get in the way of a professional investigation Neil was beginning to think that everyone was against him, but he remained relaxed and calmly explained that Harry Bowen was actually his Uncle and that he's real name was Bartholomew, he didn't add that only an idiot wouldn't know that but wanted to. They then dropped their bombshell and said that the investigation would be ongoing for a minimum of six months and to protect racing's integrity, they would have to stand him down for that period. Finally, they said, "Could you please hand your jockey's licence in on your way out".

He was assured by a small, nervous-looking, weasely little man that if he was found to be innocent that he would get his licence back straight away, but whilst it was ongoing, he was banned from all horse racing establishments, stables and racecourses.

Neil was dumbstruck and enquired, "What about my livelihood? What do I do for money?"

Oliver said, "You should have thought of that when you were stopping horses, we've spent ages trying to improve the image of racing, and your actions have set us back by years".

Neil was getting angry now and reiterated that he'd never stopped a horse but realised that nobody was listening, and he thought that they'd branded him guilty before he'd even entered the room. Raising his voice, he said, "I'll prove my innocence however long it takes me and get my licence back".

He thought that he heard Oliver mutter, "I doubt that", but decided that it was best not to respond.

One of the stewards raised his morale slightly by saying that he'd get a fair hearing and no stone would be left unturned to get to the truth, but Neil doubted this, he was beginning to wonder if some of them were in Lez Allen's payroll. No sooner than it started the meeting was all over and he was dismissed and he walked outside in something of a daze, it was a long silent journey home with his cd collections staying firmly in their boxes as he ruminated what on earth he was going to do, on nearing home his phone rang and he answered it , hands free of course, it was his mum asking him how the meeting had gone, he was just beginning to explain when out of the corner of his eye he caught sight of a cyclist coming towards him swaying from side to side, with his concentration slightly lacking he failed to give it a wide enough berth and it wobbled as they drew level and made contact with the side of his car and disappeared out of sight as the bike and rider scraped along the side of his car, his mother could hear the strange noises and said, "Neil, Neil, are you OK?"

But he just said, "I'll have to go, I'll tell you later".

He stopped and got out quickly to find a mangled bike and moaning cyclist lying crumpled on the road. As the figure got up, he was shocked to see that it was his one-time lecturer Dudley Cook smelling strongly of alcohol. He didn't look badly injured, just bruised and shaken up, but when he saw that it was Neil, all hell was let loose.

"You swerved towards me, you tried to kill me," he said accusingly, "You were on the phone," and then, as an afterthought, "you've been drinking".

Neil didn't like where this was going but tried to calm him down and asked if he was okay and offered to call an ambulance for him, and tried to help him up.

"Keep away from me!" he shouted, "I'm calling the police," and he did.

Neil had had very little contact with the police up to now in his life. They'd called in at the stud a few years ago concerning a team of poachers who'd been seen in the area, they'd been friendly and relaxed, but this time, their attitude was totally different.

"You've been accused of attempted murder," they said. "We'll have to take you to the station".

This was the last thing that Neil wanted after the day that he'd had, but he had no option. At the station, he was breathalysed, and his protestations that it was Dudley that they should be doing fell on death ears. He was then taken to a room and left to his own thoughts for a few minutes before a scruffy little chap arrived who reminded him of Columbo and who introduced himself as DC Ted Abbott, who grimaced when he saw Neil's attire and started off the conversation.

"Have you been to a fancy dress party as a New York gangster?" and smiled at his own joke. Neil calmly explained that he'd been at the Jockey Club headquarters.

"Dressed like that?" DC Abbott exclaimed, "I'm sure that didn't go down well amongst that conservative mob?"

"No, you're correct. It didn't" Neil conceded. DC Abbott then reeled off what he was being charged with.

"Attempted murder." He said, "In all my 30 years as a police officer, I can instantly tell a wrong un, and as soon as I clamped eyes on you, I knew that you fit that bill".

"What about a fair hearing?" Neil pleaded. He was asked to tell his story, so he calmly and patiently explained what had happened, said that his only error had been to keep on his side of the road and not take evasive action and finished by saying, "It's not a story but the truth".

But DC Abbott had the bit between his teeth, "It's alleged that you hold a vendetta against the injured party Dudley Cook".

"We just didn't get on. We're poles apart," Neil replied, "and I was only at the college for half a day".

"Well, Mr Cook tells a completely different story," DC Abbott said.

"Well, he would, wouldn't he?"

"Have you got any CCTV evidence to back your story? Have you got a dashcam in your car?"

Neil ignored the jibe about "story" and said, "No, I've no camera, and the incidents were on the outskirts of town in a dimly lit area, so I doubt that there will be any street or shop cameras".

"It's not looking good for you," came back the reply.

Neil was then told that the incident would be thoroughly investigated and that he'd be hearing from them in due course.

"I can't wait," he cheekily replied.

"You can go now," DC Abbott said, and as he was leaving, he shouted, "but try and keep out of trouble for the foreseeable future!"

Neil's car had been photographed from all angles, so it was cleared for him to take it. He looked at all the bumps and scratches on it and wondered who would pay for the repairs. He drove off, not sure whether to go to the stud farm or his house but decided on his house as he didn't fancy facing the interrogation that he'd get at the stud, and he needed to check his house as he hadn't been there for a few weeks. As soon as he parked up, his next-door neighbour Richard, on spying him through the window, sprang out of the door with amazing alacrity for someone of his age but stopped in his tracks and looked at him puzzled.

"Why are you dressed like a gangster?"

Neil was no longer in the mood for humour and just briefly told Richard the events of his long day.

"Oh dear," Richard said, "but sadly, I've got more bad news for you".

Neil didn't think that he could take any more but just stood stoically, thinking that bad news always came in threes, and listened as Richard continued, "You know that we were having problems with our floorboards?" Neil hadn't remembered but let him continue, "Well, we've had someone out today to look at it, and it's damp rot. The whole ground floor will have to come out and be replaced. I just don't know how we can afford it?" Before Neil could answer, he continued, "And as we're semi-detached, it's ninety-nine per cent certain that your ground floor will be in a similar state!"

Neil had had more than enough for one day and blurted out without thinking, "We'll just have to have a fire and burn them both down and claim on the insurance".

He'd have usually added 'only joking' but just went into his house without the courtesy of saying good night to Richard, who shuffled off slightly perturbed. Neil slumped into a chair and fell asleep, waking a few hours later in the middle of the night stiff and cold and in no better frame of mind.

CHAPTER THIRTY-TWO

Clutching at Straws

The next day was dull and dismal, which matched Neil's mood, he intended to go and see his next-door neighbours Richard and Lilly to discuss the damp rot problem and explain that he was only joking about having pyromaniac tendencies and burning the houses down to claim on the insurance, but they were out probably shopping or visiting their son he supposed, sending them a text was out of the question as, like most people of their generation, they didn't do texting, they each had mobile phones and would have taken them with them, but they'd be turned off! He sat down in a chair with a cup of green tea and wondered what he was going to do for the next six months and, if the result was unfavourable, what he was going to do for the rest of his life.

He was still contemplating all this but reaching no conclusion when there was a knock on the door, he was a bit mystified as he rarely got any visitors and wasn't expecting anyone, the only people who came were his mum with clean clothes and his neighbours Richard and Lilly usually with food for him, he opened the door and was pleasantly surprised to see Dawn stood there, she explained that she'd been for a job interview in the locality, but didn't think that it had gone too well, as the interview had stalled when she'd mentioned where she was working at present. As she was nearby, she said that she's decided to call in on Neil to see how he'd got on with his Jockey Club meeting. Neil briefly told her about his terrible day, finishing off by telling her about the bad news he'd received about the damp rot.

"So what are you going to do?" She asked.

"I'm going to prove my innocence."

"How?" she asked.

"That I have absolutely no idea," he replied. They then put their heads together and started thinking about the situation he was in and what could be done about it. Neil was convinced that Lez Allen was stopping horses, but how and why were the mysteries that he had no answers to.

"Is he a big gambler?" Dawn enquired.

"No idea," Neil said, "but I suppose that I could ring my Uncle Harry, the bookie, and see what he knows".

Uncle Harry was pleased to hear from Neil and wanted to talk about many subjects, and it was a good ten minutes before they got onto the subject that he'd rung about. Uncle Harry confirmed that as far as he knew Lez Allen wasn't a big gambler but said that someone could be betting on his behalf, and Bleak House wasn't known as a gambling yard, and he'd never heard of them landing a touch (gamble) or a coup (winning a race with a horse specially prepared for it). So no joy there, Neil thought.

Sadly this is how it went on for many hours, and all that they'd worked out was that money must be involved in some way or another. But then Dawn said, "But everything revolves around money".

They wondered if drugs were involved but concluded that these were generally used to improve performance, not reduce them and if they were using them, how and when were they doing it as neither of them had seen anything suspicious, but more importantly, why hadn't the yard failed drug tests?

They then mulled over other options, "What about blood doping?" Dawn said (removing blood and then replacing it a week or two later when the horse had already replaced it).

Neil shook his head and said, "But that would improve performance. The opposite is happening here".

They were clutching at straws now and coming up with bizarre and unusual ideas, "What about giving them a great big drink of water just before the race?" Dawn said.

"Well, I suppose that might work, but how do you get a horse to drink extra water, and I'd have thought that you might be in danger of causing colic."

"How about carrying extra weights," Dawn said.

"That also might work, but how do you do it unseen at a racecourse with officials and cameras watching your every move," Neil concluded. They'd run out of ideas, and Neil said morosely, "If I don't find out, I'm finished".

With nothing to go on, they hatched a plan to watch carefully what went on at Bleak House, Dawn was going to go back and observe and report back to Neil with any evidence that she could find, but neither expected that anything would show up.

"But be very careful and leave straight away if you feel that you're in any danger."

She said that she would and was going to hand in her notice and leave as soon as possible anyway.

"And what will you do?" Neil enquired.

"A bit like you," she said, "I've absolutely no idea, as my dad has no intention of retiring yet and of letting me take over his training operation just yet".

It was getting late now, so Neil suggested that they go for a meal at his local, The Hunter's Arms.

"They do a great meal there," he said, "and," he casually added, "you can stay the night if you like".

"But you've only got a double bed," she replied.

This was followed by an unusual and awkward silence punctuated when Neil said, "But I'll sleep on the couch, obviously". He had had a lot of teasing from Richard when the double bed had arrived.

"What do you need that for when you live on your own?" he asked, winking at Neil, and most times when he saw him, he'd enquired if he'd slept okay on his own.

Neil had a few pints of the Black Stuff with his meal, but Dawn refused to drink any alcohol and turned down his offers of a Jagger Bomb, saying that she was going to drive back to Bleak House as she had an early start and didn't want to create any suspicion by not being there, so they parted and promised to text each other regularly with any information either of them might find, and Neil again asked her to be careful. She was very late back as it was a long journey, and she was a careful driver, or in Neil's words, a slow one.

She quietly crept into the stable lad's hostel, and as soon as she entered, her phone went off. It was a text from Neil, and she started reading it, "Just checking that you've got back okay, see what you can find out about how they're stopping horses, but be very careful and try not to evoke suspicion. I'll be…" but she didn't get to the end of the sentence as the lights suddenly went on, and shielding her eyes from the sudden glare, she saw the Boyles standing there.

"Where've you been to this late hour?" Frank demanded and roughly grabbed her phone.

"Oi, give that back," she said, but she was wasting her words.

As Frank started reading her text with Derek peering eagerly over his shoulder, she knew that as soon as they'd finished reading it that she'd be in trouble, so whilst they were both avidly scanning it, she quietly backed away towards the door, praying that it was unlocked, thankfully it was, and she was out, and she locked it, and as an afterthought, she left her key in the door, which she knew would slow their progress down if as she expected they came after her, they could use the door out into the yard, but that would take longer, and gave her enough time to make her getaway, if she'd stayed she would have heard shouting and her phone smashing against the door where it had been flung in a fit of pique, but she wasn't hanging around and got in her car and drove off faster than she usually drove, into the dark night but where she was heading she had no idea. The Boyles picked up her broken, useless phone and instantly realised that they'd made a mistake.

If they'd kept it, they could have sent Neil all sorts of texts portraying to be from Dawn sending him on wild goose chases or, as Frank said, "Leading him down a dark alley where we could give him a good going over".

"Or worse," Derek said, and they both laughed.

They, however, weren't in a mood for humour and decided that it was time that Neil got a warning not to mess with their affairs. Neil back at home was oblivious and unaware of what had happened and had gone to bed very tired and was able to sleep really well, understandably since he was in an extremely comfortable double bed, which was pure bliss compared with his little lumpy, damp thin mattress in the caravan. He'd always been slightly concerned that whilst in the caravan, the Boyles might have hitched it up in the middle of the night and towed it away and left him in the middle of a lake or somewhere similar. He'd had nightmares as a youngster of the dark and fast-flowing water, and the incident he'd had with his horse Golden Simba in the ford hadn't helped matters. Even driving past a river in the dark made him feel uneasy.

CHAPTER THIRTY-THREE

Smoke Gets in Your Eyes

Surprisingly considering the day that he'd had, he soon got off to sleep and quite quickly started dreaming, sweet dreams to start with. He was riding the favourite in the Derby and cruised to victory without breaking a sweat in a similar style as the great Shergar, then slowly the dream started turning darker and frequently flitting on to other subjects, he was back at the Jockey Club meeting, and all the stewards were his sworn enemies, Lez Allen, the Boyles and the Connollys and Dudley and Jan Cook and they were all chanting "Bent jockey, bent jockey", and it was getting louder and louder until he suddenly woke up and instantly knew that something wasn't right.

His bedroom was warm very warm, which wasn't normal as he was too tight to leave the heating on, and it wasn't just hot but an intense and smoky sort of heat, but even so he couldn't really be bothered to stir that was until a loud explosion and a shattering of glass caused him to sit bolt upright in his bed, he could smell burning, he jumped out quickly like an Olympic athlete and made his way to the window, he could see a ball of flames coming out of where his garage window should be, he quickly realised even in his bleary eyed state that his house was on fire, he opened his bedroom door and peered tentatively down the stairs, the first thing that hit him was the billowing smoke and as the heat slapped him in the face, he deduced that there was no way out that way, he'd tried to put the lights on to get a clearer view but no joy, so he ran back into his bedroom and stuffed bedclothes under the door to try and reduce the smoke from seeping underneath and started weighing up his options.

The house was built on a slope and was higher at the front than at the back, so he decided that his best way out was through the back window and attempt to slide down the drainpipe to safety — it sounded simple but in the heat of the moment, wasn't quite so straightforward. He pushed the window wide open and breathed in the cool fresh air, gingerly stepped onto the sill, and tried to grab the drainpipe and managed to just reach it, but his grip wasn't strong enough, and he tumbled down, thankfully landing on his back lawn, but awkwardly on his left ankle causing pain to shoot up his leg, he lay still for a second or two breathing heavily and inched himself up and stood up swaying as couldn't put too much weight on his damaged ankle, he looked at where his garage window had been and could see a molten mess that was all that was left of his much loved Suzuki Vitara, Hairdresser's car on fire he thought in a moment of dark humour. He could hear sirens in the distance and hobbled around the garden corner to survey the scene from the front of the house, and it wasn't a pretty sight. Fire engines were pouring water on the flames that were surging out of the windows of his and his neighbour's houses. Sparks, ash and smoke were everywhere, and it was hard to see exactly what was happening clearly. He could, as well as the fire engine, see a police car and an ambulance.

As he got round the corner, he was approached by a policeman who said, "Keep away, sir, as this is a crime scene, please let the firemen get on with their work unhindered. They think that there's someone still in this house," he said, pointing at Neil's house.

"There isn't," he said, "as this is my house, and I've just fallen out of the top window".

The policemen looked at Neil, who could tell that he wasn't sure whether to believe him or not as Neil continued, "What's caused it?"

"I can't tell you much, but they think that it was deliberate."

Just then, Neil could see a stretcher with a body on it being loaded into the awaiting ambulance, and through the smoke haze, he could just make out another figure standing next to it and shouting loudly, "It's my neighbour's fault. He told me yesterday that he was going to set fire to his house and claim on the insurance. He's done this to my Lilly; he's the bloody arsonist".

It was Richard Secombe shouting, but before he could walk over and speak to him and protest his innocence, Richard had been ushered into the ambulance, and it sped off into the dark gloom. Neil stood with the policeman who'd heard all the accusations and who told him that he'd have to go to the hospital for a check-up. A First Responder who was just about to leave came and escorted Neil to his car and took him to the same hospital, which was only a few miles away. Neil felt fine apart from his throbbing left ankle, but he just wanted to go home and said so, though he wasn't sure if he still had a house to go to. His protestations went unheeded, and he was taken to a hospital bed, thankfully without passing the Secombes on the way. After a few tests and X-rays of his ankle, he was left alone and slept soundly. He suspected that they'd given him something to assist sleep as he didn't wake until 10 o'clock the next day. He was given a clean bill of health but told to rest his ankle and was discharged, though they suggested that he should stay in bed for a few more hours. Forget that, he thought, and intended that as soon as the nurses left, he'd get dressed and scarper. It then struck him that he had no clothes, he had arrived in his torn and smoky pyjamas, and they were nowhere to be seen. So reluctantly he rang his mum to see if she could bring him some clothes and pick him up, but she couldn't as she was off to a bowls match so couldn't help him, he forgot to ask if he could stay at the stud farm now that he was homeless, he asked about his dad, but he was at a Breeze up sale (young horses going through their paces) with Steve, so she suggested that he got a taxi before he did he asked the nurse to find him some clothes from the hospital lost property, all they could find him were drab and ill-fitting, but he didn't want to appear ungrateful, but just as he was about to leave the door swung open, and somebody that Neil didn't really want to see strode in DC Ted Abbott and he wasn't smiling.

"What did I tell you last time we met?"

"That in 30 years you'd...."

"No, not that. I told you to keep out of trouble, and only a day or two later, I find out that you've been accused of arson by setting two houses on fire for insurance fraud and could also be charged with manslaughter".

Neil was alarmed now, "What do you mean, Richard and Lilly are fine, aren't they?"

DC Abbott softened, "Richard is fine but very angry and throwing all sorts of accusations your way, and Lilly inhaled a lot of smoke, but after a few days' rest, she should be ok, but at her age, you can never be sure".

Neil was relieved, but DC Abbott went on to say that initial investigations strongly suggested that the fire was started deliberately. Neil agreed to go to the station tomorrow and make a full statement.

He then repeated his warning for Neil to keep out of trouble and then, in a lighter mood, said, "Go on then, tell me, what are you dressed as today?

I can tell that you're not a gangster but no idea what you're meant to be?"

"I'm dressed as a police DC," he cheekily replied and hobbled out of the room before DC Abbott could reply and made a swift exit from the hospital, thankfully not bumping into the Secombes. He intended to visit them, but not for a day or two when he hoped that Richard would have calmed down.

Back at the family home, after paying the taxi driver, he slumped in a chair in the empty house in deep thought. He was sure that the fire was started deliberately and was sure that the Boyles were involved in some way. He tried texting Dawn but got no reply. He was beginning to wonder if she was part of stopping horses scheme but was sure that she wasn't, but was becoming desperate as all his friends were disappearing or not speaking to him, Dawn, The Twins, The Coopers and their staff and now The Secombes who he'd thought of as surrogate grandparents, and his jockey friend Gilbert French-Saunders had ignored him since the race blocking incident, in fact, he realised that he had no one left to turn to and was on his own which was a sobering thought, his dad's suggestion of a job on a stud farm in Australia was beginning to look like an appealing solution to his problems, but would that be thought of as running away?

CHAPTER THIRTY-FOUR

On My Own

Neil set off the next morning, thankfully dressed in his own clothes in a battered old Landy that had been used around the stud for many years, which his dad had reluctantly agreed to let him use. Luckily when he got to the police station DC Abbott was nowhere to be seen, so he filled in his statement without any problems and left in next to no time. The Police had informed him that they would be in touch, which for some reason, he didn't find reassuring. Back at the stud, his next problem was where to live, he didn't think that it would be fair to his parents to ask them if he could move in with them, especially since what had happened to his house, and he didn't want anything happening to his parent's house, or God forbid to them. It was decided that he could move into the old stud man's cottage down by the ford.

It was being converted into a holiday cottage and stud student accommodation and was nearly finished, and in his dad's words, "It'll do for Neil". It had most of the basics like electricity though the plumber hadn't been to connect the water yet, there were some old-fashioned furnishings in, though his mum, who was overseeing the changes, had yet to fit the curtains or, in her words, make the cottage cosy and homely. Neil, however, was pleased with it as it was and thought that it was fine for him. He was now understandably getting paranoid about future attacks and thought that he'd be safe here as he reasoned that no one would know that the cottage existed. The front and back doors both had working locks, there was an old barn joining the cottage, full of very old hay recking of cats and rats and had a hatch joining the two together, so the first thing he did was to find some old bolts in the stud's workshop and fix bolts to both sides of the hatch to completely secure it. That afternoon he settled in and pondered what his next move would be. He realised that the stark reality was that he was on his own. Even his sister hadn't calmed down after the Lady Calamity affair and still ignored his texts.

The gamekeeper Pete Wisdom just mouthed the words, "Bent jockey" when their paths crossed, and when Neil asked if he was needed for the next seasons beating, he got no answer. What worried him most was the silent treatment that he appeared to be getting from Dawn. As every text he sent received no reply, he began wondering if she'd joined forces with the gang of four or if all along she'd been spying on him on their behalf but couldn't bring himself to believe it. Brooding on his own, he was beginning to reach the conclusion that he was beaten and that it was time to admit defeat and move on. He finally decided that he'd fill in the Australian Stud farm application form, and if getting it, he'd flee the country and start a new life. If it didn't work out, he could always come back when the dust had settled, but then again, he thought I might not get the job even with my dad's backing coz who wants to employ a bent jockey? Before putting pen to paper, he decided to go to the local, The Hunters Arms, where the food could always be relied on to be really good and would be far better than anything that he could prepare himself, especially since his cupboards were bare apart from a few tins of Guinness. He decided to walk there or hobble as his ankle was still giving him a fair bit of pain. It was only about half a mile away, and after walking down to the ford and crossing the bridge where the water was flowing fast, nearly at the level when he'd nearly drowned when coming off his horse Golden Simba long before he became a jockey, after crossing a few fields where the stud's horses were grazing contently and hardly bothering to raise their heads to look at him, he arrived at his destination, It was unusually quiet as he sat down at a corner table with a pint of foaming Guinness, he was served by a petite girl who he'd never seen before and who appeared to struggle with the English language, and he was worried that she hadn't understood his order but half an hour later a tender very appetising steak arrived supplemented with a large bowl of chunky chips and he settled down to enjoy it. His head was full of his troubles and woes when the quiet was interrupted by his phone ringing, hoping that it was Dawn finally contacting him he quickly picked it up, but it wasn't her as it was a reporter from the Sporting Life, who'd tried in vain to get an interview from Neil on the day that he'd been warned off, but he'd declined but now he thought what the hell I'll hopefully soon be far away from here so what does it matter. He told the reporter everything, all his allegations against Bleak House and the Lez Allen stable staff naming names. He said that he'd never stopped a horse and never would; in fact, once he'd opened up, it was like a release, and it all flowed out, and perhaps he thought afterwards, he'd gone slightly over the top with his accusations. The reporter was amazed as jockeys tended to be quiet and keep things to themselves, and he usually had to embellish the articles, but this was totally different, and he thought that he'd probably have to tone it down. He told Neil that they would have to be careful with unfounded accusations as there could be trouble with libel, but he promised to do his best to convey Neil's strong feelings about being treated unjustly and how his fall from grace was unfair. After the reporter had hung up, Neil started having misgivings and wondering if he was doing the right thing as this article was bound to antagonise all those mentioned in it and could possibly lead to more repercussions as he was still sure that the fire was deliberate though he knew that he had no way of proving it. He still had an uneasy feeling and wondered if he should ring the reporter back and tell him that he'd changed his mind, but after a few more pints, his worries miraculously vanished, and he walked back home in a happier mood than he'd been in for a very long time, and even his ankle didn't seem to be aching quite as much, the skies looked heavy, and he was pleased to get home just before the rain started falling. The next morning, he woke up a little stiffly but surprisingly, his head was okay.

He rang his mum to ask her when the plumber was coming as he was getting fed up with his frequent walks down to the ford to collect water. His mum informed him that he kept strange hours and would turn up unannounced when he was ready to and not before. He then remembered the Sporting Life article and wandered up to Steve's house. He was out, but his wife Lynne was in. She always seemed pleased to see him and made him a cup of tea whilst he poured over the Sporting Life, but on reflection, he realised that his article wouldn't be in as he'd only spoken to the reporter the night before, but he enjoyed reading all the racing news as had been out of the loop recently, he was a little concerned when he read a piece about Tom Cooper's promising two-year-old Galileo Girl, the horse that fell with him, it had flopped in its very next race ridden by Mark Williams, the article suggested that she'd lost her confidence and mentioned Neil's reckless actions as being the probable cause of this, and had probably scarred her for life. Rubbish, Neil thought, it's due to jockey error, but there was little chance of him ever getting the chance of riding her again in the near future. He thought that she had the potential to win a classic race, the 1000 guineas or the Oaks or both, and he smiled to himself. That evening his mum, knowing his culinary limitations invited him for a meal, and it was a very enjoyable evening with his dad on good form, especially after a few bottles of fine wine from his extensive wine cellar had been consumed.

When he was leaving slightly unsteadily, his dad enquired if he'd filled the job application form in.

"Not yet" he replied, "I'll do it tonight when I get back".

His dad then surprised Neil by saying, "It's not that we're trying to get rid of you, son, but I think that it'll be a good experience for you, and it'll keep you well away from any trouble here," he then added, "we've always hoped that you'll take over here one day when the time was right".

He'd never said that before and Neil had never really thought that it was an option. He got back intending to apply online, but as usual, the internet was non-existent, probably due to the cottage being situated down in a dip, he thought, so he abandoned it until another day. He slept well, safe in the knowledge that his abode was secret and hidden from public view, or so he thought. It rained heavily in the night, but he didn't hear it and rose early and went up to Steve and Lynne's after having a packet of crisps for his breakfast. He'd have to go and buy some proper supplies soon, he thought.

As he arrived, Steve was reading the Sporting Life and, in particular, the article about him and kept saying, "You shouldn't have said that". When he'd finished, he handed the paper to Neil as he had to dash out as a mare was in the process of foaling. Neil's article took up a full page entitled Jockeying for support. It gave a brief history of Neil's rising up the ranks and then explained what had led to him being warned off and finally, his account of his innocence, only slightly watered down, and his allegations of wrongdoings from the Lez Allen yard without actually naming names, but it was clear who he meant. There was an editorial that he thought for once was quite balanced, stating that the charges against him were harsh and that he was innocent until proven guilty, and that the Sporting Life would make no judgements until the case was over. They'd thought that he was about to break through as a jockey for the future but wondered now if his career had come to a premature end. On balance, Neil was pleased with the slant of the article, but he thought that it might be like a red rag to a bull for his antagonists and wondered if they were planning anything else but said to himself, "They'll never find me here" and smiled contentedly.

That night he again headed to the Hunters Arms and sat in his usual seat and had gammon egg and chips and perhaps a few too many pints of Guinness but reasoned that his weight wasn't a worry at present as he wasn't a jockey and the outlook of ever becoming one again was looking bleak.

As he was leaving, the landlord called him over, "There were some lads looking for you earlier".

Neil's heart missed a beat, "What did they look like?"

"Three scruffy, rough, surly lads, two looked very similar."

"Oh heck," Neil said, "What did they want?"

"They asked where you lived." The landlord could see that Neil looked worried. "Don't worry, lad; I didn't tell them anything, and they just glared at me and left. I don't think that they paid for their drinks either".

Neil was worried as he was sure that he knew who they were, Frank, Derek Boyle and Jason Connolly.

CHAPTER THIRTY-FIVE
In the Middle of the Night

Neil crept home cautiously without the Joie de Vivre of recent nights, it was getting dark, and without streetlights, menacingly looking shadows appeared round every bend. He started imaging figures ready to pounce on him behind every tree and bush. A cow suddenly loomed up, which gave him the fright of his life, the water in the beck was nearly up to the little footbridge, and yet more rain was forecast for the night ahead. When he got near the cottage he stopped and surveyed it from a distance everything appeared quiet and still, he'd left a light on, and he could tell that the cottage appeared empty, then suddenly a vehicle arrived which he didn't recognise, and a figure got out and banged on the door, it was a tall and burly chap, nothing like who he feared might turn up, he moved a little closer and suddenly realised who it was, it was the long-awaited for plumber.

He shouted out, "Don't worry as I'm here, I've just been at the pub!"

"If I'd known, you could have bought me a pint" came back the jovial reply.

"Next time," Neil said, "I know it's late, but you're mum said that you've moved in, so I've come to connect your water. It'll only take a minute or two," replied the plumber.

Well, it did only take a few minutes, but then Neil was probed about all his recent events, and it was a good two hours before they said their goodbyes, and he was once again left on his own, feeling a little as if he'd just been interrogated. The silence really hit him as he wearily picked up the stud job application form from the kitchen table, but the words as he read them just wouldn't sink in, so frustratedly, he threw it down back on the table, promising himself to get back to it tomorrow, and by now very tired he headed upstairs to bed. A few hours later, he awoke with an urgent need to go to the toilet; too much Guinness, he thought, so he went downstairs, fumbling in the dark, as he never put lights on in the middle of the night, bumping into objects which he was sure had moved since daylight was lost, he'd just flushed the toilet and was returning towards the stairs when he thought that he could hear the faint and distant sound of a car engine slowly getting louder and louder, he looked out of the kitchen window, and he could see lights snaking down the track towards his cottage. Surely the plumber hadn't come back, he thought, as he watched the vehicle being driven cautiously as if the occupants didn't quite know where they were going. When it got to level, the vehicle stopped, the lights went out, and he could hear voices and could see torches being shone around. He swiftly moved out of sight and hid behind the front door, where a thin beam of light shone through a narrow gap in the rusty old letterbox. He managed to catch a few of the words that were being said, and he instantly knew who the unwelcome visitors were. It was Frank, Derek Boyle, and the third person he presumed was Jason Connolly.

He heard them say, "Well, this is the place the geezer in the pub said, but it looks empty, go and look round the back". He heard footsteps leaving as someone continued talking, "If he's here, we've got to make it look like an accident and leave no evidence that we've been…" then a sudden gust of wind made what was being said temporarily inaudible.

Neil knew that he was in trouble, outnumbered three to one but thought that if he remained quiet, then they'd give up and just go away. Wishful thinking, perhaps, but it reassured him to hold on to that thought.

He heard footsteps reappearing and a voice, clearly Jason Connolly saying, "I can't see anything through the back windows, but there's an old Landy parked there".

"Well, someone's here then," said a voice that he could clearly recognise as Frank, who continued, "go and shine a torch in all the windows, and one of you ring Bartholomew's phone and see if it rings".

233

Neil realised that his phone was on the kitchen table and still turned on. He would have to move quickly. He fumbled his way in the pitch darkness and got to the kitchen door but couldn't see much, but that soon changed as his phone suddenly lit up and started playing its ring tune, the infectious Birdy Song.

He lunged at it but got to it but too late as he heard a voice shout, "I heard a phone ringing, and it's Neil's stupid tune". A light shone in the window, and he was spotted, "and I can see a figure".

Neil had been rumbled, and his escape was looking highly unlikely. He moved as quickly as possible up the stairs, and as he did, he could hear a splintering of wood as the back door gave way. With fear coursing through his veins, he rushed into his bedroom and bolted it turned his lights on so that he could locate his clothes, quickly put them on and slipped on a pair of jodhpur boots and turned the lights off as he heard a banging on the door, he knew that it wouldn't take them long to break a second door down, but he had his escape route planned, he unbolted the hatch clambered through and bolted it behind him in the nick of time as he could tell that the door had burst open and they'd got into the room, he imagined the look on their faces as they looked round and found nobody there, he landed softly on the damp, musty old hay and clambered down until his feet met with the ground, the dust made him want to cough, but he managed to supress it, and he peered out of the rotten door with its peeling paint and all appeared silent, he presumed that all three of them were still upstairs, but doubted that they'd stay up there for too much longer, he quietly crept out and a torch shone out from the window and surveyed the perimeter , so he crept back inside and waited until the light ceased and moved out again, he walked past the Landy, cursing that the keys were hanging up on a peg on the back door, otherwise he thought he could have made a quick and effective escape.

He reluctantly moved past the vehicle, keeping out of sight as best as he could, walked up a walled track until he came to a copse of trees and hid behind them where he would be able to see most of the cottage, then daring to look back, he could see that the lights had now moved to the outside and he smiled to himself again thinking that against the odds he'd made a miraculous escape. He moved along, keeping behind the trees, and he could still see lights frantically darting around but obviously finding nothing, or at least not what they were searching for. After a few minutes, he presumed that they were getting ready to abort their operation and leave when a thought suddenly struck him, why are there only two lights? Where's the third one? Just at that moment, he thought that he heard a faint snapping of twigs behind him and turned a fraction too late as Thwack a branch connected with his head with force and he fell unconscious to the ground like a felled tree, landing unceremoniously in the mud face down.

LESTER BOYD

CHAPTER THIRTY-SIX
Nightmare, Nightmare

He slowly came round after the attack with, not surprisingly, a splitting headache. In a semi-conscious state, he realised that he was being driven and in the passenger seat, and was shocked when it dawned on him that it was his old Landy and his blurred vision could just make out that it was Frank driving, the Landy was bumping along and being driven at a speed that he didn't think it had ever reached previously, he played dead whilst he weighed up his options, but in truth, he did feel half dead, he managed to glance in the mirror and could see that there was no one else in the vehicle, so he was wondering about grabbing the steering wheel when suddenly Frank veered off the road and dipped the headlights but hardly slowed down as they appeared to be in a field, and he could see the blurred outline of a fence approaching, just before the inevitable collision the Landy slowed a bit more and Neil took a double look as Frank suddenly jumped out and disappeared from sight.

Neil didn't have time to puzzle out what was going on as the Landy free wheeled into the wooden fence, and he heard the now familiar sound of splintering wood, but this time it was a lot louder, and a broken fence rail came flying up and shattered the windscreen showering Neil with many tiny shards of glass, he bent down and put his arm up to shield his eyes from the glass, and when he looked up all was dark, and the Landy appeared to be airborne and then one of Neil's worst fears was about to be realised as a loud splash announced that he was in the water and his nightmares became a reality as he was in a fast flowing river, and one that was in flood after all the recent rainfall, and the only sound he could hear was the roar of the water. The Landy was floating downstream rapidly.

Neil knew all about winding windows down slowly so as to let the vehicle fill up with water before opening a door and making an escape, but this was irrelevant with a smashed windscreen, and he knew when in the water not to thrash around as the cold water would take his breath away, but to let his body acclimatise before trying to move, this and other thoughts were clouding his mind when he should have been concentrating on getting out alive, but the memories of his childhood dunking under his horse kept coming back, but this was a lot worse as this time he was in a fast flowing river and under attack by three assailants. As all this was going through his head, stones were reigning down and bouncing off the Landy's roof; luckily, this isn't a soft top, he thought.

He was still relatively dry though he couldn't see the water rapidly rising inside the vehicle. As it reached the top of his legs, he guessed that it wouldn't be too long before the Landy made a passable impression of the Titanic and disappeared under the water. He, therefore, decided to make his move and slid quietly out through the driver's side, away from his assailants and slipped into the cold water and clung onto the side of the vehicle, it was colder than he remembered from his previous incident and it did indeed take his breath away, the stones were still reigning down, fending himself he actually caught one and instinctively threw it back and heard a faint ouch and smiled briefly to himself until he realised that this was a mistake as they now knew that he was conscious, and would carry on their attack. He could now see lights pointing in his direction and dim and distant shouting, and then suddenly, the Landy went under with his leg caught under the front sill. He was pulled down with it, and suddenly all was dark, quiet and very cold. He quickly freed himself and rose to the surface, gasping for air.

He was in a bad way; his head was pounding, the cold was getting through to his bones, his numbed muscles were losing strength and his ability to use his limbs was diminishing, and without the Landy for protection, the stones were bound to soon hit him with a near-fatal blow, he noticed that the lights were lessening and saw what he presumed was their car racing along the side of the river and then across the bridge to the other side, so he presumed that they could carry on the attack from both sides of the river, things were looking bleak now, and the odds were stacked against him.

He was beginning to feel really cold now and knew that if he didn't try and get out of this freezing foaming water soon, it would all be over for him, and he started imagining the headlines in the papers, saying that it had been a tragic accident on the way home from the pub. He made his move, and he headed for the far bank, hoping that there was only one assailant at that side. His feeble attempts to swim made little progress, and he was getting swept further downstream, but finally, he made it, and he dragged himself out and just lay there for a moment shivering uncontrollably, but he knew he'd have to move quickly as he could see lights to the right and heading his way, so he tried to climb the bank and away to freedom, but it was too steep, and he kept slipping back and was in danger of falling back into the river again, the very last thing that he wanted to happen, so he had to head towards the lights and finally managed to climb to the top of the bank and brushed against a barbed wire fence and gingerly stepped through it into a field with the intention of running across it. However, he could hear stampeding cows or perhaps horses. He wasn't sure which, but that didn't matter as he wasn't going to risk getting flattened by them. In daylight, he'd had risked it, but in pitch darkness, it wasn't worth it. So he edged along the perimeter of the field towards where he presumed their car was parked and where one of his assailants probably was, but then he suddenly got a change of luck as he could hear shouting and cursing below him on the river bank and he could just make out a figure thrashing about, and who looked to be stuck in a barbed wire fence, this was Neil's chance and he took it, as he knew that the stuck man would probably free himself shortly, and the other two would probably be coming over to this side. So he, as quick as he could, carried on towards the lights that he presumed came from their car, and if they did, he had formed an escape plan.

He climbed the fence again, and there at the end of a track that stopped abruptly at the river was the Boyle's car, lights on full and the engine still running. Without a second's thought, he jumped in, slammed the doors and locked them and engaged reverse and tried to make his escape but the car wasn't moving, he could see a light approaching and knew that he hadn't got long, and frantically pumped the accelerator, then out of the corner of his eye he noticed that the handbrake was still on so he swiftly released it and the car shot backwards faster than intended and in next to no time he came to the road, and all lights were now tiny distant specks. He engaged first gear and raced towards the town, which he knew involved crossing the bridge, when he had another stroke of luck as he could see lights in the field of stampeding animals and presumed that they'd gone in there looking for him and he wondered what fate his assailants would meet.

He sped over the bridge unhindered and headed towards the town, which a road sign informed him was five miles away. He was really cold now and tried to put the car's heater on but couldn't find it, frantically looking for it he took a corner far too fast and with the tyres covered with mud, the car slid off the road and slammed into a tree that just happened to be stood in his path, and he was knocked unconscious again. Unbeknown to him, this was a blessing in disguise as the tree was on the banks of the very same river, and if he hadn't hit it, he'd have probably ended in the water again, and his chances of surviving a second dunking would have been very slim. He woke up the following morning unsure where he was, but it soon became apparent that he was in the hospital again.

His heavily bandaged head was feeling a little better, and he was told by an attractive young nurse that he'd been found soon after the crash by a farmer off to milk his cows early in the morning and was swiftly transported to the hospital. Luckily, he thought before his three assailants had managed to find him and afflict yet more physical damage, he was told to get plenty of rest and wasn't going to be discharged until the following day, so he relaxed and tried to get some sleep. The following day just after he'd had an enjoyable lunch, well a lunch, a policeman arrived and said that he needed to accompany him to the station immediately, fair enough he thought surely this time they'll believe me, but alas sadly they didn't. He was taken into a room and advised that along with the outstanding charges, they were adding unlawfully taking a car and crashing it and GBH against three lads and driving under the influence, and that's just for starters. He was going to be questioned under caution this time, and a duty solicitor had been assigned to him. Sam James, the man in question, appeared in an ill-fitting suit, and Neil knew all about ill-fitting suits! Sam sat down, looked at his watch and yawned.

"I suggest that you just plead guilty, and you'll get off with rapped knuckles Nevin."

"Who's Nevin? I'm Neil," Neil said, already losing confidence.

Sam hastily looked at his papers and said, "Yes, Neil, that's what I meant to say".

"Well, I think that I'll get more than rapped knuckles for all the charges they'll level at me. Have you actually read your notes?" Sam James looked hot and bothered and started turning page after page over, but all too late. "Don't bother," Neil said, "I'll defend myself; you'd obviously rather be somewhere else. Goodbye".

Neil walked off into the interview room alone, where a familiar figure was waiting for him, DC Ted Abbott, who Neil thought was looking a lot smarter than on previous occasions. He looked at him and, without any of the usual repartees, read out the charges.

"It's alleged that you went for a drink with the three defendants at the Hunters Arms, and after a few too many pints, you all fell out," he looked at his notes and continued, "but it doesn't say what over, and then you attacked them and took their car, what do you have to say for yourself?"

"How could I attack all three of them on my own" Neil said in defence.

He then told his version, which he hastened to add was the truth, how he'd never been in the pub with them, how they'd driven his car into the river with him in it, how he'd escaped by taking their car.

DC Abbott wasn't impressed and said, "All very feasible, but how can you account for all their injuries?"

"Easily," Neil replied, "they were lobbing stones at me, and I threw one back, and I think that it made contact, and one of them got stuck in a barbed wire fence, and then I think that they got knocked down by stampeding animals, I'll take you back to the scene if you like and run you through it all".

"That won't be necessary right now, but we'll look into it all, and we'll be back in touch." He then turned the tape off and said, "You can go now, but I don't suppose that there's any point in me saying keep out of trouble, is there?" He then shook his head and left the room, preceded by Neil, who phoned his mum, who came and took him back to the stud farm.

"What have you been up to this time?"

Neil told her briefly, and she looked shocked, saying, "You better take that job in

Australia; otherwise, you're going to end up six foot under".

Neil was a little surprised as his mum wasn't known for dark humour. He had unsurprisingly forgotten about the job offer, but it did suddenly sound very inviting compared with what his life was like at present.

CHAPTER THIRTY-SEVEN
State of Confusion

The next few days went quietly as he recuperated, and he still hadn't filled in the job application form. He decided to ring the Jockey Club to see how the investigation into his alleged wrongdoing was going, as he reasoned that if they were going to clear him completely, then he would be able to return to the life he loved, as a jockey, though pessimistically he wondered who would now give him any rides on their horses as mud sticks. Only Sue Henry had remained loyal, and she only had a handful of horses and a retained female jockey already, who just happened to be very attractive. He rang the Jockey Club not expecting much, so he wasn't disappointed and wasn't surprised with the outcome, he spoke to a number of people before anyone even knew who he was, and when he finally got through to someone who had heard of him, he was put on hold whilst they checked for him, instead of playing tinny repetitive music, he could actually hear talking in the background.

"It's Neil Bartholomew on the phone."

"Who?"

"That apprentice jockey that we stood down, he wants to know how the investigation is going?"

"Investigation? I don't think that it's really started, but all signs point to him being guilty can't see him getting his licence back anytime soon."

"Yes, well, I can't tell him that. What shall I say?"

"Just tell him that investigations are ongoing and that we're making good progress and that he'll be one of the first to know when we have a result."

Neil had heard enough, and before they came back to him to relay what he'd heard, he put the phone down. Feeling depressed, he decided that the only way to clear his name was to do the investigating himself, but he had no idea where he would start and how to keep himself safe from any further attacks. He decided that a good place to start would be to go and speak to the last apprentice to work for Lez Allen before he was employed there. He knew his name was Kevin Dee but had no idea where to find him. He decided to ring Sarah Howerd and kill two birds with one stone, find out if she'd heard from her sister Dawn and see if she knew the address of Kevin Dee. She answered her phone straight away and seemed pleased to hear from it.

"Neil, who?" she said, "Didn't you used to be a jockey?" Neil laughed it off and took it in the friendly tone it was spoken. On the subject of Dawn, she was very guarded, but when Neil suggested that she'd, perhaps, joined the dark side and was now in with the Boyles.

She quickly refuted this, saying, "All that I can tell you is that she's safe but lying low, and if you ask any more, then I'll put the phone down".

Fair enough, Neil thought at least he needn't worry about Dawn anymore. He then asked about Kevin Dee and wasn't surprised when he learnt that she did know him.

"You know all the eligible young men, don't you?"

She just laughed and replied, "I don't know what you're insinuating, but we both started out at the same time, so I got to know him, but what happened was a tragedy".

"Why? What did happen? I've not heard a full account?" Neil asked, and Sarah explained that he'd had a mystery car accident when his car went off the road and ran into the side of a house, leaving him badly injured and now in a wheelchair.

Neil explained that he wanted to go and see him and ask him a few questions and see if he could find out what happened at Lez Allen's yard when he was based there.

"I don't think that he'll speak to you," she said.

"What about if you come with me?" Neil asked, but Sarah said that she didn't want to go saying that she was too busy, but Neil knew that there was more to it but didn't want to press her.

He thought that she didn't want to see him in his present state. She agreed to speak to him and pave the way for him by ringing him first and putting in a good word and trying to arrange a visit for him. True to her word, she did this, and a meeting was organised in two days. Kevin Dee lived with his parents, who were effectively his full-time carers, in a modern house in the suburbs of Birmingham, which thankfully wasn't too far away. The two days passed quickly, and he was soon setting off on his way in a hired car as he'd run out of options of vehicles to borrow. He'd asked his dad if he could borrow his Range Rover but was told that he'd rather lend it to Nigel Mansell, so this was why he was in a very basic Ford Fiesta, which surprised him by being a nice smooth drive and the petrol tank didn't seem to be going down which was always a bonus, if he had borrowed the Range Rover then he'd have been doing frequent Formula One style pit stops for fuel top-ups.

The hire car had satellite navigation, so he found his destination with ease — a brick-built house at the end of a cul-de-sac with neat hedges and tidy mown lawns and twitching curtains, which made him feel a little uneasy, but it was just what he expected suburbia to be like. He was met at the door of number six Meadow View, though Neil thought that you'd need a strong pair of binoculars to see any meadows by Kevin's parents, who were cheerful and of good humour. Neil thought inwardly to himself that anyone who calls their son Kevin must have a good sense of humour. Kevin's mum led Neil into a small warm room where Kevin was sitting in his wheelchair glued to a large TV screen which, not unsurprisingly, was showing the day's racing. Neil introduced himself, and Kevin started talking about the day's racing and all the recent racing news.

"I may be in a wheelchair," he said, "but hopefully, one day, I'll be back racing again".

"Is that realistic?" Neil asked without really thinking as he watched the overweight lad scoffing crisps.

"The doctors are hopeful, but it may be a few years down the line, and perhaps I won't be able to participate in race riding again, but as long as I can get involved in the industry in some way, then I'll be happy."

Neil thought that now was the time to steer the conversation around to what he'd really come to talk about, but before he had a chance to start, Kevin said, "I know why you're here, but I can't comment about my time at Lez Allen's yard".

Neil explained that he was trying to clear his name and would be very discreet with anything he was told. Surprisingly, this was all it took to reassure Kevin, and he started talking, and once he started, there was no stopping him.

"I've told no one else this apart from mum and dad. When I started at the yard, Mrs Allen was still there, and she was really nice and friendly, in stark contrast to everyone else there. She did the training and was hands-on. Lez Allen was rarely seen except when entertaining owners at the races. When she left, it all changed; my rides all but dried up, Brian and the Boyles arrived, and Angus

Connolly became the stable jockey, with his son Jason becoming the other apprentice. It wasn't long before I started to hate being there."

Neil interrupted him and said, "I know the feeling. You lived in that dingy caravan, didn't you?"

"Yes, I did, and on the way back from the pub, the Boyles used to turf me out of bed thinking it was a great hoot."

"How hilarious," Neil said as Kevin continued.

"As I was only getting a few rides, I jumped at the chance of riding anything that I was offered. At a lowly racecourse in Yorkshire, Ripon racecourse, I think, I was asked to give a horse an easy ride. I didn't ask what that meant but rode it normally to finish placed. The next ride I got, just as I went out to the start, Brian growled at me, 'Just make sure that this one doesn't win'. I was obviously shocked but did as I was told, by getting into traffic problems and finishing unplaced, and have regretted it ever since. For the next few rides, I was ordered to do the same, and this time they spelt it out as I was told to stop them from winning. They thought that they had a hold on me now as they threatened that if I didn't do as they said, then they'd go to the Jockey Club and tell them that I'd been stopping horses and I'd be finished. I didn't really think it through as I'm sure that it was only a threat, as they'd have probably implicated themselves. I hated doing it so hatched a plan to try and make it look that I wasn't trying to win when all the time trying my best, but this didn't work and more threats followed and got more violent and I was beginning to fear for my safety, so at the end of my tether I wrote a letter to Lez Allen detailing everything that had happened and informed him that I was sending copies to the Jockey Club and the racing papers, and set off in my car to post them I was now getting paranoid and didn't use the local post box as thought that they'd be able to tamper with it or set it on fire, so I drove to one a few miles away, before I got there I noticed a car coming at speed in the other direction it looked vaguely familiar and the next thing happened was that it swerved towards me and I was forced off the road and hit the side of a house head on with force and came to a shuddering halt, I was in unbelievable pain and knew that I'd sustained a serious injury, before I could try and get out Frank or Derek Boyle I can't remember which one, appeared at the window, didn't try and help me just threatened me and said if I didn't keep quiet then not only would I regret it but my parents would be in grave danger as well, and of course the letters that I was about to post were snatched. So I just kept quiet and have been ever since I've been watching the yard, and I think that there's a pattern building up, they seem to have horses that run up a sequence of wins, and before their handicap goes up, they run a really bad race with an apprentice on board, and then in next to no time with Angus Connolly back on board they win a big handicap easily off an artificially low handicap and at much better odds, I've got it all written down on a sheet somewhere, I'll give you a copy before you leave, I think that they've found an undetectable way of stopping horses which works temporarily and leaves no trace and which the horses soon bounce back from. All the old gentlemen and titled owners that were there when Mrs Allen trained have long since left, and all that appears to be left is some shady dodgy owners. Sadly, I can't prove any of this, and you want to be careful if you get the wrong side of them. You'll end up like me or a lot worse."

Neil told him that he'd already got on the wrong side of them, big time. He told Kevin about the Milligan twins and their car crash after they had crossed the Boyles and how they were remaining silent as well. They both agreed that there was a pattern emerging, and Kevin told Neil to be very careful driving back home.

Finally, Kevin said, "It appears to me that they've moved on from just stopping horses to more sophisticated methods, but what they are and how they do it, I've no idea".

Neil said, "Well, it's up to me to find that out, though, at present, I've no ideas".

Neil had been there for a long time, and Kevin was getting tired, so it was time to leave. So they said their goodbyes, and Neil promised to keep him in the loop of any developments he made and hoped that one day soon, they'd both be back at the racecourse together, Neil free of the stigma of being a bent jockey and Kevin free of pain and disability, though sadly this seemed a tall order. Neil decided that his next move was to go to a few race meetings when Lez Allen had horses running and observe the goings on and hopefully make a breakthrough, but the big problem was how was he going to go when he was banned from every racecourse in the country.

CHAPTER THIRTY-EIGHT

Lola

On his way home with his cheery music playing, Neil was relaxed though he was occasionally glancing at his rear mirror to see if he was being followed, though he convinced himself that he was being paranoid. Neil started formulating a plan of action. He decided to go to the three-day race meeting at Newmarket and observe closely what went on; he'd checked the race entries and noted that the Lez Allen stable had a number of runners on every day and thought that if he watched them closely, something might show up, even if he didn't really know what he was looking for. He gave his Uncle Harry the bookmaker a phone call to see if he could help him; his uncle, who lived on his own, was pleased to hear from him, as they rarely met up and invited him to go for a meal with him that night, and Neil readily accepted. An hour or two later, Neil and his uncle were sat at his uncle's local, The Moorview Arms, with a large bottle of red wine already half empty. Neil had heard that his uncle was a heavy drinker, and the proof of that was being played out in front of his eyes. Neil knew that he had no chance of keeping up with him in the drinking stakes.

They talked about mundane and general things and a catch-up with family matters, and as the drink relaxed their tongues, the conversation got more personal. Neil asked him why he and his Aunt Emily had never got married; Uncle Harry said that his sister never had any intention of splicing the knot and was far too busy with village life, the WI and all her local groups and committee meetings, and her cat was the only company that she needed. He himself, he said, hadn't avoided marriage but that it had never happened, he'd thought that he was perhaps getting a bit old now and set in his ways.

As the second bottle of red wine was opened and the drink continued to flow, Uncle Harry began to wax lyrically, and he said, "Life is like a piece of theatre; you spend a lot of your life acting. When I'm bookmaking, I'm putting on a show trying to entice the punters to spend more money. I treat them as friends laughing and joking with them, but it's all a front. Getting married or having a partner is similar as you're still acting even behind closed doors even if you don't really realise it; you're having to bend to someone else's will and do what they want. You've got two people with completely different mindsets wanting totally different things from life, and that can cause friction, and tensions can build up. I bet that you've seen your parents arguing on numerous occasions?'' Neil conceded that he had.

Uncle Harry hadn't finished yet and carried on, "When you care for someone, and they do something that you think is letting you down or themselves, then that can cause arguments but only because you care. If no one cared, then they wouldn't be bothered by what you do, so the closer you get involved with someone, the more problems that can develop, the highs are higher, and the lows are lower. Living on my own, I have none of these issues. When I close the front door, it's just me on my own, and I can do exactly what I want; I can even leave the toilet seat up. I will admit that the silence is sometimes deafening, but on the whole, I prefer the single way of life".

"But what about the physical side of a relationship," Neil cheekily asked.

"You mean all the DIY that they make you do." Uncle Harry replied, quick as a flash. The alcohol certainly wasn't slowing his humour down. As he topped up his own and Neil's glass, he continued, "I'm my own boss. It's just me and the goldfish".

Neil couldn't recall seeing any and asked, "What goldfish?"

"That's another thing," Harry said, "the silence of living on your own makes you lose your marbles". They both laughed.

Neil hoped that his uncle would eventually find someone or at least get a pet but something more interesting than a goldfish. He found his company very entertaining and his humour funnier than his dad's, but then he reflected that if he heard it every day, then it could become repetitive, as in the well-known saying, familiarity breeds contempt. He was beginning to realise what that meant.

His uncle finished by saying, "You're still young, you've a lot still to learn in life, but you need to try and get your jockey's licence back and then worry about the finer things in life".

It was now getting late now, and they were too far gone or as his uncle said, "Four sheets to the wind", to discuss his racing problem and just carried on with light banter and general subjects until the bell rang to denote the final orders and they left and staggered home.

As the cold air hit him, Neil was feeling a little dizzy and light-headed but tried to hide it as he didn't want his uncle to think that he was a lightweight in the drinking stakes. When they got back home, he reluctantly agreed to a nightcap and sipped his large glass of port very slowly. It had been decided earlier that he'd stay the night and was shown to a dimly lit spare bedroom that smelt a little damp and fusty and looked like it had rarely been used, but the bed was comfy, and he slept really well, and when he awoke in the morning he only had a slightly thick head but surprised himself by managing to eat the large fried breakfast his uncle had prepared for him.

"Great," he said, "I thought that you couldn't cook".

His Uncle smiled and said, "I can, but after a long tiring day at the races, I usually can't be bothered".

His Uncle was setting off to Newmarket in a couple of hours, so they didn't have much time. Neil told him all that had happened to him since he'd joined Lez Allen's yard. His Uncle listened intently, especially when he mentioned Kevin Dee's stopping horses' admission. They decided to watch some previous races featuring Lez Allen runners on the enormous TV screen in Harry's living room. They watched horses winning under Angus Connolly, and then the same horse losing with either Kevin, Neil or Jason Connolly on board and tried to spot any differences, but nothing came to light.

Neil said, "They look like two different horses. Could they be switching horses, and perhaps these other horses live behind the steel doors?"

"No chance," Harry said. "Not nowadays with all the racecourse security, and all horses been microchipped and regularly checked. It used to happen in the good old days. There have been a few famous cases over the years. Flockton Grey was a ringer, or a ringer replaced him of which I just can't remember, but nowadays, this just doesn't happen". (A Ringer is where they swap a horse for another one.)

They all but ruled out drugs as they would show up. Neil told his uncle that he'd gone through all the possible options with Dawn.

"Oh yes, who's Dawn?" Uncle Harry enquired, suddenly getting very interested.

"She's a stable lass who used to work at Lez Allen's, but I've no idea where she is now?"

His uncle told him that he always stayed in rented accommodation near the races for the three-day meeting and asked if he wanted to stay with him, Neil jumped at the suggestion, and they set off in convoy though Neil had great trouble keeping up with his Uncle's top of the range Jaguar, so he gave up and stopped a couple of miles before Newmarket to do some shopping as he'd come up with a plan, he was going to get into the races unnoticed as he was going to go in fancy dress in drag as a woman no less. He thought that it was the perfect way to get around the racecourse ban and hoped that no one would recognise him, especially the Boyles. Therefore as he entered a charity shop he knew exactly what he wanted to buy, he told the two old ladies behind the counter that he wanted some women's clothes for a fancy dress party that he was going to, they eyed him suspiciously so he nervously blurted out that he wasn't a crossdresser and that this was the first time that he'd ever dressed as a woman, which wasn't actually true as he'd won a pony club fancy dress competition dressed as a Royal princess.

He told them that he wanted to look like a typical racegoer, so they found him a tweed skirt, a striped top and a jacket, and long leather boots, and he finished off his outfit with a scarf and a hat that covered most of his face, and he nervously went to look at himself in the mirror, he was shocked at the apparition that glared back at him, "I don't fancy yours," he said and smiled to himself, but the main thing he thought was that no one would recognise him.

He kept the clothes on, and as he left the shop, he was aware of the shopkeepers sniggering behind him as he wandered back to his car, feeling mildly ridiculous and rather unsure of himself if my friends could see me now, he thought. His nerve began to fail him when he reached the races, but he parked in the car park, took a deep breath and got out and strode purposely in the direction of the entrance hoping that he was blending in with the crowds, he walked past Sue Henry and her jockey Sarah Howerd, and they didn't give him a second glance, he nearly blows his cover as without thinking he walked up to Sarah intending to enquire after her sister Dawn but just in time he checked himself, he wandered around the betting ring and winked at his Uncle who was smiling and laughing with the punters and Neil (or Sheila as he was today), realised that he was very good at his job. He went to a quiet corner to study his race card and check out the runners for the day, Lez Allen only had one horse running, and it was just Neil's luck that it was down as a non-runner, so there was no one present from the yard, so nothing for Neil to observe. He went up to the Owner's stand and had an enjoyable day watching from there, training his binoculars on the proceedings. He got a few strange looks but wasn't quite sure why. The champion trainer Henry Aske won the first two races, and after the third race, Neil just happened to be stood near him and was amazed when he came over and started talking to him, and Neil suddenly got the horrible feeling that he was being chatted up, and by another man, and certainly didn't enjoy the experience, Henry's breath smelt of alcohol and Neil presumed that he'd been in the bar celebrating his two earlier victories.

Neil started moving away as quickly as was politely possible without appearing rude, and Henry shouted after him, "If I see you in the Owner's and Trainer's after the last, I'll buy you a drink". Neil knew that one thing for certain was that he was going nowhere near that bar. Well, certainly not in his present guise.

That night over a meal, this time washed down with pints of local ale, too many pints in Neil's case, he told his uncle that he'd made no progress and told him about the incident with Henry Aske.

His uncle started roaring with laughter and said, "He's got a roving eye, that one, but he's harmless". Then he added with a smile, "But young ladies like you need to be careful when you're out on your own". When the laughter had died down, Neil said that he was going to watch Lez Allen's runners and stable staff getting the horses ready prior to the start to see if anything untoward happened, and if anything was administered to the horses, highly unlikely he thought but worth watching, just in case he saw something unusual. Neil woke the next morning with a thick head again, and even though he greatly enjoyed his uncle's company, he was in a way quite pleased that tomorrow night would be the last one as all the heavy drinking was beginning to take its toll on him, and at a time when he really needed to be at his sharpest. At the races again, he still went unrecognised and found a good place to stand where he could observe all that occurred in the pre-parade ring and the paddock. He saw his ex-colleagues leading horses around and carrying the racing equipment, but when they went to tack the horses up, they went into a box and closed the doors so Neil couldn't see anything that was going on. There was nothing unusual about this, as a lot of trainers did it to keep horses calm by blocking out all the racecourse sounds, but it didn't help Neil's quest for information. Angus Connolly was down to ride all the runners, and it was with a touch of resentment that Neil watched him confidently stride into the paddock to ride the first horse, which managed to finish a very close third, and Neil could tell that he was trying to win, the second runner won very easily even with Angus easing down when he knew that he'd won and obviously trying not to win by too far, the third one was a strange result as it started as favourite and Neil could see that Connolly was trying, but the horse just didn't fire and trailed in about tenth place.

Neil noticed the huddled group of a trainer, jockey and Frank Boyle in deep animated discussion and thought that something had gone wrong. Perhaps their corrupt system still had flaws. Neil discussed it all with his uncle at the pub in the evening. This time, they washed the meal down with some old-fashioned, mild ale, which Neil found easy to drink, too easy.

Neil said that he was going to watch the bookmakers in the betting ring tomorrow to see if any clues would surface as so far, he'd had a wasted two days, "Oh, I don't know" his uncle said, "You've got a potential date with a leading trainer".

In the morning, they both had a look through a trainer's book, which listed all the trainers, their horses and their owners. Uncle Harry pointed out that all the old owners had left, something that Kevin Dee had already told him, and they noticed that a lot of the horses were owned by obscure syndicates and surprisingly, a lot were owned by Lez Allen himself, and the rest were owned by a company calling itself BB racing.

"Do you know who they are?" Neil asked Uncle Harry, who shook his head.

"I've no idea."

"We don't seem to be making much progress," Neil said despondently.

Neil went to get dressed in his now familiar ladies' attire, and it worried him slightly that it was becoming second nature to him. A part of him was upset that this would be the last time, but he put it down to the adrenalin caused by being in disguise and not the thrill of dressing up. At least, he hoped that was the reason. He drove to the races and parked in a similar spot and was just about to get out after studying the Lez Allen runners in the paper and noting that they were all owned by this mysterious BB racing. Interesting, he thought but wasn't sure why. He glanced at the car parked next to him and did a double take as it was the Boyles. They looked at him, but he didn't think and hoped that they hadn't recognised him. He waited a good five minutes after they'd gone before he dared to get out and cautiously enter the racecourse. The three Allen runners were called Cracked Eggs, Jam Butty and Captain Confusion, Neil noticed that they were all being ridden by the apprentice Jason Connolly, so if his theory was correct, then they were all due to lose. He stood in the stands and watched the betting ring for Cracked Egg's race. He noticed Derek and Frank Boyle darting around from bookie to bookie, he noted that one bookie was giving better odds for Cracked Eggs than the rest, and this was Bentine Bros Bookmakers. He studied them with his binoculars, and he knew instantly that he'd seen them somewhere before but where he just couldn't remember. Cracked Eggs had won his last race but was ridden very quietly and found nothing near the finish to end up fifth. Jam Butty started favourite, and Neil thought that a trend was developing as the Bentine Bros were offering much better odds on this

Lez Allen runner and making a great trade with a big queue of punters doing business with them.

In the race, Jason was almost motionless on the horse, and when he appeared to be trying near the finish yet again, the horse found nothing and finished unplaced. Neil noticed that after the race, Bentine Bros were hardly paying out compared with the other bookies, including his uncle. Captain Confusion was the second favourite but never appeared to be travelling, and the horse appeared tired, almost worn out and found nothing at the finish to also fail to make the frame. Neil's theory was correct as none of the horses won, and in his opinion, they'd run a long way below their true form, just like what had happened to him when he'd last rode for Allen, and ridden these horses, they'd found nothing when asked to go and try and win their races. Bentine Bros seemed to know what was going on, and Neil suddenly had a thought, I wonder if Bentine Bros are the same as the owners of BB racing. He thought that it was highly possible; this would explain a lot, but then what does it actually explain, he thought.

Just then, Pete Wisdom walked past and caught Neil off guard. He said, "What are you doing here, Neil? I thought that you were warned off?"

"Sorry you're mistaken, young man. I'm Sheila. Who's Neil?" he said in a high-pitched voice and quickly walked away. A few minutes later, he was alarmed to see Pete talking to the Boyles in the betting ring and saw him pointing to the place where they'd briefly met. Oh, heck, he thought my cover had been rumbled. He swiftly moved away and went to the back of the stands in the silver ring, where he could see all the way around the racecourse, including the car park. After the last race, he watched as the Boyles strode over to their car, they stood near it and his car for about ten minutes, but he couldn't quite work out what they were doing. Why aren't they leaving, he wondered.

When the car park was almost empty, they finally left and sped off, so Neil slowly and cautiously made his way down to his car, had a quick look around it, but everything seemed okay, so he got in and quickly drove off, thankful that he hadn't had a confrontation with anyone. He was driving back to the stud, so with his music playing and himself singing along.

"I've been driving in my car. It's not quite a Jaguar."

Quite apt, he thought, thinking about his uncle's plush Jag. He was relaxed now as he thought that he was in no immediate danger. He started thinking about what he'd found out. He wrote all his findings down, and with Kevin Dee's information, he was beginning to build up a picture, but crucially he had no proper facts to back it all up. He intended to put all the information together that night and send it all to the Jockey Club but thought that they probably wouldn't even look at it. He had a trouble-free journey home, which certainly couldn't be guaranteed for him in his present situation. As he approached home, he thought that his brakes were getting a little spongy but was getting very tired and thought that it wouldn't matter as he was nearly home, just before he got to Shiloh Farm, the home of the twins' Tilly and Dilly and the Milligan family, he went round a sharp corner and braked, and nothing happened, in a bit of a panic he pressed again but still nothing, a large tractor was looming large coming the other way on the narrow road, and there wasn't room for both of them. Neil swerved left and went straight through a dry stone wall, with stones flying everywhere and the sickening sound of bending metal. As the car came to a halt on a pile of stones, Neil hit his head on the steering wheel, and slightly dazed, he looked up to see the tractor driver peering in through the driver's window. It was the twins' brother Jim Milligan, and he looked understandably shocked.

"What the hell?" he said, "Is that you, Neil?"

Neil carefully and gingerly got out.

"What on earth, why are you dressed like that? Is there something that you need to tell me?"

When Neil regained his composure, he explained that he was undercover investigating the racing world, trying to clear his name. He wasn't sure if Jim believed him just said, "Wait till I tell the twins that you drive round in women's clothes".

He arranged to get the car towed away, another write-off, he thought, and it was going to be tested to find out what had gone wrong. The hirers were annoyed as they said every car, they hired out was checked meticulously before they went out. Neil was pretty sure that the brakes had been tampered with but knew that he'd have difficulty proving it. He agreed to help Jim repair the wall the following day, as it was one of his fields and reasoned that wall building couldn't be that hard, but how wrong was he? He got there the next morning, and Jim had already started. He'd taken it all down and laid out all the stones in different piles, small, long and large stones.

Jim was a man of very few words, but after saying, "You look different today".

He explained how to build the wall, "It's like a giant jigsaw puzzle; if you put one stone in incorrectly near the base, then the whole wall could fall down". He said that he'd build the roadside and Neil could do the inside, which very few people would see; as soon as they started, Neil realised that it was a lot harder than he expected.

He picked up a stone and put it on the wall, Jim took it off, and this continued until Jim said, "I'll tell you what I'll do the walling. You just put the middle filling stones in and help me lift the heavy ones".

Neil marvelled at how talented Jim was at walling and what a hard job it was. When it was finished, they both stood back and admired their work, well, Jim's work. Neil got invited back to the farmhouse for a meal; it was just himself and Jim. Neil asked how the twins were and explained that they were ignoring all his text messages.

"They blame you for their accident" Jim said, "They think that you told the Boyles the derogatory remarks they made about them".

"Nothing could be further from the truth," Neil said.

Jim continued, "They've told me what happened, but nobody else. The Boyles forced them off the road and threatened them that if they didn't stay silent, worse would befall them and their loved ones".

"I'd guessed that was what had happened," Neil said. "I never said a word to the Boyles, but I told Dawn, and I think that the foreign grooms unbeknown to us were listening and informed the Boyles."

"I'll tell them that it wasn't your fault then, I don't think they really thought that you had done it, but they weren't thinking straight. I've never seen them so scared; it's taken them a long time to get over it, physically and more importantly, mentally." Neil told him that the Boyles had previous form and told him what had happened to Kevin Dee and how badly it had finished for him.

A day or two later, the results came back on the hired car, it was a write-off, and the brake fluid had leaked out through a frayed pipe. Neil was pretty sure that it had been helped on his way, and he was sure he knew by whom, but as usual, he had no proof, or not yet anyway.

CHAPTER THIRTY-NINE
Infiltrate

Neil had kindly been invited to stay with the stud manager Steve and his wife Lynne in their modern bungalow for a few days. Lynne spent the whole time fussing over him and feeding him extremely well, so much so that Neil settled in very quickly and decided that he could do with a girlfriend like her.

"Has Lynne got a sister?" he asked Steve one day.

"Yes," he replied, "she's married to a rugby player, has three kids and lives in South Africa". So that was the end of that discussion.

In the evenings, he went through the events of the past few weeks with Steve, showing him his notes and the ones that he'd been given by Kevin Dee. They both came to the obvious conclusion that there were huge sums of money involved in the deception, but he still had no proof of any wrongdoing. Neil said that he was sure that the Bentine Bros bookmakers were behind it somehow and that they were the same as BB racing that owned many of the horses at Lez Allen's yard. He decided that his evidence wasn't anywhere near enough to clear his name and that his only option was to infiltrate the enemy and go behind enemy lines.

"What do you mean?" Steve asked.

"I'm going to go to the stables late at night and somehow get behind the locked steel doors and see what happens there."

Steve and especially Lynne didn't like the idea, but he was determined to go and hopefully gather evidence. He sketched a rough plan of the stable layout and decided that he could probably get to the locked part from the second floor above the stables. He transferred all of his and Kevin Dee's evidence onto his phone with the intention of sending it to the Jockey Club and the Police with the expected extra evidence that he was hoping to obtain. His next problem was transport as he was running out of available wheels, so he asked Steve if he could borrow his treasured Royal Enfield classic motorbike. Steve was reluctant to lend it, but he hadn't ridden it much recently since he'd fallen off it in icy conditions in winter and slightly lost his nerve. Lynne was constantly nagging him to sell it, so eventually, he agreed to let Neil borrow it.

That evening after a brief lesson on how to handle it, he was off. It was a long journey, but luckily it was a clear, dry night; but even so, Neil didn't arrive until after 11 o'clock. He turned the engine off and wheeled it behind the detested caravan, which he'd hoped that he would never see again. He then walked through the dilapidated old wooden stables and reached the exterior of the locked area; he walked around trying to find a way in, but as he'd expected, it was all solid walls with no access. Undeterred, he carried on round until he got to the other side just below the main house at the top of the yard where he knew there was a side gate which he'd used before on many occasions, as he expected it was bolted, but he easily scaled the wall dropping down silently in the yard and unbolting it so that it was ready for him to make his escape when the time came, which hopefully it would. All was dark and very quiet. He rounded the corner and could hear the contented and soothing sound of the horses munching hay and also a distinct and distant mechanical sound which he'd heard many times before and was hoping to find out very shortly what was causing it. He climbed the stairs above the top stable and gained access to the room above as the door, as he knew, was never locked; it was a rug-drying room. He turned his torch on and surveyed the scene, which consisted of a few rugs draped over rails, the room was warm, and there was a distinct but not unpleasant smell of wet horses.

There was no time to stop and linger. The longer he took, the more likely it was that he'd be discovered. He moved to the end of the room where there was a door that led through to another one that he thought must adjoin the building that he was aiming to get into, he'd never been in this room before, but luckily the door opened unhindered once inside he found that the room was full of large bales of shavings (used for stable bedding), but they looked like they'd been here for a long time as they were covered with a deep layer of dust, he made his way to the far end and shone his torch on to his dismay a solid wall, with what appeared to be no way through, however near the eaves he could see a slight gap where the new building's beams had been slotted in, and it looked like there was just enough room for a slim person to fit through and even though he'd been piling on the pounds due to his recent inactivity, he still was of small stature, so he climbed up on a bale of shavings and just managed to squeeze through the narrow gap and slipped down, landing on a tatty old sofa, he was in a sparsely furnished room with a few chairs and a table with some heavy tea stained mugs strewn on it and some old Sporting Life papers and a few old girly mags, and a strong smell of tobacco, the room was obviously used a lot and quite recently and he thought that he knew by whom. He located the door that he presumed would lead down to the secret yard below. It, however, was locked, so he was blocked again, tantalisingly so close to where he wanted to get to. It was a solid new door, so the brute force would be fruitless. He sat down in one of the chairs, thinking that he was defeated and would have to go back none the wiser. He absentmindedly shined his torch around the walls and jumped up as the beam landed on a bunch of keys; surely, one of these wouldn't open the door, but the second one did, and he was soon out into the dimly lit secret yard. He swiftly descended the wooden stairs and looked around. The mechanical sound was a lot louder now and appeared to be coming from a stable nearby. He looked in and was astonished to find two or three stables had been knocked together, and inside there was a horse walker (a cage with a number of compartments which each can hold one horse and is used for automatically exercising horses), nothing unusual there, Neil thought, as nearly every training establishment has one, but what was astonishing was that when he looked in over the stable door, he could see that the horse walker was in use, and three horses were walking round and round in the circular walker.

Neil couldn't understand it; why would this be happening this time at night? Nothing made any sense. A board in front of the stables had three horses' names chalked up and different times for each. He'd just read the first horse's name, Caught in a Trap, and it said five hours. He took a few photos and was just about to explore further when he heard voices and a rattling of door latches and bolts, and the big steel door started to open. Neil quickly ran for cover as the lights came on. He took refuge behind a stack of straw bales and breathed heavily, hopefully wishing that he hadn't been spotted. But he had, he could hear bales furiously being moved, and before he knew it, he was stood with his back against the last of the bales, and Derek Boyle and Jason Connolly stood glaring at him and brandishing shiny gleaming pitchforks before he had a chance to speak a pitchfork came flying through the air and pinned him against the straw by his neck, and two more swiftly followed and pinned his legs also, a little too high up for his liking, blood started trickling down his neck, but he knew that it could have been a lot worse, and was probably just about to become so.

He was well and truly pinned securely like a cheap fairground knife-throwing act. Derek motioned to Jason and said, "Watch him closely and check to see if he's got a phone. I'll go and get Brian, and then the fun can begin".

Neil thought that it certainly wouldn't be fun for him but knew that with only the not-so-clever Jason watching him, this was his best, and perhaps only, chance to escape. He said something to him but very quietly.

"What's that?" Jason gruffly said, trying to appear tough.

Neil repeated it but even more quietly, and as Jason lent in close and bent his head to listen to him, Neil quickly grabbed hold of the top pitchfork and forcibly whacked Jason on the head, he staggered back, giving Neil time to free the pitchfork and whack Jason again for good measure, and he freed himself, and as he heard voices returning he jumped up the steps two at a time and soon reached the top when a sudden pain in one knee stopped him in his tracks, he cried out but managed to limp through the door quickly locking it and leaving the key in. That should give me breathing space and a little time, he thought. He looked down to see a pitchfork sticking out of his knee. He bent down and swiftly pulled it out, gasping in pain. Luckily there didn't seem to be too much blood, so he quickly wrapped his scarf around the wound and tied it tightly and set off to try and escape. Even though the odds were against him, he could hear the door rattling as he limped off using the pitchfork as a walking stick cum crutch, his progress was slow, but he made it through the narrow gap into the next room and then finally into the drying room, he looked out of the door, and all appeared silent, though he could hear sounds in the rooms behind, so as quick as possible he descended the steps to ground level, and he foolishly allowed a smile to spread across his face, as he thought that he'd escaped, but alas he'd been counting his chickens as when he reached the door to freedom, he heard voices.

Sounds like Frank Boyle and a girl's voice, possibly Jan Cook, he thought, they're the last people I want to see, and as he saw the door handle turn, he swiftly ran in the dark around the side of the house, and he found himself by the coal hatch, where he'd been thrown in for his stable initiation, and without time to think he quickly opened it and slid in intending to hide there until the coast was clear. He walked through the bunker into the boiler room and could see a light shining from the next room, the underground office. He was surprised to see that Lez Allen was there on his landline phone.

He could just hear him say, "The horse's tomorrow are Caught in a Trap, Last Chance and Baler Twine," then he put the phone down as his mobile phone vibrated on the table. He quickly answered it, and Neil could hear the odd word, and it sounded like he was being told about the intruder in the stables. Lez slammed the phone down and left the room and disappeared up into the house.

Neil took his chance and entered the room and took a few photos of it though it was just a bare-walled bland office. He dialled the last number on the phone called and recorded the reply, which was as he expected an answer phone.

"You're through to Bentine Bros; please leave a message..." but he put the phone down before the end of the message as he could hear the door to the house opening.

He swiftly retreated into the shadows as someone went back into the office but only briefly as the lights were turned off, the door locked, and the steps retreated back into the house, and all was quiet again. Neil waited a few minutes before going up the steps and, with a little difficulty leaping into the little secret room that he'd found previously, he sat down and took the scarf off the injured knee. There was a lot of dried and caked blood, and his knee was beginning to swell, he then reapplied the scarf under his trousers, and he settled down for what was left of the night. He couldn't really sleep due to the pain, the cold and the hard floor but most of all, the fear of being found. He managed to slip into a very light sleep, and he awoke in a drowsy state when a loud explosion outside shook the building to its foundations. I bet he thought that's my motorbike gone up in flames; what will Steve say? He looked up at the grid at the top of the wall to see daylight seeping through. His phone was turned off so that he couldn't be traced, so he had no idea what time it was, but he had a vague feeling that it was early morning.

He tried to stretch out his injured knee, but it had seized up and took a lot of massaging before he could get it to move. A little later, he heard a clatter of horse's hooves, the familiar clip-clop sound of metal shoes on the tarmac, and he realised that the first string of horses was going out to the gallops. Now he thought it was the time to make my escape. He gingerly eased himself up and jumped through the narrow gap and winched with pain as he landed awkwardly, and as quick as he could, he went down the steps through the boiler room and clambered up the coal, and peered out of the bunker hatch, it appeared that the coast was clear, so with difficulty, he hauled himself out and walked slowly back to the gate where he'd tried to leave the night before, he got there without being seen and was able to open it and escape. He walked round the back to where he'd parked the motorbike what seemed like a very long time ago, but it wasn't there as all he found was a smouldering mass of twisted metal; Steve's pride and joy was unrecognisable.

LESTER BOYD

He didn't have time to worry about that now and hatched another plan. He'd take the bus into town and go to the police station, and all his troubles would be behind him, or so he hoped.

CHAPTER FORTY

On a Bus

Neil knew where the nearest bus stop was, though he'd never used one. It was on the opposite side of the road to the stables; he took a detour to get to it and entered the wooden bus shelter unseen, or so he hoped and sat down with his mind full of the previous night's events whilst he waited for a bus unsure when one would come. He looked at the faded timetable posted on the wall, but as he still didn't have his phone turned on, he peered out of the cover of the shelter and could just see the time on the clock in the market square and could see that it was nearly 8 o'clock, according to the timetable the next bus was due at 8:10 am and took twenty minutes to get to the town centre. The time dragged whilst he waited, and every person who walked by caused an intake of breath as he worried who they may be. An old lady arrived and sat down.

"Should be here soon," Neil said, but she just looked him up and down and said something to herself about the lack of dress sense of the young nowadays. Neil was inclined to tell her the reason for his unkempt state but thought that if he mentioned that he'd been attacked by some pitchfork-wielding maniacs, he might scare her. Finally, the bus appeared. He let the old lady get on first and followed her closely so as not to stand out. He strode to the back of the bus past a few unfamiliar faces and sat down. Just as the bus was about to leave, someone jumped on and sat at the front, and to his horror, he instantly realised that it was Derek Boyle. Neil grabbed an old newspaper off the floor and opened it up to cover his face; it was the Sunday Sport, so the old ladies who got on frowned and tut-tutted.

The bus set off on its long, winding, tortuous journey, they passed the racehorse string returning, and he wondered why Derek wasn't with them, the bus stopped at many places with people getting on and off, but Derek resolutely stayed where he was, the bus twisted and turned around the narrow country lanes, but finally reached its destination of the town centre where everyone got off apart from Neil who still sat wondering what to do.

The bus driver shouted to him, "Wake up, sonny, we're there. You'll have to get off".

Neil reluctantly put down the paper, having not even read one line or looked at the many pictures. He tentatively stepped out into a thankfully deserted street, and there was no sign of Derek, so he strode off towards the police station. As he passed a narrow dark ginnel, he was suddenly grabbed from behind and pulled into the ginnel, and he was face to face with Derek. Before Neil had a chance to think, Derek had hit him, and they both fell to the floor heavily together, with Neil hitting his head on the ground and rolling around in the dust and grime, with neither really getting any blows in as they were too close to each other, they were near a back entrance to a café and Neil spotted amongst the rubbish stacked outside an old broken chair, he quickly grabbed it and battered Derek with it, as he fell back Neil was able to get a better swing and hit him again and made heavy contact, and he fell back heavily dazed.

Neil took his chance and made his escape through the side door of the café. He must have looked like he'd been dragged through a hedge backwards as a waitress looked at him in disgust. Thinking quickly, he said, "Undercover Police" and reached into his pocket to show her an imaginary police warrant card.

She gasped in horror and dropped her tray with cups and plates flying everywhere. I bet she thinks that I'm going to draw out a gun, he thought, but there was no time to explain as he knew that Derek could soon be up and after him, so he left by the main door and hobbled down the street passed a number of shops before crossing the road and walking back up towards the police station but out of sight, when he got near he peered round the corner to see if the coast was clear, but of course, it wasn't as Frank Boyle and Jason Connolly had positioned themselves discreetly at either side of the entrance, so that there was no way of getting in without passing them, and in his weakened state he didn't think that it was worth trying.

He stood for a few minutes undecided about what to do, hoping that they'd leave soon, but they didn't, his head was aching, and his knee was throbbing, and on top of that, he hadn't eaten since the early evening before. He then saw another bus pulling up and obscuring his view of the police station, and its destination was the hospital, and an idea pinged in his head. He jumped on at the last minute and hoped that no one would follow him. He still had no idea where Derek had gone, but as the bus chugged off in the direction of the hospital, with none of his fears being allayed, he tried to relax in his seat but couldn't. Apart from the underlying fear, he was becoming light-headed and a little dizzy.

As soon as the bus arrived at the hospital stop, he got out and scanned the area but couldn't see any immediate dangers, so he started limping across the hospital car park, thinking that if he got through the front doors, then all his worries would cease, but that would be too simple. He carried on up the car park and suddenly noticed the Suzuki Jimny belonging to Brian Cougan parked under a tree, but there was no sign of him, so Neil kept going on towards the entrance, and just as he reached the steps, he saw Brian coming out and heading in his direction. He turned sharply and headed back down the car park but with no idea where he was going and no idea if he'd been spotted. As he reached the row of shops, he entered the first one without knowing what it was. When he got in, he instantly realised that he was in the Post Office, and yet another idea pinged in his head.

All his evidence was on his phone, so he grabbed an envelope and Biro and scribbled his address, Lazy Horse Stud, on it, put the Biro back on the shelf, inserted his phone in the envelope and sealed it and headed, in an unstable fashion, to the counter and said, "First class please".

"Are you okay?" the worried assistant said as the dizziness reappeared, and his face was drained of all colour.

He heard a loud click as the door opened and fearing that it might be Brian or another member of the gang of four, he turned too swiftly and fell to the ground banging his head on the counter, saying as he went, "Keep the change", before landing on the floor out cold again.

When he woke up, unsure how much time had passed and slowly came around, he instantly knew where he was and that he was back in the hospital. As he stirred, he noticed that there was someone searching through her personal belongings, even though there weren't many of them, it was a girl, and when he looked closer he realised that it was Jan Cook, so he pretended to still be sleeping, and she soon gave up and left, and he just caught her saying to herself, "It's not here".

Neil realised that they would go to whatever length it would take to stop their little horse-stopping scam from getting out. He realised that they'd found the perfect risk-free way of stopping horses; putting horses on the horse walker the night before their race would stop them from performing at their best and prevent them from winning. It was a drug-free way, without any risk of injuring the horse or souring it and putting it off racing, and there would be no future detrimental effects on the horse. They would have an easy race, and after a few days' rest, they'd still be fully fit and ready to show their true form. At enhanced betting odds, it was a win-win situation for whoever the mastermind was behind it.

It could possibly be Lez Allen, but he doubted it. It definitely wasn't the gang of four, as in Neil's mind, they just didn't have the intelligence. It was still all a bit of a mystery. He looked around the room and saw a policeman standing outside his door. Good, he thought, they're finally protecting me. He wandered to the door and waved at the policeman as a sort of thank you but was surprised by the response he received.

The policeman opened the door and sternly said, "Get back in bed; you're going nowhere except to the police station". Neil was stunned. He'd thought that he was being protected when it was the opposite.

Mystified, he went back to his bed as a nurse came in with his breakfast; there wasn't much of it, but he wolfed it down, and it only slightly eased his hunger pangs. Afterwards, he got his jacket off the chair and looked in the pockets until he found what he was looking for, DC Abbott's calling card and dialled the number on the hospital phone above his bed, desperate to find out what he was being accused of this time, after a few rings it was answered gruffly by DC Abbott.

"It's serious this time; a prison sentence beckons."

"Why?" Neil asked.

"You're being accused of breaking into Lez Allen's stable yard late at night and brandishing a gun and threatening," he stopped for a few seconds, and Neil could hear him shuffling paper, "just checking my notes; we've got so many pages on you. In fact, enough to write a novel. You're accused of threatening Brian Cougan, Derek and Frank Boyle and Jason Connolly".

"How could I overpower four of them," Neil asked exasperated.

"In their words, you didn't as they say that they managed to knock the gun out of your hands, and it harmlessly fired into the night sky."

"It's all fairy tales and complete rubbish," Neil said. "Have you checked the gun for my fingerprints?"

"Not yet, but we will be doing it in due course. Do you deny that you broke in?"

"I was there, but I didn't break in; you can't believe a word they say."

DC Abbott then said grimly, "Well, if I was you, I'd get a lawyer quick sharp, and when you've recovered, you'll be escorted to the police station, and I'll be waiting for you," and he put the phone down with none of the usual banter.

Neil now realised the seriousness of the situation. He had trespassed into the stables but with a gun that was completely preposterous. He rang home, and his dad answered. Neil was expecting a tirade of abuse but was pleasantly surprised when the opposite happened.

His dad, after asking what he'd been up to, quickly took control of the situation and said, "It's looking bad for you with all these allegations mounting up".

"Not a word of which is true," Neil quickly added.

"I realise that," his dad said, "but proving it is going to be extremely hard, breaking into someone else's property in the middle of the night is asking for trouble".

"Well, I'm hardly likely to break into my own property, am I?" he foolishly said.

His dad ignored the comment and said, "What you need is a good lawyer, and one of my long-standing stud clients just happens to be a lawyer, so I'll give him a ring straight away and sort something out for you, but in the meantime just try and keep out of trouble".

Neil was feeling a little brighter now, and after putting the receiver down, he was beginning to think that it was just possible that the whole world wasn't completely against him. He felt relaxed, and after a good lunch, well, it felt good to a hungry man, he fell asleep, to be woken by a doctor who came in to inform him that he was being discharged on the following day.

As soon as he'd left, the phone went again; he answered it and was just about to say hello when an unknown voice said, "We're watching your every step, so don't say anything that you'll later repent, or you might not live to regret it".

Neil was about to say something but didn't get the chance as the line went dead, something he sincerely hoped wouldn't be happening to him. If they're trying to scare me, they've succeeded, he said to himself, but I'm not giving up my quest to clear my name now, especially as I think that I'm getting near. He'd hardly had the chance to get himself comfortably back in bed when the phone went again.

Apprehensively he answered it, and a loud booming voice said, "Walsh, Miller and Armstrong lawyers here. We're sending out someone to see you; expect them in about an hour".

"Thank you," Neil said and was about to ask a bit more detail, but they'd gone, saving my money, he thought, but they'll need someone very good to extract an idiot like me from the mess I've got myself into.

He went back to bed, hoping that the phone would finally remain silent, put the radio on but promptly fell asleep and woke an hour or so later to find a stocky beefy young girl nervously coughing at the side of his bed as she tried to wake him.

"I didn't like to disturb you," she said.

"School's out early today," Neil rather foolishly said.

She flushed slightly and looked annoyed, and said, "I'm Suzie Walsh; I'm your solicitor". There was an awkward silence, and then they both laughed when Neil quickly said that he was only joking, and she admitted that she'd only recently qualified and that this was her first case.

CHAPTER FORTY-ONE

Big Girls Don't Cry

After they'd done the introductions, Suzie explained that she was a big racing fan and often attended the races. She knew who Neil was and had admired him — as a jockey; she'd hastened to add.

"I used to ride horses," she said.

"Did you ever want to be a jockey?" he innocently asked but realised instantly that it was a rather crass insensitive question, especially if she worried about her weight, but she either ignored his slight or didn't realise and carried on.

"No, not a jockey. I never thought of that, but I got into show jumping instead, and I managed to reach quite a high level. I even won a big class at the Great Yorkshire Show."

Neil was impressed and said, "So why did you stop and become a lawyer?"

"Well, I was the clever one in the family; school was a breeze for me; everything was so easy. Didn't you find that?"

"Yes," Neil said, lying through his teeth, then added, "I just spent all my school days looking out of the window, and there's nothing easier than that".

She gave him a strange look but continued, "My dad always wanted one of his children to join the family firm of lawyers. He'd already given up on my brother, who's just a gardener".

"Just a gardener?" Neil enquired.

"Well, he's not made much effort all his life, and mowing lawns is about the limit of his abilities," Suzie said. Neil thought that it was best to drop this line of enquiry and let her carry on. "I had to make a decision, Show Jumping or become a lawyer, and the decision was sort of made for me. I started having a bad run of form for no perceptible reason, then I had a bad fall and had to spend time on the sidelines, so I lent my horse to a friend who straight away started doing a lot better than me, and I realised there and then that show jumping would be a fickle perilous career with more lows than highs and no financial security, so I opted to become a lawyer".

"And regretted it ever since," Neil said.

"Surprisingly not," she replied, "and strangely, since that day, I've never sat on a horse again, and that was four years ago before I started my university course".

Neil found this surprising, but then he was the complete opposite as he'd never sat on a horse until his late teenage years and didn't want to stop anytime soon. He was enjoying his chat with Suzie but realised that it was time to finish the pleasantries and get down to business, especially if she was charging the normal extortionately high lawyer's hourly rate. She told him that there were some serious allegations being thrown in his direction, and unless they could prove otherwise, then it didn't look good for him. She agreed to go through it all with him that evening, and then she said that she would return in the morning and accompany him to the police station, where she said that she was confident that she'd be able to get him out on bail.

"I've not lost a case yet," she brightly said.

"I hope not, especially since this is your first one," Neil replied. They painstakingly went through all the allegations, and there was a long extensive list of them.

Suzie said, "You've been busy. They didn't mention this in our training".

"What do you mean?" he replied, puzzled.

"Someone with so many allegations against them in such a short period of time."

"This is a baptism of fire for you," Neil said and then added, "can we go somewhere where we can talk in private?"

The policeman had insisted on keeping the door open, and a multitude of people kept walking by.

"Anyone can overhear what we're saying," Neil said and was worrying that his enemies could listen.

Suzie said, "OK, we'll go and stand in the hospital courtyard. We should be OK there. I'll go and square it with PC Plod out there". She went and spoke to the policeman, who wasn't happy about any derogation from his orders, but Suzie was very persuasive. "I'm just having a briefing with my client, and then I'll escort him straight back. We'll just be over there; you'll be able to see us at all times."

He still wasn't pleased, but her best flirtatious smile did the trick, and he assented and offered no more resistance. They went into the brightly painted courtyard, which was a cheery oasis and thankfully away from the clinical odour and smell of the hospital. It was in the centre and had a few doors leading to it and a few plants and bushes next to a food and drinks dispenser. Luckily no one else appeared to be in. They could see the policeman at the end of the corridor, and he looked to have lost interest in Neil and appeared to be taking a nap. Neil started talking and told her what he thought was going off at Lez Allen's yard and all the evidence that he'd acquired concerning their stopping of horses and race fixing. He explained to her how he thought that they were doing it.

"Ingenious," Suzie said when he explained to her about the horse walkers. She was easy to talk to and understood all the racing jargon, which made his descriptions so much easier. He said that he thought that they'd been planning this for years, starting by just using bent jockey's to stop the horses, but he thought that this perhaps became too obvious to the watching stewards, and finding bent jockeys wouldn't be easy, he explained that he thought that they then probably came up with the horse walker method by accident, he expected that they had some teething problems like the time when he won on one on his first ride for them that obviously wasn't meant to win. Getting a horse to win a race is difficult enough but getting them to lose is equally difficult. He said that he thought that the idea was just to take the edge off the horse's performance by giving it a number of hours on the horse walker the night before the race, just enough to impair its performance, but so it looked like it was trying, but looked like it lacked ability, and after a few days rest the horse would still be fit and come out and put up a winning performance when unfancied at much better odds. It was a perfect untraceable way to fix racing and a licence to print money.

He explained how he thought that the Bentine Bros bookmakers were the masterminds behind the whole operation and could be raking in vast amounts of money.

"Fascinating," Suzie said, "I can see now why they've been trying to stop you, but can you prove any of this?"

"Well, I hope so," he replied.

He told her about Kevin Dee and the Milligan twins and their car crashes and repeated the details of all the scrapes he'd got into. Suzie was horrified.

"You could have been killed or seriously injured; these thugs need locking up. Why didn't you go to the police?"

"Oh, I did," he replied, "many times. I'm on first-name terms there and have my own reserved parking places".

She gave him one of her strange looks but pressed on, "Where is all your evidence?"

"I'm not sure," he replied and got one of her strange looks yet again, and then explained how he had put all the evidence on his phone, including photos and how he'd actually recorded the pitchfork attack, and that he thought that he'd posted it to his home address.

"And where is that?" she asked.

"Lazy Horse Stud," he replied.

"Well," she said, "we need that ASAP if we're going to stand any chance of getting you off all these charges".

Just then, they were distracted from their intense discussion by a sound from the food and drinks dispenser, and Neil said, "I think that there's someone standing behind it listening to all our conversation".

As he said this, a figure darted out and quickly exited through one of the doors and was gone. Neil turned to Suzie and said, "That's one of them; it's Jan Cook, and she'll be off to tell the rest straight away".

"Do you think that she overheard us?" Suzie rather naively asked.

"Yes, every single word. She's probably been there all the time we've been speaking, and now they will all know."

She interrupted him, "Who do you mean?"

"Frank and Derek Boyle, Brian Cogan and Jason Connolly — and once Jan Cook tells them what she's overheard — they will now know what to do to make matters a whole lot worse."

CHAPTER FORTY-TWO

Country House

Suzie tried to take control of the situation, "I suggest that you ring your dad and ask him to check to see if your phone has arrived in the post, and request that he puts it in a safe place and to lock the house doors".

"OK," Neil said, but can I borrow your phone, please?"

She looked at him quizzically, "Well, you know where mine is?" She quickly lent him her top-of-the-range smartphone.

"Nice," Neil said. "Can you ring the number for me as this phone is far too clever for me?"

She dialled for him, but as Neil expected, no one answered. He was beginning to panic now and pace around, "My family will all be at a horse sale or another stud. Goodness knows what time they'll be back".

Neil tried ringing both his dad's and mum's mobile phones, but both went straight to answer the phone, "They'll check them in about a week," he said sarcastically. "There's only one thing we can do," he said with a sense of panic in his voice, "we'll have to go there and get my phone before my enemies do".

Susie was unsure, "You're meant to be going straight to the police station tomorrow morning".

"Well, we'll have to make a little diversion then," Neil said.

"Okay," Suzie said, "I'll drive you there and then straight to the police station in the morning. I'll just go and tell that policeman".

"No time for that," Neil said, "come on, let's go".

They darted off and jumped into Suzie's shiny little gleaming yellow sports car and sped off, but Suzie was having second thoughts.

"I don't like it," she said, "helping a police suspect abscond; it could be the end of my career before it's even started".

Neil could tell that she was worried, so he said, "Why don't you ring your firm and tell them what has happened? They should be able to sort it all out with their legal clout".

"That's not a bad idea, except for one thing; they'll have all gone home at this time of night, and the answer phone will be on."

"Oh well," Neil said light-heartedly, "I'm sure it'll all sort itself out in the long run".

"It's alright for you to be so blasé," she snapped, "this is all your fault."

"Don't lose your shirt," Neil said, trying to calm the situation, but she was getting annoyed now.

"What?" she said, "It's don't lose your rag or pull your hair out".

"Thank you, teacher," Neil said, and she calmed down a little. "Anyway," Neil said, "it's a nice shirt".

"What do you mean?" she enquired.

"The one you're wearing; it's very classy and looks expensive."

"It's a blouse and wasn't cheap."

"OK'," Neil said, "it's a very nice blouse".

The conversation carried on like this, a little banal and juvenile, but it served the purpose of helping to while away the time and stopped them from thinking about the situation they could be driving towards.

"I could be in big trouble for helping you abscond," Suzie said.

"Don't worry," Neil said, "I'll vouch for you".

"That's great," she replied, "I'm sure that will help when an absconding police suspect who's got more charges against him than the Kray twins vouches for me".

They both laughed, but it was a hollow laugh. They became silent now, apart from Neil's occasional directional pointer. As they got nearer, Neil realised that he could be leading her into danger.

"If you like," he said, "you can drop me at the top of the drive, and I'll pop down and collect my phone".

"No chance," she said, "I'm not letting you out of my sight". So as they approached Lazy Horse Stud, "Why Lazy Horse?" Susie asked.

"I'll tell you later," Neil said, "when this is all over," which he hoped wouldn't be that far away. They drove down the long, impressive drive with smart timber fencing on both sides, and they arrived at the stud farmhouse.

"Wow. That's big," Suzie said while looking up at the big three-storied country house. Neil nearly replied with a racy comment but thought better of it, as now wasn't the time he thought.

"Park at the front, and I'll nip in and get my phone, but keep the engine running just in case." Neil ran round the side where the spare key was always left and quickly entered the dark and silent empty house, on the kitchen table he found what he was looking for a package addressed to him in his handwriting, thinking quickly he ran upstairs and grabbed his phone charger and was soon outside after locking the house, as he nearly got back to Suzie's car thinking to himself that he'd been panicking about nothing when he saw car lights coming down the drive. Neil thought that it was probably his dad's Range Rover, but he soon realised that it wasn't as a Suzuki Jimny skidded to a halt and Brian Cougan leapt out brandishing a baseball bat.

"Quick, get inside!" Suzie shouted.

Neil didn't need telling twice and jumped in as the baseball bat came crashing down on the boot of Suzie's car.

"That's great," she said, "I've only just got this car".

"Better than my head," Neil grimly said. Suzie had set off but didn't know where she was going.

"Keep going down this track," Neil said, "the track's a little rough, but you should be okay, and we can..." he stopped in mid-sentence.

"What is it? What's wrong?" she said worriedly. He knew that he'd have to tell her the bad news.

"It comes to a ford, but I've just realised that there's no way you'll get through, especially after all this rain."

"Great," she said, "so you've led me to a dead end?"

"Don't worry," Neil said, trying to hide his concern, "I've got a plan, if you carry on past the cottage and then round the corner and then if you turn sharp left and pull in behind the trees and turn your lights off, then hopefully Brian will drive straight past us and before he knows what's happening, he'll have driven into the ford".

"That sounds a good plan," she said, reassured.

"It's the only one that I've got," he replied.

Luckily it worked a treat as Brian shot past their unseen vehicle, and in the dark, he didn't see the ford before it was too late and was soon in it. As they reversed out from their hiding place to retrace their steps, Neil laughed and said, "I think that his car is floating downstream". But it was a short-lived reprieve as when they got near the cottage, they both suddenly could see distant car lights, and they were coming their way.

"Heck, Brian must have called for backup," Neil said, "quickly, drive behind the cottage and turn your lights off, and hopefully, they'll drive past". Neil strained his neck to watch the car speed past down towards the ford from where they'd just come from.

"There's two in the car," he said, "but I'm not sure who they are, but I've got a jolly good idea?" When the lights faded out of view, he said, "Quickly, let's go, as I presume that they'll pick up Brian and they'll soon be back".

Suzie set off again, but as it was slightly uphill, the sports car was struggling to gain purchase on the loose gravel and was making painstakingly slow progress. As they got near to the stud house, they suddenly came to a gate closed across the track, that's strange Neil thought how and why is that closed, he quickly got out to open it and promptly fell flat on his face in the mud, he pulled himself up, and a shriek from Suzie alerted him to a figure in the shadows pointing a shotgun straight at him.

"What the hell?!" he said and instinctively put his hands in the air in submission. It looked like it was all over now, but as the figure moved closer, he let out a shout, "Steve, what are you doing? It's me, Neil?"

Steve Carson, the stud manager, came closer, put the gun down and explained that he'd seen three cars racing down here and had come down to inspect. Neil quickly and as clearly as possible explained what was happening.

"Keep out of sight when they come back; they're a dangerous bunch, and can you phone the police, please?"

"I've already done that," Steve said, "ten minutes ago," and he retreated into the shadows.

Just then, the car lights could be seen approaching up the hill, and as Neil shouted, "I'll drive!" and Suzie shifted across into the passenger seat, the car was suddenly right behind them. Neil could see that Brian was driving and noticed the doors opening and two figures jumping out.

"Lock the doors!" he shouted at Suzie as he saw Frank Boyle grab the door handle on his side and noticed Jason Connolly grab the other side whilst leering at Suzie.

He engaged first gear, and nothing initially happened as the wheels spun frantically and attempted to grip, the doors were now rattling, and Brian was bumping their car from behind, which unwittingly helped them, and the little sports car surged forwards and as the wheels met the metalled road, they sped off leaving the now tiny figures in the distance.

Suzie looked shaken, and Neil apologised for involving her in his troubles. They sped past the stud house over the speed bumps, with Suzie complaining about the damage he was doing to her car. At the stud entrance, they turned left and disappeared into the moonlight when they saw flashing lights approaching. It was a police car, and it turned down into the stud drive.

"Great," Neil said, "that's three out of the gang of four soon to be rounded up and caught".

"Gang of Four; wasn't that the four politicians that set up their own party?"

"That's before my time," Neil said, "this gang of four is the four from Lez Allen's yard. But I'm still worried as there's still one of them out there".

"Who's that?" Suzie asked.

"Derek Boyle," Neil replied, "and I don't like it. I'm worried. Very worried".

CHAPTER FORTY-THREE

Behind the Green Door

"Where now?" Suzie asked.

"We need to go somewhere quiet to write all my evidence up and then send it to the police and the Jockey Club, and then I'll hand myself in."

"OK," Suzie said, a little unsure of herself, "let's go to my flat. It's not far away, as it's on the outskirts of Cheltenham".

"Thanks," Neil said as he kept looking anxiously in the mirror.

"No one's following us," Suzie said, reading his thoughts. "They'll all have been caught by the police at your stud and will be helping them with their enquiries."

That made Neil smile, but he wasn't completely convinced, as Derek hadn't been involved in the stud attack, and it was very strange for him to be apart from his twin brother Frank.

"I just don't like it," he said, "something doesn't seem right".

"He's probably gone to the pub," Suzie said, trying to reassure him, but it didn't work.

When they got to her modern exclusive flat, Neil exclaimed, "Wow, that's very upmarket".

"Says the man that comes from an upper-class horse stud," Suzie said.

Neil persuaded her to drive past to check that no one was following them. On the second circuit, Suzie was getting fed up and remotely opened the garage door and drove inside as the door quickly closed.

"Feel safe now?" she said.

"Not really," he replied.

The garage led to a door, then to some steps and at the top of them, another door opened into a small but tastefully laid out, impeccably clean flat. Neil darted around, checking that all the windows were secure.

"Make yourself at home," Suzie said sarcastically.

"I'm just checking that no one's here or can get in. Where does that door lead to?" he said, pointing.

"That's the back door that leads to the yard."

"OK," Neil said, and he started to relax but only a little. Suzie looked at him, covered head to foot in mud and worried about her décor.

"Strip off," she suddenly said.

"I thought that you'd never ask," Neil replied cheekily.

"Let me finish my sentence," she snapped, "strip off in the bathroom, and you can have a shower if you like, and then I'll find you some clean clothes to wear. I've got some men's clothes somewhere".

"From an ex or present boyfriend?" Neil asked.

"None of your business, but actually, I went to a fancy dress party last year, and the theme was eighties pop stars."

"Oh no," Neil said, "please don't tell me that you went as Boy George?"

"No, that was a very popular choice, but I went as Shakin Stevens."

"Phew," Neil said, "that's not too bad".

"You have a shower," Suzie said, "and I'll hang the clothes in the spare bedroom behind the green door for you, and after that, we'll start looking at your shaky evidence".

"There's nothing shaky about it," Neil replied more in hope than expectation.

His shower didn't take long but helped to refresh him and ease his tired and aching body. He grabbed a dressing gown in shocking pink hanging on the door and reappeared to find that Suzie had prepared them a meal.

"And help yourself to my clothes as well," she said, but he could see that she was struggling to suppress a smile.

"Sorry," Neil said, "but you didn't want me to appear in my birthday suit, did you?"

"Well, I expect that would have kept any intruders away."

After they'd eaten and he'd got dressed as Shakin Stevens. "Actually, this isn't too bad," he said, "I look like a Teddy boy".

They sat down and started to assimilate all the evidence, the notes from Kevin Dee, and all of Neil's, including videos and photos. Neil seemed content, but Suzie just shook her head and said, "It doesn't make any sense". Neil could, fortunately, see a pattern developing and tried to explain it to Susie in layman's terms.

"Simply, the horses win with a professional jockey on, then before the horse's handicap rises too high, Lez Allen books an apprentice jockey and deliberately loses the race, and then the next time out at better odds and with a lower handicap and a professional jockey on, they win again."

"Someone could make a lot of money out of knowing all this," Suzie said.

"Exactly," Neil said, "and that, I think, is where the Bentine Bros come into it. Simply they offer better odds than their rivals on the horses that they know are going to lose and vice-versa. They have a big advantage over the other bookies, and that's what my Uncle Harry told me, that it was getting harder to make a decent living at bookmaking nowadays, and I now know why this is".

"Well, can any of this be proved?" Suzie said, sounding concerned and putting on her lawyer's hat.

"Well, I expect that the Jockey Club can look into betting patterns, and I'm sure that something will show up."

Suzie said, "That's all very good, but how did they stop the horses?"

"That's the interesting part, and actually, it's very easy. They use horse walkers."

He was about to explain what a horse walker was, but she impatiently said, "Of course, I know what they are. Carry on, and anyway, you're getting forgetful as you told me yesterday".

"Well, everything is a bit of a blur at the moment," Neil said, "horses are usually given an easy, relaxing day before their intended race day; you'll have heard the old adage about losing the race on the gallops, caused by training too hard".

"Yes, I have. Please get to the point," she said, interrupting him again as the midnight candle burnt even lower.

"What they do is put the horses on the horse walkers the night before for, I believe, up to seven hours, sometimes I believe with weight cloths on full of weights, and simply that's all it takes to stop them winning, as they run like tired horses, which is what they are, whilst it appears that the jockeys are trying their best and they finish down the field, looking to all watching that they just were not good enough, and in a few days when fully refreshed they go and win a race, and at no time will any illegal substances show up because none have been needed."

"Brilliant," Suzie said, "it's so simple if it works as well as you say".

"It does," Neil replied.

"Well, no wonder that they've been trying to stop you from blowing their cover and put a stop to their money-making scheme," Suzie said. With his safety in mind again, he asked her if she had a burglar alarm.

"No," Suzie said, "this is a quiet neighbourhood; I don't need one".

Neil still wasn't convinced and looked out of the window to see if he could see anyone prowling about outside. She looked at him and sighed and said, "You've been reading too many Dick Francome racing thrillers".

He smiled and said, "You mean Dick Francis or John Francome?" and they both laughed, but he was still ill at ease and couldn't relax, however hard he tried.

They started writing out all the evidence and reports when Suzie suddenly said, "I should have rung the police and let them know that you're here".

"They'd have come straight round before we got all the evidence sorted out, ring them in the morning. That's not too far away now."

They tidied up all his evidential reports and sent it all via email, one copy to the police, one to the Jockey Club and one to Suzie's firm of lawyers, Walsh Miller & Armstrong. At least they tried to, but they wouldn't go.

"Slow broadband," Suzie said. "Don't worry, they'll go, but it'll take an hour or two. They'll be there by morning". Suzie then got up and came back in a minute's time with two tumblers full of neat whisky. "A nightcap will do you a load of good and help you sleep," she said, passing him one.

Neil wasn't really partial to whisky but gratefully accepted the kind gesture, and they sat in silence, each deep in their own thoughts, until Suzie said, "Do you know what time it is?"

"No idea," Neil replied.

"It's past 3 am. Time we went to bed."

Neil was given the spare bedroom, and Suzie said, "Goodnight. I'll see you in the morning in about four hours, and then I'll take you straight to the police station".

"Something to look forward to," Neil said sarcastically.

The spare bedroom was very small but was all he needed as despite all the recent events he soon got to sleep and started daydreaming, he was riding Galileo Girl, and about to win the 1000 guineas as she was clear of the field, then it all turned swiftly and with no warning into a nightmare, just before the horse crossed the line to a sea of adulation, she jinked, and he fell off and hit the sodden turf, and suddenly Derek Boyle was stood above him jeering and cursing and jabbing at him with a pitchfork, how dare he invade my dream Neil thought, can I never get away from them? And then, with a chilling realisation, he woke up to find that it wasn't a dream. Derek really was there and really was jabbing at him with a pitchfork. He sat upright, and the jabbing continued, and he had to swiftly move left and then right to avoid being impaled on the headboard. Derek was delirious and shouting but not making a lot of sense.

"You've been nothing but trouble ever since we first met you. Well, now is the time to settle this once and for all!"

Neil didn't like the sound of this but couldn't think of a response as he kept dodging the pitchfork, just clinging on to the hope that he'd soon get tired. Out of the corner of his eye, he caught sight of Suzie standing in the doorway in a fetching pair of tightly fitting pyjamas that were straining to keep everything in. Funny, he thought, how he noticed this when he was in the middle of a life-threatening situation. He realised that she had her phone out and was filming the incident.

I'd rather she just save me, he thought but decided to try and get Derek to incriminate himself and said, "It's all over, Derek. The police have got the others and know what's been going on; they know about the Bentine Bros running the operation".

This stopped him in his tracks for a second, but then he said, "They can't know anything. We've been very careful and covered our tracks".

Neil realised that he'd hit a nerve and carried on, "They know how and why you've been stopping horses, so the games up".

Derek cursed and jabbed at Neil again, this time with more force, and said, "Well, it's you that's ruined it, and you'll have to pay".

Suzie had disappeared now, and before Neil could wonder where she'd gone, she reappeared with a frying pan and with alacrity, she moved silently across the room and hit Derek with the frying pan with such force that he was sent flying and landed in a crumpled heap at the side of the bed, and the pitchfork fell harmlessly nearby. Neil looked up at Suzie, red in the face with the exertion, but he noticed that the force of the action had popped open her pyjama top, and she'd suffered a wardrobe malfunction. Neil got an eyeful, and a broad smile radiated across his face.

"What are you smiling at?" she said as she subconsciously pulled her top tightly closed, "I should have just left you to your fate," and she turned to go. "I'm off to get some rope, and we can tie him up until the police arrive".

Neil was feeling very relieved now and quipped, "Shame to not use that frying pan. A full English would be nice, and don't forget the fried eggs". But perhaps luckily for Neil, she'd gone and didn't hear him fully.

Suzie returned with a rope, and they tied up a now groggy Derek, and Suzie went to phone the police, "Right, get dressed now. They'll be here soon, and it could get ugly".

And it did. They arrived a few minutes later, and Neil was arrested for absconding from the police, even though Suzie protested his innocence. He was driven to the now familiar police station and put in a cell awaiting the arrival of DC Abbott.

CHAPTER FORTY-FOUR

Grey Day

Neil was thinking; surely they'll soon realise that I'm innocent of all charges. I'm the good guy here.

A policeman came to the cell door and said, "Would you like a cup of tea?"

"Yes, please," Neil replied, "I'll have an organic green tea with a slice of lemon, please".

A weak milky cup of ordinary tea was slapped down on the little wooden table spilling over the sides, and the door was closed again without comment. Soon afterwards, before he'd touched the cup of tea, he was called into the interview room.

"It's this way," he was told.

"Don't worry," he replied, "I know where it is as this station is like a second home to me".

A grim-looking DC Abbott was waiting for him but didn't acknowledge Neil's entrance, but when he looked up to see Neil standing there in his Shakin Stevens suit, he let out a surprised gasp.

"Oh, god," he said, "it's Showaddywaddy!"

Neil didn't bother to correct him and just sat down to listen to the charges as DC Abbott started reading them out.

"Firstly, attempted murder to a Mr Dudley Cook by driving your car at him deliberately."

"Nonsense," Neil said. A Police Sargent gestured to him to keep quiet, and DC Abbott continued.

"Secondly, deliberately setting fire to your house for attempted fraudulent financial gain and damaging neighbouring properties and endangering life." Neil was about to speak but got glared at, so he remained quiet as the charges continued to be read out.

"Thirdly, taking a vehicle violently and crashing it and writing it off and beating up its occupants."

Neil couldn't stop himself muttering, "Rubbish," but the charges kept coming.

"Fourthly, breaking into a property and threatening the residents with a gun." The Sargent looked at Neil, but he remained silent. "Fifthly, absconding from the police and sixthly, kidnapping and holding someone against his will."

Neil was dumbstruck by the whole charade and especially mystified with the last charge. What had Derek said? Surely he couldn't turn it round in his favour? He was beginning to feel uneasy and wondered why DC Abbott hadn't read his report.

"Have you anything to say?" he asked.

"Yes, where's my solicitor?" They obviously didn't know, and he was beginning to wonder if she'd abandoned him.

The Sargent said, "You can go back to your cell now, and when your solicitor arrives, we'll discuss bail, but I wouldn't get your hopes up".

"Haven't you seen my evidence in my report?" Neil asked.

"What report?" came back the reply.

Back in the cells, he peered out of the small window high up on the far wall, and he could just see the dark foreboding clouds threatening rain. It's a grey day, he thought, just like my mood, feeling totally deflated and very low and numb. He stared blankly at the floor. All I ever wanted to be was a successful jockey. How had all this happened, he slumped onto the hard, uncompromising mattress and put his head in his hands as his mind started spiralling out of control with so many different thoughts flying around and crashing into each other, but he just couldn't concentrate on anything, and he had the feeling that any minute now his brain was about to explode. The past few days were beginning to catch up with him, the stress, tension, lack of sleep and food, and bodily injuries had been taking their toll on him, and it was all too much for one man to take. He wondered where it had all gone spectacularly wrong, and he started dredging up recent events in his cluttered mind. What if I'd ridden Galileo Girl with more restraint and not recklessly gone for that gap? I might have still been riding for Tom Cooper and looking forward to riding Galileo Girl next season and quite possibly in the classic races. Neil was sure that she deserved her place at the top level, but it was no use him thinking about her as he wouldn't be involved with her anymore. His mood was getting dangerously low as he continued on a downwards spiral of negative thoughts. Look at me now, he mused, stuck in a police cell facing a multitude of charges, all of which I'm innocent of, but can I prove it? If I'm charged, he thought it would be a miscarriage of justice in the realms of previous ones like he thought Nelson Mandela's incarceration and the song came to his mind.

"Twenty-seven years in captivity, are you so blind that you cannot see? Free Nelson Mandela."

How did he survive that long imprisonment and come out the other side with good grace and humility and then go on to lead his country for many years? He obviously never gave up and lost faith. If I spent twenty-seven years in prison, he thought, when I came out, I'd be approaching fifty years of age, and that's ancient.

His mind was beginning to settle as he started thinking about lesser injustices like in the pop music world when Ultravox's stunning song Vienna was kept off the number one spot by the throwaway song Shaddup your face by Joe Dolce or when Gareth Gates got beaten by Will Young in one of the biggest shocks in Pop Idol. Whatever happened to those two, he wondered? His mind was always full of eclectic complex thoughts, but he'd never known it to be overflowing with so many random and bizarre notions. He started thinking about horse racing and the travesty when The Giant Crisp got beaten in the Grand National, Crisp had led them all on a merry dance treating the fences with disdain and building up a big lead until near the finish when he began to falter due to the huge weight he was lumbered with, and the little terrier of a horse Red Rum carrying about two stone less gradually closed the gap and past a leg-weary Crisp to get his head in front on the line, it must have been heartbreaking for everyone connected with Crisp.

It seemed so unfair that he had to carry so much weight, but then Neil pondered life isn't always fair, and you just have to get on with it and make the most of the chances that you get given and, like Mr Mandela, never give up. He then smiled for the first time in a while, and his mind seemed to be calming down, and his sense of humour returned.

So when a knock came on the door, and a policeman said, "Lunch has arrived" Neil said, "I'll have my steak done rare, please".

A plate containing a sandwich was placed next to the cold undrunk cup of tea, he ate it, which he thought was surprisingly quite good, and he washed it down with the cold cup of tea, and his melancholic feelings diminished.

He lay on the bed and promptly fell straight asleep until he was rudely awoken by a smiling

Suzie who said, "Come on, wake up Sleeping Beauty. Get your things; you're out on bail".

"How on earth have you managed that?" he said.

"Trade secrets," she said, "but hurry up; you don't want to stay here a minute longer, do you? Let's go before they change their mind".

"Okay," Neil said, not needing to be told twice.

"Well, hurry up. I'll drop you off at your home, and I'll explain how I got you bail on the journey."

He left with her, hoping that he wasn't going to see the inside of the police station again sometime soon. They got into her mud-stained battered car.

"You could have cleaned it," Neil said and got one of her looks.

She went through all the charges with him again and told him that the police had now got hold of his report, and she'd shown them all the evidence from the night before."

"I expect," she said confidently, "that we'll be able to get most of the charges dropped, but I'm not sure about the first one with the bicycle as we've no evidence, and I'm worried about the arson one unless you can get your neighbour to change his statement".

"I've forgotten what he said," Neil replied.

"He alleges that you told him that you were going to burn your house down for financial gain due to the damp rot."

"Well, I was only joking," Neil said.

"Well, sometimes your jokes just aren't funny," she said harshly. "I suggest," she continued, "that you should go and look at your house and see if you can find anything. I know that it's a long shot as the fire investigators will have been through it with a fine tooth comb and speak to your neighbours".

"I'll do that tomorrow," he said.

Suzie continued, "I'll ring you with daily updates. Apparently, they've preliminarily booked your court case for the same day as your former workmates from Lez Allen's yard".

Neil thanked her for all she'd done and apologised for dragging her into danger, and as she left, she said, "I'll get you off the charges," then added with a hint of mischief, "well, most of them." And then she was gone, and Neil could just hear Shakin Stevens's dulcet tones over the roar of her engine as she disappeared up the drive.

CHAPTER FORTY-FIVE

Things are Looking Brighter

He was pleased that his Mum had invited him to live back at the stud house as he couldn't face going to live on his own at the cottage at the present time, even though the back door had been repaired and the cottage was secure again, so he returned to his childhood room and was soon settled and enjoying his mum's great home cooking again but started to worry about his weight, but then he mused to himself that he might not be a jockey again. Suzie, the solicitor, rang most days with an update on how the case was going and was always bright and cheerful.

"Good news," she said, "the police have dropped two charges, so we're down to four".

"Great," he said, "which ones have been dropped?"

She then explained that she'd argued that he hadn't absconded as he had been with his solicitor all the time and that she was bringing him in, but circumstances had intervened.

"Well done," he said, "what's the other dropped case?"

"You're friendly lecturer Dudley Cook has shot himself in the foot."

"Oh," Neil said, looking slightly shocked, "is he okay?"

"No, not literally, you fool, but he's crashed his bike into another car, and this time he's broken his arm."

"Couldn't have happened to a nicer man," Neil replied.

"But on this occasion," she continued, "he was breathalysed and was way over the limit, and the car driver had a dashcam fixed to his windscreen, which proved that Dudley was at fault. When he was questioned and admitted his guilt, your case was referred to, and he agreed with the police that he could have been mistaken and withdrew all his accusations against you. Between you and me, he's having a bad time at present as he was found drunk in the lecture theatre."

"Sounds like Educating Rita," Neil blurted out, but she ignored him and continued.

"And he's in danger of losing his job, but you don't need to know that. All you need to know is that the charge has been dropped."

Neil said, "Two down, four to go".

"Have you been to your house yet?" Suzie enquired.

Neil had been putting this off as he wasn't looking forward to seeing his fire-damaged house and was also a little worried about bumping into his next-door neighbours, Richard and Lilly. He, however, agreed to go there the following day but wasn't sure how he was going to get there as he'd run out of vehicles to use, with one a molten mass of metal, one missing in a river, one a write off and another one a burnt out shell, and the goodwill for borrowing one had vanished, he'd thought about walking there but didn't fancy doing that with his dodgy knee not making any significant improvement. The problem was solved when his mum said that she was off to town visiting the hairdressers and the accountant and would drop him off on her way. The following morning, he sat in his mum's Mini as she sped along the narrow country lanes, but he couldn't see much and enjoy the views as they were so low down, and when they met a big tractor, he thought that she was going to drive right underneath it.

"Do you think that you should perhaps visit the Optician as well?" he cheekily asked.

"If you want to walk," she said, "just carry on with your quips".

So he shut up, and they carried on in silence and soon arrived. When he was dropped off, he found himself walking up the drive to his house, fearful of what he might find. He was pleased to see that it didn't look too bad, the garage had taken the biggest hit as this was where the fire had started, but the rest of the house didn't seem too bad, mainly superficial smoke damage, his Suzuki Vitara was still there, well in name, as all that he could see was a mangled mess of metal, it was beginning to rust and all around it was debris, and it was all wet through from the fire hoses and that rain was able to get in where the windows and garage doors had once been. He sifted through the debris, not expecting to find anything, and he didn't. Nothing in the car had survived. All he could find was a couple of copper coins that he'd kept in the ashtray for emergencies, he was sure that the fire investigators would have done a thorough search, and if anything had been there, they would have found it. He looked across to Richard and Lilly's side of the semi-detached house, over the charred dividing fence and could see a caravan peering out from round the side of their house. Their house, thankfully, didn't have as much damage as his but was also presently unhabitable. Work hadn't started on repairing Neil's house due to the insurers refusing to pay out since it was thought that he or someone had started the fire deliberately, quite understandable, he thought, and he realised that this was probably usual practice. He decided that he'd go and see if his neighbours were in and walked round but could see that the caravan was being lived in, but no one was at home, he was about to leave when he heard a click on the front gate latch, and Richard and Lilly appeared, thankfully both looking a picture of health and laden down with shopping bags, but they weren't pleased to see him, especially Richard.

"Nice to see you're looking so well," Neil said to them both, but Richard frowned and replied, "After you tried to murder us in our sleep?"

"Now then," Lilly said, "I'm sure that's not what happened. Come in for a cup of tea, lad, and we'll hear your story". It's not a story Neil thought but let that rest.

"Thank you," he said, whilst Richard just snorted and shook his head.

"You're too soft, woman," he said to his wife.

Neil went into the very neat compact caravan and noticed all the smoke detectors dotted around. He was about to make a joke about them but thought better of it. Lilly busied herself making the tea and bringing in a plate of homemade scones laden with thick cream and jam. Richard had calmed down a little and explained that they were living in the caravan until the house was sorted out but that they were having trouble with the insurers.

"Same here," Neil said.

When the tea arrived, they all sat down, rather too close together for comfort as there wasn't much room, and Neil told them the full story of what had been happening to him since the fateful day when he'd joined the Lez Allen yard, and how he was sure that it was someone from that yard who had burnt their houses down.

"You poor mite," Lilly said, "you could have been killed".

Richard reached over and put his hand on Neil's shoulder, "Sorry, lad. I think that we've misjudged you, but you did talk about burning the house down before the fire. It seemed too much of a coincidence, but I believe what you say".

"Thank you," Neil said, "that means a lot to me, as I've always regarded you highly, like surrogate grandparents".

"What can we do to help?" Richard asked.

Neil explained about all the charges that he was facing, six to start with but now down to four. He told them that the fire investigators had proved that the fire had been started deliberately, but obviously, they didn't know by whom.

"I need to find evidence," Neil said, "about who started the fire. I'm pretty sure that it's someone from the Lez Allen's yard, and if I can prove that, it'll clear my name".

"OK," Richard said, pleased to have something to do, "we'll ask around. You never know, but something might turn up. We heard nothing on the night until we were dragged out of our beds by two muscular firemen".

"I enjoyed that," Lilly said, and they all laughed, and they parted on good terms just like they used to be on, and that really was a relief for Neil, and in a much better frame of mind, he rang his mum to say that he'd start walking home and she could pick him up when passing, and he set off slowly hobbling as he went and hoping that his mum would see him and not just drive past.

The next day when Suzie rang, she was even more cheerful. "The case is beginning to go our way at long last. Your Land Rover has been found in the river under the weir quite a long way from where you had nearly been drowned. They hadn't found it before because they had concentrated their search further upstream, and also the landlord of the pub where they said that they'd met you for a drink, said that only three came in and he recognised from the photos shown to him Frank and Derek Boyle and Jason Connolly and luckily when shown a photo of you he said he admitted that he knew you but had never seen you in the presence of the three. It now looks like the police are beginning to suspect the three of them and are perhaps at long last beginning to believe that your recollections are nearer the truth than what they're saying."

"Great," Neil said, "you're worth your weight in gold".

When she put the phone down, he wondered if that had been a slightly insensitive remark, as she was quite a big girl and perhaps a very expensive remark if taken literally. The next day brought even better news as Suzie rang, bubbling over.

"Tilly and Dilly Miligan and Kevin Dee have been interviewed, and both have told the police what happened to them, and their incidents were remarkably similar. They all said that they'd been too scared to come forward before. Kevin also mentioned that he'd been specifically told to stop horses winning and regrettably had obeyed orders, and the police have told me that they're bringing in Lez Allen for questioning."

"Great," Neil said.

"No problem, skinny lad," she replied, "I'm only doing my job". Neil realised that perhaps his previous comments had hit home.

"Bingo" Suzie said when she next rang, "Lez Allen has done a deal with the police and has spilt the beans. He's admitted everything; he's really put the boot into the Bentine Bros, who are one and the same as BB racing".

"I knew it," Neil said.

"Stop interrupting," Suzie said, "do you know how much I charge per hour?" Neil thought that this was said tongue in cheek but wasn't really sure. Suzie continued, "Lez Allen said that all was fine until his wife left".

"Why did she leave?" Neil asked unwisely, interrupting again.

"He didn't say, and it's not important, so do stop interrupting!" Neil didn't answer and let her continue, "His wife really did all the training, and when she left, she took a lot of the owners with her".

Neil risked interrupting her again. "But she didn't carry on training, did she?" and he knew if she was stood next to him, he'd be getting her special look of disdain and annoyance.

"No," she continued, "but she recommended other trainers for them, and as Mr Allen had just started a big expansion plan building new stables and had bought a number of young horses speculatively that he was unable to sell on and with the cost of divorce proceedings, he had a sudden cash-flow problem, when the Bentine Bros, who'd only just started having horses in the yard, offered him a loan, he jumped at it, but it solved nothing, so the loans had increased and as expected their interest rates were a lot higher than conventional loan methods, and his debts mushroomed out of control. The Bentine Bros came up with a solution, which he ruefully admitted was probably their aim from the beginning, and you've probably guessed what this was. They wanted a few horses stopping, and Mr Alen thought that he was powerless to say no to them, especially as the bankruptcy was looming large, and he thought that agreeing to them would be an end to his problems, but of course, it wasn't, and he was stuck in a classic conundrum, if he refused to stop any future runners they'd told him that they'd shop him to the authorities, and he'd have lost his training licence, he now realises that this was just an idle threat as doing so would have implicated them as well, but Mr Allen was in too deep to think straight and just sank deeper into the mire. He did, however, say that getting jockeys to stop the horses in the races was too risky, and they'd have to find another way. He explained that Brian Cougan and Frank, and Derek Boyle had been brought in by the Bentine Bros and took over most of the running of the yard and the race fixing so that Mr Allen became a trainer by name only. He knew that these three were getting paid extra money from the Bentine Bros but never interfered. All he had to do was relay to them which horses were being stopped on the night before. Using the horse walkers, he'd explained, was a stroke of genius as anyone looking around the yard and checking it wouldn't give the machines a second glance as every yard has them".

"I bet," said Neil, "that they hit upon their idea by accident, leaving a horse on the machine for too long and noticing the effects on it, and being of a devious nature, they'd realise how they could use this to their advantage, no wonder that they wanted to silence me".

Suzie agreed with him and continued, "Anyway, the police are now shifting their attention to the Lez Allen yard, and you'll be pleased to hear that every case against you has been dropped except the arson one. Did you find anything on your visit to your house?"

"No," Neil replied, "but I'm working on it. I presume that the gun didn't have my fingerprints on it?"

"Of course not," Suzie said, "they were getting desperate then as you appeared to be always one step ahead of them".

"It didn't feel like that," Neil said with a shudder remembering suddenly all that he'd been through.

"Well," Suzie said, "if we can link the Mr Allen stable to the fire, then you'll be completely in the clear, and then all you'll have to do is sort out the

Jockey Club, and you could be soon back on horseback as a jockey wowing the crowds".

"As simple as that," Neil replied.

CHAPTER FORTY-SIX

Things Can Only Get Better

Neil rang his Uncle Harry with the good news and updated him on the Lez Allen yard's wrongdoings.

His uncle said, "I knew that there was something going on at the racecourses. I'd always wondered how the Bentine Bros rose up the ranks so quickly, they started at Point to Point tracks and then progressed to the gaff tracks (small racecourses), and before long, they had some of the best pitches at all the top tracks. I'd also heard that they were about to venture into buying a load of betting shops, but I presume that this will all come to a sudden end".

"As long as they're found guilty," Neil said, and then rather pensively, he added, "I suppose that when they've gone, you are wanting all your money that you gave me back to buy your pitches back now you should be able to compete on a level playing field again?"

"Don't be daft, lad. That money's yours now, and anyway you've spent it, I'm beginning to wind down, and retirement is getting closer."

"So you'll be getting a dog then and going for long walks soon?" Neil asked.

"Or a goldfish," Uncle Harry replied, "They take less maintenance". They both laughed and said their goodbyes.

Next, Neil rang the Jockey Club and had an illuminating conversation with Oliver French-Saunders, who was charm personified completely different to the character he portrayed at their last meeting.

"Great to hear from you, Neil," he said, "how have you been keeping?"

Not Mr Bartholomew this time, Neil thought. He told Oliver exactly what had been happening to him, the full story in great detail. When Oliver started speaking again, Neil could tell that he was shocked by what he'd heard.

"We owe you a very big apology, Neil. I'm afraid that you've been used as a minnow to catch a big fish, we've been investigating Mr Allen and the Bentine Bros undercover for a number of months, but the Jockey Club security department was making little progress. So we decided to go along with Mr Allen's accusations that you were stopping horses so that he'd think that we didn't suspect him of anything, and we could continue investigating him unhindered and hopefully gain evidence."

"So whilst this was all going on, I was left financially struggling and at the mercy of the criminal fraternity and a group of desperados," Neil said.

"Well, you do have a point there, Neil," Oliver said, "perhaps we hadn't thought it out very well, but you must admit that you were getting a bit hot-headed and that your race riding was getting dangerous and putting yourself and others at risk of serious injury, and that you needed your wings clipped. The plan was to only warn you off for a couple of weeks before reinstating you with your reputation unblemished. However, the big breakthrough against Mr Allen never came, that was until we got your evidence".

"Well, perhaps I need compensation," Neil said, "I bet that your security men are all on a big wage with many perks, and I've solved the case for you at a huge risk to my life and all without any cost to the Jockey Club".

Oliver agreed wholeheartedly with him but said, "We obviously can't give you any compensation, but I've sure that we can reward you in other ways. The Jockey Club are planning to sponsor a few jockeys next season mainly by providing them with a car emblazoned with the Jockey Club logo'.' Neil liked the sound of a free car, especially since the only transport he could lay his hands on at present was a rusty old bike.

"You'll be coming back as a jockey, won't you when all this has concluded?" Oliver asked, but Neil hadn't had a chance to ponder about it. Without thinking, he replied, "Yes, of course, when my knee has fully recovered".

Oliver asked him to keep quiet about the sponsorship until after the court cases, and then if Neil was completely cleared, the Jockey Club would make an announcement completely exonerating him. As the call was coming to an end, Neil asked, "How is your son Gilbert doing?"

"Oh," Oliver replied, "he's in France race-riding and trying to improve his jockeyship. Give him a ring; I'm sure that he'll be pleased to hear from you".

Neil decided that he'd do just that. But before he could, there was a knock at the door, expecting it to be someone for his dad on stud business, he didn't look up until his mum said cheerfully to him, "Neil, you've got visitors". Neil looked up to see Richard and Lilly Secombe coming through the door.

"Hello, Neil," Richard said smiling, "we've had a breakthrough, I saw our neighbour from across the road in the Post Office yesterday, and we got talking about the fire and how we had no idea who had started it, and he said that a scruffy youth had knocked on his door early that evening of the fire, and had asked where you lived, well he didn't like the look of him but believed his story that he was one of your work colleagues, so he pointed him in the right direction. As he left, he saw him talking to someone parked outside in a car, so just to be sure, he wrote the number plate down. He always has arguments with people who park outside his house, and what's more, he found an empty petrol can discarded in his garden the next morning".

"Great," Neil said, "I'm sure that will be the Boyles. Can you thank your neighbour and tell him that I'll go and see him after the court cases are all over?" Neil was really pleased with this breakthrough and was beginning to think that things were finally going his way after many weeks of everything taking the wrong route.

Suzie rang a day or two later and said, "Well done. The neighbour across the road has been to the police and identified Frank Boyle in a photofit, and if that wasn't conclusive enough, the car number plate was the Boyles, and you've probably guessed that the fingerprints on the petrol can were of both Frank and Derek Boyle, so that's more than enough evidence for the police. You'll therefore be pleased to hear that that's another charge against you dropped, so you're completely in the clear now, and your court case has been cancelled. Your only role now will be as a witness against the Lez Allen yard, and what's more, you'll be pleased to hear that you don't need me anymore, as this, my very first case, is now finished, and I certainly hope future cases are nothing like this one".

Strangely Neil wasn't pleased to think that he wouldn't be hearing from her again, as he had got used to her regular phone calls and their jocular banter, but he didn't say so.

She continued, "But don't worry, I'll come and see you and bring my report, and I'll probably come to the court to make sure you don't say the wrong things, and anyway, I'm sure that you'll be in need of my services again before too long".

"What do you mean?" Neil enquired.

"Well," she said, "you're bound to get yourself into some more scrapes, aren't you? You just can't help it, can you?" and they both laughed and said their goodbyes.

Neil then sat down and started thinking. More scrapes, indeed, definitely not. I'm going to keep out of trouble in the future and not even cross the road on a zebra crossing when the lights are flashing telling me not to. But then he started worrying, what if Suzie was right? He knew that she was semi-joking, but it started gnawing away at the back of his mind. He wondered that if he came back as a jockey would he end up in trouble again, he certainly hadn't been looking for it, but it had found him. Would history repeat itself, and he knew if it did that, he wouldn't be able to cope with it all happening again. Getting back as a jockey and perhaps challenging Gilbert French-Saunders for the jockey's title in the coming season had been the aim that kept him going through all the dark times, and there had definitely been some dark times.

He was suddenly unsure of what he should do and started wondering if a stint in the stud in Australia or somewhere else if as he thought that job was no longer available, would be a better, safer option for him, but was he ready to give up his career before it had really started? He just didn't know and decided to do what his mum always advised him with difficult decisions, and that was to sleep on it.

CHAPTER FORTY-SEVEN
Close Escape

The day of the court case was grey and gloomy, but Neil was full of high spirits as he was hoping that his ordeal would be finally reaching a happy ending. Suzie met him at the court, saying that she'd come to make sure that he didn't say the wrong things and, as she put it, to see the Lez Allen mob put behind bars for a very long time. Neil was feeling nervous when entering the building but didn't really know why as he wasn't on trial but just giving evidence. He, therefore, headed off to the Gents as soon as he arrived, before the case started, deep in thought, wondering why nervous feelings always made his bladder feel like it needed emptying. He was drying his hands using the automatic dryer, though all it seemed to be doing was wafting cold air around and having little effect on his wet hands. When someone walked in, he paid little attention to them until he turned round to leave, and he found them standing in front of him, effectively blocking his exit. Neil tried to sidestep him, but the man did the same, and Neil got the feeling that he could be in trouble yet again.

The man stared at Neil and said, "You needn't know who I am, but I know exactly who you are".

Neil stared at him and knew instantly who he was as he looked just like the Boyle twins, but an older meaner, and more menacing version and said, trying to keep the conversation light-hearted, "Morning, Mr Boyle," as he'd guessed correctly that it was Mr Boyle senior. "Sorry, but I haven't got time to chat," and tried to brush past him.

Surprisingly he let him pass but soon realised why as there was a large chap built like a brick outhouse blocking his exit, and there was no way that he could force his way past him. He turned back towards Mr Boyle senior, wondering what was going to happen next, and soon found out as Mr Boyle said, "This is how you're to proceed today. You're going to go into the courtroom and say that all your previous statements were all false and you'd like to retract them".

Neil would have laughed if he hadn't been locked in this dire situation and replied, "Why would I say that?" Mr Boyle senior had it all worked out.

"Because you're a drug addict and have spent most of your time at Lez Allen's yard in a drug-induced haze, Frank and Derek will confirm this."

Neil was confused and worried at the same time, "I've never taken a drug in my entire life," he said.

However, it soon became clear what Mr Boyle senior's plan was as he said, "If you don't agree, wouldn't it be a shame if you were found in here suffering from a drug overdose?"

"I've…" Neil started to say as alarm bells began ringing in his head, but the unnamed beefcake started moving slowly towards him and put his hand in his pocket as if to get something out as Mr Boyle senior continued, "What if you're found slumped in a cubicle half alive with your survival hanging in the balance".

This was followed by an almost pantomime laugh as Neil tried to stall for time, "Look up there" he said, pointing at the ceiling.

"It's a CCTV camera; all this will be recorded. You'll never get away with anything untoward." Mr Boyle senior smiled, but it wasn't a warm, reassuring one but a cold and scary grin.

"That's a bloody air freshener." All the time, they were slowly moving closer to him, invading his personal space.

Neil said as a last resort, "Oh, OK, I'll do what you say. In fact, I'll leave the courtroom instantly and not give my evidence, but it won't matter what I say or don't say as your boys are going down anyway".

He wished that he hadn't added the last quip, as a hard, determined look appeared on his assailant's face, they had him surrounded now, leaving an escape virtually impossible, and his options were diminishing rapidly. Just then, the door swung open, and two court officials walked in, and as quick as a flash, his two assailants vanished. It was almost as if they'd never been there at all. The court officials asked Neil if he felt okay as he'd gone a very pale shade of white, he assured them that he was fine and hung around until they'd finished, which got him some strange glances so that he could walk out between them for safety, but the men had totally vanished. He quickly went up the stairs to the courtroom, breathing heavily and was met with Suzie pacing around.

"Where have you been?" she angrily asked. Neil explained what had happened to him, and she said exasperatedly, "You're not safe to be left on your own, are you?"

"Well, I could hardly take my solicitor in with me, could I?" he said, regaining his sense of humour.

"It's not funny," she replied, "you're dealing with dangerous men, and they're not guilty yet!"

Neil's parents could be seen approaching, and Neil retold them his adventure in the Gents' toilet. His mum said, "You're not James Bond, you know; you'll get injured if you carry on like this".

Carry on like what Neil thought? "I only went in for a Jimmy Riddle."

"More like Basildon Bond," Neil's dad said, and Suzie laughed.

"Don't encourage him," Neil said, "he'll only get worse, and that's probably one of his better so-called jokes".

Suzie then turned to Neil and said, "Now go inside the courtroom and try and keep out of trouble".

Neil had relaxed now and said, "Are you going to straighten my tie and pat me on my head and give me a peck on the cheek and say run along, dear?"

This didn't get a reply, just a withering look, but once inside the courtroom, he felt safe and looking round in the gallery, he was reassured that there was no sign of Mr Boyle senior or his musclebound friend, and Neil hoped that he'd never bump into either of them again. He wondered why Suzie and his parents treated his recent incident so light-heartedly. If he'd been injected with drugs which he was sure is what they were threatening to do, then it could have been very bad for him. He wondered if they didn't believe him, did they think that he was a fantasist, or did they joke about it to hide their concern for him. He hoped that it was the latter.

His enemies were all there, Frank and Derek Boyle, Brian Cougan, Jason Connolly, Lez Allen and the Bentine Bros. Surprisingly, the court case went like clockwork, with his evidence helping to convict them all. It emerged that the Boyle twins had spent various stretches at different Borstals and had previous convictions for stealing cars and many minor criminal activities. The Bentine Bros were the most interesting, as information came out that they had been in court before under many different names but had always seemed one step ahead of the law, that was until now, they had convictions for everything from money laundering to rural crimes. Neil started wondering what these rural crimes could have been. It emerged that all except Les Allen had many previous convictions. The evidence against them came from many different sources, the police, the Jockey Club, Kevin Dee and the Milligan twins and of course, Neil. The Jockey Club produced evidence of irregular betting patterns and estimated that over the period that they'd been operating, they had made at least 3 million pounds out of stopping horses and that this didn't take into account the money made when the horses won at better odds next time out when they were allowed to perform at their true level or monies gained from unregulated betting exchanges (where the punter acts as a bookmaker and offers odds on the horses), and they reckoned that this easily had doubled the money that they'd illegally gained.

Neil, who was at present strapped for cash momentarily could see the benefits of a life of crime, but he'd been brought up, to be honest, and intended to stay that way. It was a long case as the court meticulously went through all the evidence, and it was fully conclusive against the accused. Their defence fell apart as they could offer no explanations for all of the charges against them, they tried, of course, but the explanations convinced nobody.

As the judge was about, to sum up, Neil looked at the very old frail gentleman and asked Suzie, "Who's the Judge? He looks a bit of an old relic?"

"Don't be fooled. He's very good and well-regarded. He's called Lord Heathfield."

In his summing up, he said that they'd obtained money from illegal activity and endangered life. Neil got a special mention, as the judge said they could easily have been facing a murder charge from all their attempts of trying to silence him. The jury was shown a video obtained from Lez Allen's yard CCTV showing the pitchforks being used to pin Neil to the straw bales and Brian Cougan throwing one at Neil, which landed embedded in his leg. Neil turned away whilst this was being shown as watching it would have brought back too many bad memories, but hearing Suzie gasp next to him brought home to him how serious it had been and how it could have ended so differently. The video failed to capture any evidence of Neil waving a gun which was yet another one of their claims that failed. Neil looked across at the gang of four.

The Boyle twins had their usual sullen impassive look, which was hard to penetrate, Brian Cougan looked resigned to his fate, and Jason Connolly looked scared to death. He'd obviously got in out of his depth. He'd have never made it as a jockey, Neil thought, but he could have achieved honest and regular employment in the racing game.

The only one who looked regretful was Lez Allen, who it appeared had been cajoled into the operation against his better judgement and wishes and had little part in organising it. Neil also looked across at DC Ted Abbott and could see that he was enjoying himself, a professional at work, Neil thought. So it came as no surprise when the jury found them all unanimously guilty with prison sentences of various lengths for the main protagonists, Derek and Frank Boyle, Brian Cougan and the Bentine Bros and suspended sentences for Jason Connolly and Lez Allen, and suddenly it was all over.

On his way out, Neil got a hug from Suzie, and she promised to keep in touch, as an attractive, well-dressed lady came over and shook his hand.

"Well done, Neil," she said, "I don't suppose that you know who I am?"

"No," was all that Neil could answer.

"Well, I'm Celia Allen. I was married to that weak, easily led man in the dock over there," she said, pointing to Lez Allen as he was being led away. "He never was any good at training, managing money, or anything really. He's just a waste of space. "An amicable divorce then, Neil thought but dared not say so, and she's still bitter, but it sounds like she has every reason to be. She continued, "It was fine at first, but I did most of the training, and Lez just went out drinking with the owners. He helped with the entries a bit but not much else. He can't even ride a horse, you know." Neil was wondering what had ever attracted her to Lez. She carried on talking,

"When everything has settled down, I'm planning on coming back to the yard and start training there myself. I never got all my divorce settlement paid, so the yard is still partly mine anyway. I've lined up Tom Cooper junior as my assistant trainer''.

"I didn't know that he was giving up riding,'' Neil said, surprised.

"Yes,'' Celia said, "he hadn't really made it as a jockey and said that he wasn't enjoying it and had struggled since his injury, and training seemed the ideal solution. I suppose that he hopes to take over from his dad eventually''.

"Well,'' Neil said, "he knows a lot about racing, and his dad's a good trainer of horses and people, but isn't he a little quiet to be a trainer?''

"Don't worry, I'll bring him out of his shell,'' she said with a wicked and mischievous smile.

As she was leaving, she added, "And once I'm set up back as a trainer, I'll throw a few rides your way, and I'll be looking for a stable jockey''.

"You won't be keeping Angus Connolly then?'' Neil asked.

"No way,'' she said, shaking her head. Neil realised that everyone expected him to come back as a jockey, he'd even told the Jockey Club that he would, but he was still unsure but reasoned that there was no hurry to make his decision.

The next to come and talk to him was DC Ted Abbott, and he had a smile on his face as he grabbed Neil's hand vigorously. Neil spook first and started repeating DC Abbotts' favourite phrase, "In 30 years..." but he wasn't allowed to finish as DC Abbott said, "I say that to everyone who comes in. It's a tactic to try and unnerve them and get them talking. I must admit that I had my doubts about you when I first saw you as you came across as a typical bored rich kid propped up by his daddy's money who thinks that they're above the law, but as time went on and the cases kept coming to my thoughts changed, even with all the strange outfits you appeared in, but you did do some daft things, you should have left the investigations to the police, as you could have been seriously injured or worse, and absconding from the law is never a good idea". He was still smiling and patting Neil on the back as he said, "I like a day at the races. I'll come one day when you're back riding. When will that be?"

"I'm not sure yet," Neil said, realising that he would have to make the decision pretty soon. "I need to get my knee fixed first and lose a bit of weight."

"I'll see you next season," DC Abbott said as he left. He might, or he might not, Neil thought.

Oliver French-Saunders from the Jockey Club was next to speak to Neil and told him that they would be making an announcement in the racing papers the following day saying that the convicted men would be warned off from racing indefinitely and that Lez Allen would never be able to train again.

"I don't think he ever has," Neil said before Oliver continued.

"And we'll make it clear that you were warned off as a cover to help catch the wrongdoers who were becoming very clever at evading discovery of their illegal activities and that you had only deserved a few days suspension for your reckless riding." He didn't mention the sponsorship deal, but Neil was sure that he'd be true to his word when he returned if he actually did.

Driving home with his parents, Neil started wondering if the Jockey Club would give him a Range Rover but expected that it would more likely be a Ford Fiesta. His Dad pulled in at the local, The Hunter's Arms and they had an enjoyable few drinks together, which was something that they rarely did. Neil told them that he still wasn't sure that he wanted to come back as a jockey and was still mulling over the stud job in Australia. He could tell that his mum and dad didn't really believe him, and he began to wonder himself, especially when his dad told him that the job had been filled a week or two ago.

CHAPTER FORTY-EIGHT
Tying up Loose Ends

The next day he walked the short distance to Steve and Lynne's cottage to read the Racing Post and found out that he was the centrefold, which had never happened to him before, with two pages of coverage all about the court case and details about Neil's trials and tribulations and the Jockey Club's statement clearing him. After the stuffy atmosphere of the courts, Neil was in need of some fresh air and open spaces, so he took a very excited and doolally Brock out for a walk around the stud and up to the woods where he'd found him in a sorry state which after what had happened subsequently, seemed a very long time ago, as Brock chased a ball Neil suddenly remembered where he'd seen the Bentine Bros before, they were the men that had been in these very woods, the men who had callously left Brock behind discarded like a throwaway snack. When he got back, he told Steve and queried why his dad let them get away with it at the time. Steve told him that a farmer had confronted them and had ended up in a ditch, badly beaten up with threats to his family if he went to the police, so most people thought rightly or wrongly that it was best to leave them to it and hope that they didn't do any damage, however distasteful their actions were.

"Imagine," Steve said, "if you crossed them, what damage they could do on a stud farm, gates left open, stallions getting into the same fields, youngstock on the road etc., and anyway, I believe that the police apprehended them eventually but not round here".

Neil then apologised for what had happened to Steve's treasured motorbike, but luckily, he didn't appear too bothered and Lynne said, "It was a blessing in disguise as Steve was getting too old to ride it". Steve shook his head at this remark as Lynne continued, "The insurance money will come in and pay for a nice holiday".

"When do I ever get a chance for a holiday?" Steve protested.

Neil thought that now was a good time to leave. As he was walking back idly, kicking a stone along in front of him, he saw two riders approaching and was pleased to see as they got nearer that it was the Milligan twins Tilly and Dilly, and all the past acrimony appeared to be forgotten.

"We didn't recognise you in men's clothes," they said, chuckling.

When the laughter had subdued, they said that they were pleased for him that it had all worked out well and that they hadn't thought that he'd been the one who'd snitched to the Boyles, but they had been scared, very scared, all was forgotten and forgiven, and they arranged to go for a horse ride in the next few days and that they had a spare horse for him to ride, and that they had a lot of catching up to do.

As they left, they shouted out, "I hope that your dog hasn't been eating any more cakes recently," and then they were gone in a whirl of galloping hooves.

How on earth did they know that? Neil wondered and wandered on, scratching his head. His phone kept ringing nonstop with congratulatory calls from friends and trainers, including one that surprised him from Gilbert French-Saunders, who said that he was riding in France and that the jockeys there were a lot rougher than what Neil had ever been and that he was learning a lot out there and intended to come back next season stronger and fitter and was going to try and become a champion jockey.

"Not if I've anything to do with it," Neil said, "you'll have me to contend with for the title". They both laughed, and Neil was finally beginning to warm to the idea of returning.

He next borrowed his mum's mini with a promise to put some fuel in it for her and went to see the Coopers at Sunrise Farm. Sadly no one was there apart from Tracy, John Cooper's girlfriend, who just happened to be grooming Galileo Girl.

"She looks well," Neil said.

"Yes," Tracy replied, "she's really come on in the last few weeks. I think that she's finally got over the unfortunate incident".

"That's great news," Neil replied.

Tracy wanted to hear all about what had been happening to him. He was getting very good at retelling the recent events and made it even more interesting with a little added embellishment, and he enjoyed watching the reaction that the dangerous parts received.

"You want to put all this down in a book," Tracy said, "it'll be a best seller".

Neil thought this over and said, "I don't think that I'd have the patience to write it all down, and no one would believe it. They'd say that it was too far-fetched".

Tracy promised to tell the Coopers that Neil had been, and he said that he'd call in at a later day and asked her to say that if they wanted a jockey for Galileo Girl, they would only have to ask.

"Don't push your luck," she said.

Next, he went off to see Richard and Lilly, who were pottering around in their garden. It was looking overgrown and a bit of a mess, so he promised to come and sort it out sometime soon. He told them all about the court case, and they said that they were very pleased that it had all worked out for him in the end but that he needed to be careful in future with the company that he kept. They told him that things were looking promising with the insurance and that they were hoping to move back into the house in the next month or two.

"Well," Neil said, "I'll come and help you with the decorating if you like whilst I'm doing mine".

"Are you planning on moving back yourself," they enquired.

Neil didn't know the answer to that question as he hadn't given it much thought and just had to tell them that he wasn't sure. They parted as friends which gave Neil a good feeling as he'd had far too much acrimony and trouble in his life recently. As he was driving back, he got a phone call from Sarah Howerd and whilst trying to connect it through the hands-free system, he nearly went off the road and was very close to impacting with a concrete bollard. This gave him a big shock as if he'd damaged his mum's car, then going to Australia wouldn't have been far enough away to escape her wrath. He quickly parked the car and phoned Sarah back and went through his story yet again, he asked her about Dawn, but she remained quiet on that subject, but she was also pleased that he'd come through the ordeal none the worse, or only slightly battered. He returned to the stud farm and parked the Mini and went inside and watched his mum walk around the car checking for damage as if she expected the worst, and he remembered that he hadn't put any fuel in for her.

When she came in, he said, "Sorry about the dint".

"What dint?" she exclaimed and then realised that he was joking and raised her eyebrows and said, "That's not really funny after all the vehicles that you've written off recently". Would anyone ever let him forget about that, he wondered, as none of them was really his fault anyway.

He briefly told her about the Racing Post article and said, "The only one who got off with his record unblemished was Angus Connolly. Incidentally, what was your history with him you never did tell me?"

"It's nothing much really," she replied, "but our paths crossed years ago at a racing awards ceremony. He'd won an award. I can't remember what for; I think that it was for the most promising apprentice jockey".

"It must have been a very lean year," Neil said.

"Was he the only nominee?" His mum carried on ignoring his quips, "He was at the bar, and as I tried to walk past, he blocked my way and said in a slurred voice, 'How about you come up to my hotel room for a nightcap?' or something like that. I thanked him for his kind offer but flatly declined. He then turned nasty and lurched towards me and tried to grab at my clothes, but in his drunken state, he fell over, and all his mates laughed at him. He was far from amused but regained his composure as much as he could and replied, 'Don't worry, love, I've had a lot of better offers from girls who aren't stuck-up snobs like you' and I perhaps unwisely said, 'I doubt it as who would be interested in a tiny stunted ginger Scottish pillock who would make Quasimodo look attractive' and I stormed off but I caught the look in his eye as I left and realised that he would be the type who don't suffer slights with good grace and would bear grudges for years and probably intensifying the animosity, and I think that's what has happened and when you came on the scene, the grudge has continued".

"Did he ever get married?" Neil asked innocently.

"I think so," his mum replied, "or how else would you account for Jason Connolly, his son?" and they both laughed. Neil then told her that he'd tried to ring his sister but got no answer.

"Oh, she'll be too busy with her new boyfriend, a slimy bloodstock agent. I don't like him or trust him."

They were still chatting when a car drew up, and he instantly recognised it as Suzie's, the big dent in the boot was a big clue where Brian Cogan's baseball bat had made contact. She got out and came over, and Neil got a big hug.

"I bet that you're pleased that it's all over?"

"You're not joking," he replied rather lamely as, in reality, pleased didn't cover the elation that he felt. They went inside, and Neil put the kettle on. Before the tea was brewed, there was a knock on the door.

"Can someone answer that," he called out, but no one did as the knocking got more urgent, so muttering to himself, he went and opened it and got another shock.

In fact, a very big shock, as standing there was Dawn. He was lost for words for a second or two but managed to mumble, "Come inside and meet my solicitor, Suzie".

"You've gone up in the world," she said, "if you've got your own personal solicitor".

Neil had so many questions to ask her but thought that they would have to wait.

"I'm just making some tea," he said and introduced the two girls, the tall slim statuesque Dawn and the beefier pear-shaped Suzie.

"We're celebrating, aren't we?" Dawn said, "Tea won't do; let's go to the pub". Both Suzie and Neil liked that idea.

"OK," Neil said, "I'll drive".

"No chance," they both said in unison. "Not with your recent driving record."

"OK," Neil said, knowing that the jokes about his driving would run for a very long time, "we'll walk then. I'll go and get my walking stick".

"You won't need that," they said, "we'll hold you up," and with that, they each got hold of one arm and dragged him off towards the pub, down past the old stud managers cottage and towards the ford, the scenes of many of his recent incidents, but all was thankfully quiet and serene.

"I'll buy the first round," Neil said, but when they got there, that pleasure wasn't his as the landlord, pleased to see his safe return, gave them the first round on the house. They must have all been very thirsty as their glasses were soon empty.

"Second round is yours," Dawn said, handing her glass to Neil, "since you didn't actually buy the first one".

"Nothing gets past you, does it?" he replied, "but before I go to the bar, I want to make an announcement," he got up, cleared his throat and started to speak, but they drowned him out.

"Don't bother with any big speeches. Everyone knows what you're going to say — that you're going to return as a jockey." And that was exactly what he was going to say; that he intended to return next season stronger and, more importantly, wiser.

"How did you know that?" he said, puzzled.

"Everyone knows. It's a foregone conclusion." He sat down again with his grand gesture nullified. "Get up again," Dawn said, "it's your round, remember".

He got up and went to the bar accepting congratulations from a few other local acquaintances and came back with a broad smile on his face.

"What are you smiling for?" Dawn asked.

"For the first time in many months, I feel completely at ease, relaxed and more importantly, completely safe!"

(But was he really safe?)

THE END

(To Be continued)

About the Author

The author had a disrupted early life as the family kept moving due to his dad's job. He went to a lot of different schools, and friendships formed were soon lost, and he had to start out again. The first sport he showed any interest in was football, as his dad used to take him to football matches, to watch Leeds United, and his abiding memory is of at one such match, there was a pitch invasion, and the mounted police galloped onto the pitch and soon had the situation under control; he decided there and then that he'd like to be a Mounted policeman, but later this changed to a Blacksmith, farmer or Jockey, all of which met with a shake of the head from his careers advisor.

His mum kindled his interest in horses at about the age of seven, when he was taken to a local riding school, but wasn't very keen as the ponies used to suddenly get down and roll, and the pupils got told off if this happened, so he wanted to stop riding, but luckily he didn't and carried on. Not long after, he got his first pony, Mischief, for £150.00 with all the tack included, this was shared with his sister, and he used to enjoy going hacking after school. His next pony soon followed called Palo, who was a little strong and he used to bolt once past the Huntmaster, which got him bellowed at, and on another occasion, he fell off and ended up with a broken arm and numerous stitches on his face, but luckily this didn't ruin his good looks. It wasn't until he got Golden Simba that he found his feet and confidence, and with a friend, he used to race cars along the roads, which lasted until someone complained. He competed at all the local shows with had success in most events, apart from dressage. At around this time, he found the Pony Club, where a lot of good friends were made, with the summer camp being the highlight, sadly the riders weren't allowed to camp as the year before, the pony clubbers had galloped their horses round the racecourse late at night. He started taking an interest in racing while at school and joined a Tipster group, picking one horse each day, with a prize going to the one who had the most winners by the end of term. It goes without saying that he never won this, as his gambling wasn't (and still isn't) very good. In the intervening years, many local racecourses were visited, and whilst visiting the Middleham open day with family and friends. His Mum joined a racing syndicate which opened another side to racing, one he hadn't seen before. She soon had racehorses of her own and bred a few, so inevitably, he had a leg (share) in these, and some actually managed to win races.

The idea of writing a book had been around for a long time since he'd heard the old adage that there is one good book in everyone. His first attempt was a story about some boys that blew up a reservoir which caused a big flood, but on research, he found that that had already been written. His second attempt was about a lad who got involved with poachers, who beat up a gamekeeper, and the lad ends up being blamed for it, it got a little further insomuch that the chapters were planned and the story was formulated, but it floundered and went no further. His third attempt is Pitchfork. Sometime during the first lockdown, the idea of a book suddenly appeared. The hardest part was getting started, but then when he got going, it just flowed, without a hint of writer's block, and he soon had the finished book; whether the old adage is correct, we are yet to find out, but I can say that it was an enjoyable experience writing it.

Printed in Great Britain
by Amazon

45761978R00205